EXPERIENCE AND INNOCENCE

Sarah felt Mark's grip on her half-bare shoulders tighten when she accused him of having a mistress, but she did not waver. "It's no use lying," she told him. "I saw you embracing her in an open doorway for all the world to see."

To her surprise he did not even look abashed. He coolly replied, "That embrace was more or less forced on me—"

"Forced on you?" Sarah exclaimed incredulously.

The indignant cry had barely left her lips when they were ruthlessly covered by Mark's mouth. As his embrace lengthened, quite new and insistent feelings woke in her and flamed into response.

How could Sarah believe the innocence of kisses from someone as experienced as the notorious viscount? Yet how could she resist them . . . ?

DOROTHY MACK is a native New Englander, born in Rhode Island and educated at Brown and Harvard universities. While living in Massachusetts with her husband and four young sons, she began to combine a longtime interest in English history with her desire to write, and emerged as an author of Regency romances. The family now resides in northern Virginia, where Dorothy continues to pursue both interests.

ROMANTIC ENCOUNTERS

The General's Granddaughter

Dorothy Mack

A SIGNET BOOK

SIGNET
Published by the Penguin Group
Penguin Books USA Inc., 375 Hudson Street,
New York, New York, U.S.A. 10014
Penguin Books Ltd, 27 Wrights Lane, London W8 5TZ, England
Penguin Books Australia Ltd, Ringwood, Victoria, Australia
Penguin Books Canada Ltd, 2801 John Street, Markham, Ontario,
Canada L3R 1B4
Penguin Books (N.Z.) Ltd, 182-190 Wairau Road,
Auckland 10, New Zealand

Penguin Books Ltd, Registered Offices:
Harmondsworth, Middlesex, England

First published by Signet, an imprint of Penguin Books USA Inc.

First Printing, May, 1990

10 9 8 7 6 5 4 3 2 1

1

Not one but three curled ostrich plumes adorned the extravagantly high crown of the bonnet reposing in splendid isolation in the shop window. Considering the luxuriant nature of the fabrics employed in the construction of this master-piece, such prodigality seemed no more than fitting, however, as was the decision not to display it in company with lesser examples of the hat maker's art, which would certainly suffer from comparisons. True, there was a charming little posy in a pierced gilt holder and an exquisite ivory fan carelessly disposed on the drapery at the base of the domed pedestal holding the bonnet, but these elegant trifles merely served to enhance the beauty of the *pièce de résistance*. A three-paneled screen behind the display area concealed the interior of the shop from the casual glances of those passing by. A discreet sign above the door to the left of the window bore the scant information that Sarah of Boston was located within.

The younger of the two females peering into the shop window removed her hand from the arm of the elder, whom she appeared to have been towing along the street, and clasped it in its mate in an attitude of triumphant supplication. "There, Mama, did I not promise you it was the most beautiful bonnet in all of London? I must have it. Say I may have it, please, Mama. That stuck-up Jane Farraday has nothing to equal it."

"Now, now, do compose yourself, Amelia, and let me catch my breath. Dragging me away from my tea like that to come look at a hat! I declare I don't know what your Aunt Margaret must be thinking of you, dashing into her parlor like a hoyden

5

and interrupting our visit without so much as a by-your-leave."

"Oh, bother what Aunt Margaret thinks! You know she is nothing but a tiresome scold, and in any case, you may see her any day of the week, but a bonnet like this one will be snapped up in a trice. Do let us go inside, darling Mama."

This last plea was uttered in a cajoling voice that brought a fond smile to the older woman's lips that lasted until her eyes lighted on the sign above the door, whereupon her mouth firmed and she dug in her heels. "I don't like the proprietress of this shop, with her absurd pretensions to gentility, Amelia, and I'm not at all certain that bronze-green color is suitable for a young girl."

"Of course it is suitable, Mama!" Amelia's naturally high color was intensified by her passion, but she swallowed hard and lowered her voice once more. "I know Miss Sarah is rather . . . formal, but she does have the prettiest hats in town. We don't have to like her."

"Calling herself Miss Sarah as if her last name was too high to be spoken by her customers, and her no better than any other shopkeeper when all's said, despite those airs of hers. I'll go bail she's no more from Boston than I am."

And indeed, the quiet voice of the woman who came forward to greet her clients a moment later gave no hints of an origin across the Atlantic Ocean.

"Good afternoon, Mrs. Merryman, Miss Merryman. What may I show you today?"

"I want the bonnet in the window," blurted Amelia, her eagerness earning her a quelling look from her parent, whose manner had stiffened considerably since entering the shop.

A faint, not unsympathetic smile appeared briefly on the shop-keeper's lips. "Yes, of course," she replied, glancing to the still-silent matron for guidance before continuing in a persuasive tone, "though the hat in the window is perhaps a trifle old for a girl in her first Season. We have several exceptionally pretty bonnets more suitable to a *jeune fille*—"

"Oh, no," protested Amelia. "That's the one I want. Please, Mama!"

"Well, you may try it on at least, my dear, and then we shall see.'' Mrs. Merryman directed a haughty stare at the proprietress, who lowered her eyes in acquiescence and went to remove the bronze-green velvet bonnet from the display stand while the eager girl hastened to plop herself on the spindly chair in front of a dressing table containing a good-sized mirror.

By the time Miss Sarah returned with the coveted prize, Amelia had tossed her own bonnet on the dressing table and was running a smoothing hand through her crimped straw-colored locks. Her slightly protuberant blue eyes avidly followed the other's movements in the mirror and she appeared to have the utmost difficulty in sitting still while the bonnet was placed on her head.

"I'll do the bow," she declared, taking the sherry-colored satin ribbons from the saleswoman's hands and tying them in a large bow beneath her wide square chin. "There, Mama, isn't it simply beautiful?"

Mrs. Merryman, fond parent though she was, did not immediately comply with her daughter's request to confirm her own opinion. Uncertainty rather than admiration was the dominant emotion expressed by dark shoe-button eyes and pursed lips as she flashed a covert look at the curiously blank visage of the proprietress, who was staring into the mirror at the preening girl turning her head this way and that.

"Well, I won't say it isn't a pretty hat, my love, because it is, but I'm not sure but what Miss Sarah might not be right in thinking it too old for you." Her voice dwindled in the wake of the storm gathering on her daughter's face.

The shopkeeper said gently, "I fear this particular bonnet is not for everyone: the high poke is too narrow to flatter any but the most pointed-chinned female, and that odd color is not easy to wear." She smiled coaxingly at the increasingly red-faced girl and added, "We have a really lovely wide-brimmed hat in a deep-blue velvet that would emphasize the color of your eyes."

"But I don't want blue, blue is too common. No one I know has a hat like this one, and this is the one I want."

She might be young in years but Miss Merryman was a girl who knew her own mind, and she now proceeded to make up her mother's as well. When a parental suggestion to try on the blue hat at least was rejected summarily, it became obvious that youthful determination would prevail. Miss Sarah assumed a professional smile as she awaited the inevitable.

"Very well, we'll take it," Mrs. Merryman became equally businesslike. "What is the price?"

"Five pounds six, ma'am."

"That's ridiculous," blustered the would-be purchaser, sending a glance of hostility at the owner of the shop. "Much too dear."

The slim young woman in black regarded the overdressed matron before her and said with a placatory smile, "I fear ostrich feathers and satin are much too dear these days, ma'am. We are compelled to raise our prices accordingly." Her glance did not falter before her customer's accusing stare, and after an awkward pause, during which an anxious Miss Merryman tugged at her mother's sleeve and whispered urgently, the latter capitulated with an ungracious sniff.

"Very well, you may put it on my account."

There was another short pause while the proprietress seemed to gather her forces together. At the end of it she said, "In view of the fact that we have sent you two so-far-unavailing requests for payment of your outstanding account in the last three months, Mrs. Merryman, I regret that I shall have to ask for payment in cash for this purchase."

The outraged matron drew herself up to her full height, her formidable bosom swelling with indignation. "Are you daring to question my integrity, young woman?"

"Not at all, madam. I am simply stating that I cannot afford to advance you any additional credit at this moment. If it is inconvenient for you to pay for the bonnet today, I will gladly put it aside for you until tomorrow."

"That will not be necessary, Miss Sarah Whatever-your-name is. I have no intention of setting foot in this establishment again, and you may be sure that I shall warn all my friends against patronizing somone of your sort also. Come, Amelia."

"But, Mama, my hat," wailed Miss Merryman, refusing to

budge. "You promised to buy me this bonnet. Miss Sarah will hold it for us, she said she would."

"And *I* said I have no intention of doing business with this person again," repeated Mrs. Merryman, sending the silent object of her scorn a withering glance that failed in its object. "Come along, Amelia. We'll find you another hat tomorrow."

"But I don't want another hat, Mama, I want this one."

The sound of Amelia's shrill protests drifted back to the young woman, who quietly closed the door Mrs. Merryman had wrenched open and flung back in her haste to leave the shop. After a glance at the wall clock, she locked the door and walked back through the curtains hanging in the archway leading out of the front room with the disputed bonnet still in her hands.

"You heard?"

The middle-aged woman addressed looked up briefly from the riding hat she was trimming with red braid. "I heard, all right. That harpy has a voice that could penetrate steel. Never mind, Sarah, we can do without her custom."

"And that of all her friends? For, mark my words, Lottie, Mrs. Merryman is the kind to enjoy making good her threat to ruin us. Heaven knows it won't take much intervention. We'll probably manage it all on our own before long."

"Are matters that serious?" This time the seamstress put down her work and gave all her attention to Sarah, who had slumped into the other chair in the workroom, a look of weary defeat on her face. "I was under the impression that our hats had achieved some recognition beyond this unfashionable section of town. This special order, for instance," indicating the riding hat with a movement of her head.

"Oh, yes, our hats have caught the eyes of some discerning persons this past year, but I could wish gentlemen bought them for their wives and daughters rather than their mistresses. The ladies of the *haut ton* are unlikely to venture this far from the fashionable shopping districts that we cannot afford. The real problem is that, although we sell our hats, we have the greatest difficulty in getting people to pay their accounts." She sighed and raised a troubled gaze to the woman regarding her with affectionate concern. Her fingers continued to smooth a couple of small creases from the ribbons of the bonnet in her lap. "Do you think perhaps I should have permitted Mrs. Merryman to take this?"

"No, I do not," Lottie replied firmly, addressing the other's self-doubt. "She is the type who won't pay until pushed to the wall by a solicitor, which we cannot afford. You would have had to take a stand at some point or other. At least this way we still have the bonnet."

"Yes. It's the loveliest hat we've ever created, and was quite wasted on that objectionable child." A gleam of pure mischief momentarily lighted large eyes of an indeterminate color in the gathering dusk. "How I wish you could have seen her primping in the mirror with a huge bow tied squarely under her chin, looking for all the world like a squirrel with its cheeks stuffed full of acorns, though if you had been there, Lottie, I could never have kept my countenance. Even such a doting mama as Mrs. Merryman was unable to bring herself to admire her chick. I realize now that I spoke no more than the truth when I said the bonnet was not for every woman."

"No, it takes a beauty to wear it; after all, it was designed for you," the older woman said matter-of-factly. She had taken up her task again but noted with satisfaction the hint of rose that crept into Sarah's pale cheeks, though she objected laughingly.

"Oh, Lottie, I vow you are as blindly partial as Mrs. Merryman. Any pretensions I ever had to beauty—doubtful at best— are so far in the past as to be ancient history. I feel as faded as those flowers in the window will be tomorrow. Which reminds me that I must put them in some water to try to get another day out of them." And, placing the bonnet tenderly on the long worktable, she rose with an effort she could not quite conceal and went out of the room.

"Nonsense." Lottie's raised voice followed her. "Who has decreed that a woman of six-and-twenty is at her last prayers? You are feeling low at present because you have not yet recovered from the effects of as nasty a bout of influenza as I ever hope to see. Like those flowers, all you need is a little water to revive you," she added as Sarah returned with the posy and removed the holder and the wet cloth she had wrapped around the stem. "You want plenty of sunshine and good food to build up your strength again and put the roses back in your cheeks."

"I daresay your prescription would be a universal panacea if it were not beyond the grasp of a great proportion of the people, Lottie," Sarah said with a return of her somber manner. "You are no doubt correct in attributing my low spirits to that wretched influenza, but at least the enforced stay in my bed provided the opportunity for some serious consideration of our future. It was more than just confronting one's own mortality. I realized for the first time how little we two women can do for Richard. My annuity is barely adequate to keep us housed and fed. Even if this venture into trade were to become a resounding success we could not afford the fees for a decent school. We have almost no acquaintance in England to advise us, so how is Richard to prepare himself for a career?"

"Perhaps we might consider returning to America when this war is over. It is easier for an enterprising young man to make his fortune there, and you have friends there too."

"We did before this latest trouble blew up, but Father's affairs were somewhat tangled when we left. I . . . I am not entirely certain that he settled all his debts when we returned to England."

The older woman clamped her lips against anything she might wish to say about Gerald Ridgemont. No one knew better what it had cost Sarah to make this admission. She had loved her charming, improvident father devotedly as a child, and the gradual discovery of his weaknesses had been painful knowledge that she guarded even from the one person she had known closely all her life. Through all the vicissitudes of fortune into which Gerald's harebrained schemes for enriching the family had dragged them, Sarah had held her head high and preserved the image of a dutiful loving daughter, following in her mother's difficult path. Lottie could understand that; after all, her own loyalty and devotion to her mistress had been of the same order and had been transferred to Alice's children on her death. But her own loyalty had come easily, for Alice Ridgemont had been a saint on earth, and her children, though endearingly fallible, were full worthy of devotion.

So Lottie held her peace on the subject of Gerald Ridgemont, asking merely when Sarah's embarrassed glance met hers, "Does all this heartburning mean you have decided to apply to your grandfather after all?"

"I think for Richard's sake I must swallow my pride. It is grossly unfair that he should have to be flung into the working world without any patronage behind him when his grandfather is one of the wealthiest men in the country. We shall never be able to afford the hundreds of pounds it would take to apprentice him to a successful banker or merchant. Somehow I must make my grandfather accept some responsibility for Richard's education. I know I have been most boringly vociferous in the past about never asking him for a penny-piece after the shameful way he treated my father, but lying there in my bed, knowing that *I* was all that stood between Richard and the workhouse, was a frightening and humbling experience, and—"

"You forgot to mention me. Do you suppose I should simply stand by and see Richard hauled off to the workhouse?"

Lottie's dry interjection served to arrest Sarah in full flight. She blinked long lashes, and her quiet features broke into laughter with somewhat the same effect as the sun coming out from behind a cloud. "Dear Lottie, you always know how to depress my tendency toward dramatization. Very well, then, Richard is doubly fortunate to have two fierce guardians, but what he will need most in the future is a good education that will give him a start in life. And that, I fear, is and will remain beyond our ability to provide. Therefore, it must be Grandfather."

"All this noble resolution to swallow your pride is very fine talking, but what gives you to suppose that General Ridgemont will undergo a sudden revulsion of feeling when applied to for assistance? He never acknowledged your birth twenty-six years ago, or Richard's eleven years ago. He refused to see your father when he went to bid him good-bye before we went to America, and he has not written so much as a line to express his condolences in the months since your father's death. It is nearly a year now. If he was not moved at that time to a sense of remorse for his treatment of his son or even curiosity as to how his orphaned grandchildren were faring, how can you hope another letter, and this one a begging letter, will do the trick?''

Strangely, Lottie's severe practicality failed to daunt her former nurseling. "I do not plan to write my grandfather another letter," Sarah replied calmly. "I intend to go and see him myself. It is one thing to ignore a petition written by some totally unknown person and quite another to stand in front of one's own flesh and blood and deny that same petition."

"Somehow, I can still envision that response being well within your grandfather's capabilities," retorted Lottie, "and Beech Hill must be all of one hundred miles away. Are you certain you wish to gamble the cost of a ticket on the mail coach on the chance that he'll even receive you?"

"Oh, I wouldn't travel by mail," Sarah was horrified. "I'll go by stagecoach, of course, and I shall see to it that my grandfather receives me." Her delicate chin firmed quite discernibly, but Lottie ignored this sign and harked back to the first part of the statement.

"Sarah, you are barely out of a sickbed," she protested earnestly. "You cannot expose yourself to the rigors of a long uncomfortable journey in one of those accommodation coaches, especially in the winter."

"The cost of traveling by mail is prohibitive. I am quite recovered now and shall take no harm on the common stage, Lottie. All kinds of people travel that way every day. It might not be a comfortable ride, but there is certainly no danger attached to going to stage."

Lottie was not reassured by this calm pronouncement. " 'All kinds of people' is no more than the sad truth. You'll be trapped inside one of those smelly vehicles, rammed elbow to elbow with heaven knows what kind of riffraff for a whole day and probably half the night too. Why not wait for a month or two until you have regained your health? Perhaps by then the shop will be on a more profitable basis so that you'll feel able to go by mail. There is no cause for desperate haste in the matter surely. Richard is barely eleven, and the day school he attends is adequate for the moment.''

Lottie's measured words were eminently reasonable, but it became evident over the next few days that on this subject Sarah had gone beyond the reach of reason. She had nerved herself up to take drastic action and this state, once achieved, consumed her mental energy to the exclusion of all other interests. Generally the most amenable of creatures, she had on one or two occasions in the past exhibited a similar mulish determination of purpose that brooked no opposition. Her arguments proving ineffective, Lottie was eventually persuaded to bestow her qualified blessing on the undertaking despite private misgivings.

''I don't know what Richard or I would do without you, Lottie,'' declared a grateful but slightly remorseful Sarah when she had succeeded in getting her own way.

''Neither do I,'' she was told with grim humor, ''but that goes two ways. I would not like to contemplate life without the two of you either. One gets used to the incessant chattering of a pair of magpies after a while.''

At this reminder of Lottie's childhood name for her, Sarah laughed and embraced the big-boned but sparsely padded figure who had been the one unchanging element in her life. Except that her dark hair was now streaked with gray, she had scarcely altered from the loving, no-nonsense nurse who used to dress a little girl in starched dresses to bring her to the frail young woman whose delicate constitution never completely recovered from childbearing. ''I do love you, Lottie. You are our family.''

''I wonder. Would your ladyship be so quick to hug me had you lost this tug-of-war?'' came the quick rejoinder.

Sarah chuckled again. ''You know me too well. Now, let us be serious for a moment while we decide which items in my unique wardrobe will disgrace us least before my rich grandfather.'' She pulled a long face.

Lottie said promptly, ''Bring the bronze-green bonnet with you.''

''Oh, I couldn't, Lottie. It's much too grand for a poor

relation. Besides, I'm hoping we'll be able to sell it before I leave, to help defray the expenses of the journey.''

Lottie looked rebellious but forbore to argue.

The next few days were crowded with preparations for Sarah's journey. She had flatly refused to spend additional money on a new traveling dress or pelisse, but Lottie coolly appropriated some of the costliest materials from their hat-making supplies and put her clever fingers to work in refurbishing some items dating back to their days in New England. Fortunately, the period of mourning was now up, providing more scope for her efforts. She cut out the neckline of one of Sarah's plain black gowns and inserted finely pleated white lawn that she found time to embroider below a dainty collar. There was even enough of the bronze-green velvet left to make up a smart little spencer that she trimmed with the same sherry-colored satin as the ribbons on the bonnet. After some cogitation she replaced the worn collar and cuffs on the despised black serge pelisse with black velvet. No one of refined taste would mistake Sarah's modest wardrobe for the height of fashion, but her clothes were always well-cut and beautifully fitted, though she had lost weight during her recent illness, necessitating some slight adjustments.

One aspect of her appearance required no apology in any company. Sarah's hats had always been the envy of her friends in America, thanks to her creative artistry and Lottie's exquisite sewing. It gave her old nurse some small satisfaction to reflect that if her chick must demean herself to the extent of riding on the public stage, at least she would sport the most attractive headgear of any passenger thereon. Sarah would not hear of taking one of the hats from the shop with her, insisting that the black velvet bonnet they had made after her father's death was still the most suitable, and slyly laying stress on the happy coincidence of the pelisse's new velvet trim providing a stylish pairing. Defeated in her main object but determined at all costs to negate any aura of pathetic widowhood clinging to the all-black costume, Lottie removed the veiling material from the bonnet and added a white satin band around the crown, to which she attached a single large white ostrich feather, placing it to curl enticingly over the brim above one eyebrow.

Though she had supplied generous practical assistance, even packing Sarah's portmanteau, Lottie was not by any means reconciled to the desperate scheme of trying to force an audience upon General Ridgemont in his home. Nor was she taken in by Sarah's well-done but spurious air of detachment whenever the subject was brought up—as though to imply that such expeditions were commonplace in her young life. When she thought herself unobserved, her anxious eyes and a strained look about her mouth testified to a trepidation she would have denied on the rack. Even Richard, told merely that his sister had some business in Gloucestershire, was unable to express his feelings with total unfettered freedom. To a boy of eleven, any deviation from their quiet life represented adventure and was thus ardently to be desired. He did indeed offer himself as escort and companion to Sarah, but when told gently that finances would not permit this happy arrangement, he manfully concealed his disappointment and threw himself into the preparations for the trip. It was Richard who actually purchased the ticket and reserved a place for Sarah on the Bristol stage and it was Richard's persistent nagging that was responsible for their arrival at the White Horse Inn in Fetter Lane in good time for the nine A.M. departure of the coaches for the West Country. He had insisted on taking care of Sarah's portmanteau on the short hackney carriage ride and attended to its final disposal among the diverse baggage being loaded on the huge green-and-gold accommodation coach in which his sister would spend at least the next twelve hours, for the stage didn't reckon to achieve more than eight miles per hour. He even submitted good-naturedly to Sarah's loving embrace despite the embarrassing proximity of spectators.

Sarah was safely established in a corner of the coach with the basket of food provided by Lottie on her lap. At Richard's insistence her attendants remained to watch the heavily laden vehicle rumble out of the inn yard with a full complement of interior passengers plus seven or eight hardy souls perched up on the roof in defiance of threatening skies and a biting wind.

Richard chattered away on the trip home, pleasantly conscious that he had surmounted his natural disappointment and willingly assisted in getting his sister off on her adventure. That his companion was a far cry from sharing his positive thoughts about the adventure in store for Sarah never entered his mind, for Lottie took care to respond to his prattle with a convincing show of attention, reserving to herself both the nagging worry that the physical discomfort of the journey might undermine Sarah's precarious state of health and the pessimistic conviction, based on the accumulated evidence of General Ridgemont's stony nature, that the effort was destined to be in vain. Her last glimpse of Sarah's pinched features in the window of the coach when she waved a final good-bye had confirmed her supposition that the girl's determined confidence this past sennight had been in the nature of whistling in the dark.

2

Lottie's uneasy assumptions about the genuineness of Sarah's confidence in the success of her mission were well-founded, but not even to herself—especially not to herself—could the young woman have acknowledged any misgivings. Unhappily, the driving force of the desperation to act that had carried her through the preparation period and into a corner of a clumsy stagecoach began to lose impetus before the vehicle had lumbered out of the yard of the White Horse. In the instant before Lottie's and Richard's faces vanished from her sight, panic rose up and nearly choked Sarah. A little gasp escaped her lips as her hand blindly sought the door handle. At that moment the coach turned sharply into the city street, throwing the unprepared girl back into her corner with a bump she felt from her shoulder to her tingling fingertips.

"Too late, missy. You'd best learn to do without whatever it was yer forgot."

A tinge of color crept into Sarah's pale cheeks as she made belated sense of the words addressed to her by the grinning, portly man sitting in the opposite corner. "Yes," she murmured, dropping her eyes hastily as she read the interest in his. She tried to mask her instinctive shrinking into her own corner by producing a polite little smile.

"What was it?"

"I beg your pardon?" Huge amber-brown eyes returned to the jowly face across from her.

"Whatever it was that was so important yer tried to climb out of a moving coach to get."

"Oh! Ah . . . tooth powder," Sarah said, inventing madly.

"Not to fret, dearie, salt will do just as well," commented an amply padded matron with a benevolent smile beneath a brown hat whose brim sagged under the weight of artificial fruit piled upon it. "You've got very pretty teeth, dearie, just like my second girl before hers went all loose from childbearing. She's lost most of them now, more's the pity."

"I . . . I'm sorry," Sarah offered feebly, feeling some response was demanded of her. She had not given previous thought to the enforced intimacy obtaining among a half-dozen strangers confined together in a closed carriage for an extended period. She did so now and experienced another tide of anxiety. How was she to bear a whole day of being subjected to the rude stares and prying questions of strangers—strangers whom she would never choose to associate with in the ordinary course of events?

Fortunately, an eager interjection by the woman sitting beside Sarah led to a prolonged exchange of horror stories dealing with dental problems, which gave Sarah a respite in which to subdue the diffuse anxieties attacking her and reestablish her customary commonsensical outlook. How ridiculous of her even for a moment to doubt her ability to survive a day in a stagecoach when she had survived six weeks of a stormy Atlantic crossing two years before. It might not prove the most agreeable day of her life, but neither would it be the worst. One could stand any inconvenience for a few hours.

Imperceptibly, Sarah's defensive posture relaxed and she began to take an interest in her fellow passengers. Her glance slid quickly past her lumpish admirer across the way. The look in his eyes as they had appraised her earlier was one with which she had grown all too familiar since their entrance into the world of trade following her father's death. Familiarity had not overcome her distress or discomfort at being assessed like livestock for sale on market day, though she had quickly learned to disguise her reaction, knowing full well that a significant portion of the shop's business was directly attributable to her modeling of hats for their masculine customers. Initially, she had been surprised to receive any male patronage, but her naïveté had not survived the first bold offer of a *carte blanche*. In recounting her shocked outrage to Lottie after the would-be protector had been shown the door with icy dismissal, she had received a second shock when her old nurse took her to task for losing a sale.

Eventually she had learned to swallow her disgust and project an air of impersonal pleasantness that not the most blatantly flirtatious approach could dislodge. The measure of her success was to be seen in the steady growth of sales to gentlemen despite her cool refusal of even the most minimal personal involvement with her clients. Indeed, she suspected her persistent unreceptiveness to masculine blandishments had brought the shop a degree of notoriety among a certain class of clientele. She resented this situation while at the same time taking advantage of it to increase their sales, something that should have troubled her conscience more had their need not been so great. The practical side of her nature decreed that she was in no position to afford those particular niceties of a lady's sensibililty.

Sarah's eyes passed over the friendly countrywoman who was still holding forth on her family's medical history in the intervals when she could wrest the initiative from the garrulous woman next to Sarah. The man beside her was evidently her husband, though he possessed none of his rib's bonhomie. A thin, sourfaced individual, he had replied to his spouse's repeated requests for confirmation of her various statements with monosyllabic grunts that might just as well have been taken for disagreement, while his eyes never left off their rapt contemplation of the scenery rushing past the window.

Even by angling her head into the side of the carriage, Sarah could not really see the third occupant on her own side of the coach who, judging by her wavery but persistent voice, was an elderly lady of frail physique but indomitable spirit. Her nearest neighbor blocked her view, which was not surprising since her girth was considerable and made even more so by an accumulation of shawls and wraps about her person.

For the first few stages the novelty of the experience and the extraordinary conversations of her companions helped the time pass fairly quickly. Sarah replied politely when directly addressed but was aware that among a plethora of embarrassingly intimate anecdotes and personal histories aired, her own few impersonal contributions lacked any savor whatever as entertainment value.

The elderly lady got out at Reading with the man who had ogled Sarah and tried unavailingly to impress her with his status as a successful printer on Fleet Street. His place was taken by a taciturn individual whose welcome silence failed to compensate for the rancid odor eminating from his slovenly person. Sarah, who rather enjoyed modest experiments in meal preparation under Lottie's tutelage, eventually identified the main component as garlic. By the time the unpleasantly aromatic man left the stage at Woolhampton she had resolved never to get within smelling distance of that pungent bulb again.

Time had slowed to a jolting crawl and the individual rotations of the coach wheels had begun sending rhythmic hammer blows of discomfort through her temples. The stops to change horses afforded some slight respite, but none was longer than five minutes or so, barely enough time in which to take a few breaths of cold clean air into one's lungs, certainly too short to stretch one's legs or shake out muscles cramped from sitting.

Lottie's carefully prepared food was just so much wasted effort. Ever since the advent of the garlic-eating passenger, Sarah had been struggling, first to ignore, then to subdue a rising nausea that was only briefly alleviated by descending from the coach and gulping air at the various stages. As the daylight waned, all her physical and mental resources were concentrated on not being sick. She was quite literally afraid to eat, and only by staring out the window and fiercely concentrating on the darkening landscape could she ignore the odors of the various foodstuffs being consumed by her fellow travelers. Her fingers gripped her own basket with an unrelenting pressure that cramped them periodically, thus adding to her discomfort.

Having consulted Carey's *Traveller's Companion* before embarking on her journey, Sarah knew that Beech Hill was located in the vicinity of Marshfield, a thriving town a dozen or so miles east of Bristol. As night settled on the circumscribed little purgatory that was the swaying stagecoach, all thoughts of deliverance were focused on Marshfield. According to the waybill, there were only two more stops before hers. All she had to do was contain the nausea, allow her body to roll with the movement of the coach, and ignore the pain in her head. She had been clenching her teeth against any movement of her head for so long that her jaw ached also. Several of the passengers had actually dozed off from time to time. How she envied them as she noted the outlines of their relaxed bodies, their lolling heads. She attempted without conspicuous success to relax her muscles and tried to train her attention past the pain to the steady rumble of the wheels, tried to listen for a lessening of their speed as they approached a town so she might prepare herself for the guard's blast on the yard of tin to alert the coaching inn to have the new team of horses ready to harness.

When the accommodation coach finally pulled into Marshfield, Sarah was near collapse. She would have fallen to the ground had not the guard's arms been quick as he assisted her down. She stood trembling in the cold damp night air while her portmanteau was retrieved from the baggage. When she tipped the driver and the guard, she asked the latter to recommend a smaller inn where her unattended status would not draw unfavorable notice, but she was reassured that, unlike posting houses that catered to a wealthy clientele, coaching inns were accustomed to serving ordinary persons. She summoned up a grateful smile as the guard pointed out a door to her, unaware of the passing sympathy in his eyes as he climbed somewhat reluctantly back up to his perch.

Indeed, Sarah was almost totally unaware of her surroundings at this juncture. All her remaining resources were focused on achieving privacy before she disgraced herself by collapsing in a heap. The innkeeper, noting his guest's extreme pallor, eased her through the preliminaries ahead of a man waiting impatiently, and she was shown in short order to a quiet room at the back of the inn. By now each stair represented a separate and distinct agony, adding to the painful cacophony jangling in her head. There were no thoughts in her mind beyond removing the once comfortable bonnet, which had assumed all the more unpleasant properties of a vise, and laying her head on a pillow. By the time the servant had lighted the candles and thrown some coals on a very small fire, Sarah had placed the hat on a modest chest of drawers and was struggling with the buttons on her pelisse. It would have been nice to warm her stiff fingers at the fire, but the urgent necessity to ease her head dictated all her actions. She laid her gown carelessly over a chair and sank down immediately onto the bed's surface, taking care not to make any jerking motions as she awkwardly removed her half-boots and brought her legs under the bedcovers before easing her head onto the pillows.

The relief to the rest of her body was instant and palpable, but the pounding in her head was only dulled to a degree. She hadn't expected more, she told herself bracingly, not at first. Her mother had suffered all her life from migraines that prostrated her for up to forty-eight hours before loosening their grip enough to permit a rise from her bed. Sarah had never endured a headache that even approached the severity of a real migraine before, but she was in no doubt as to what ailed her at present.

The anodyne of sleep was denied her during the next several hours, but at least the accompanying nausea dissipated as soon as her body became relaxed. She lay very still, consciously avoiding the increase of discomfort that attended even the slightest movement of her head. Now thoughts of the immediate future that she was powerless to resist came crowding into Sarah's aching head. Sleep seemed an impossible goal as she lay in a strange bed in a fast-cooling room more than a hundred miles from home and faced the rashness of her proposed action. Reduced to its most basic terms, she had come to beg financial support from a man who did not wish to acknowledge her existence. It was not the behavior of anyone with a scrap of pride, and the Lord knew she loathed the necessity, but with her father's death had vanished the last vestige of security for Richard. For a time, with the exciting possibilities of success from their venture into trade dazzling their eyes, her basic fear of the future had been held at bay. But with the siege of influenza her last line of defense against confronting the bleak reality had been overrun, and the subterranean fears surfaced to torment her as they did now. She had not been able to overcome the depression of spirits that had descended upon her during her illness.

Suppose her grandfather refused to see her, what then? Sarah jerked her head and immediately regretted it as needles of pain shot through her temples to augment the ever-present pressure. A small moan escaped her lips and slow, burning tears glided over her cheekbones. She could not fail. She must not fail!

Toward morning the exhausted young woman sank into a deep sleep that lasted until nearly midday. She did not stir until a persistent knocking at the door yanked her out of a blessed oblivion.

"Who . . . who is it?" she called in a weak voice, coming slowly to a sense of her surroundings.

"The maid. Are you all right in there, ma'am? May I come in?"

Sarah called out permission, thankful that her voice sounded stronger, thankful also, as she struggled into a sitting position, that the sharp pains in her head had dulled to a manageable ache, which she confirmed by cautious movements of her neck as the maid bustled in.

"Well, now, you nigh slept the clock around, didn't you, ma'am? I checked up on you two hours ago, but you was dead under, so I let you be."

"What time is it?" Sarah frowned at the bars of sunshine coming through the room's single window and realized the motion hurt. She raised a finger to smooth her brow as she focused dull eyes on the maid.

"Past eleven." The buxom young woman in a crisp apron and mobcap was pouring hot water into the basin as her curious gaze roamed over the guest's bare shoulders.

"I . . . I felt so unwell from the long journey that I just fell into bed last night without bothering about a night rail," Sarah explained.

"Yes." The maid nodded wisely. "You do be looking as white as them sheets still, ma'am. Why not stay in bed while I make up this fire? I dessay you'll feel better when you've warmed up some and had a hot meal."

"Yes. Th—thank you." Sarah slid back under the bedcovers, shivering a little in the room's chill and aware suddenly of a deep hollowness within, not surprising when she considered that she had eaten nothing since an early breakfast in London the day before. She chided herself for an idiot as she blinked back silly tears brought to the surface by the maid's simple kindliness.

"Even Lottie could not call you a beauty today," Sarah told the pasty-faced image that stared back at her from a cracked mirror over the washstand. Dark bruised-looking areas under her eyes bore mute testimony to her recent illness. Actually they had nearly faded until yesterday's ordeal, though her cheeks still had a drawn look. "I would not blame my grandfather for not wishing to acknowledge such a pitiful-looking creature," she declared, pinching her cheeks savagely. The resultant flow of blood ebbed as quickly as it had appeared, and she turned away from her reflection in disgust.

Everything about her simple toilette was an effort that morning, and it was in an uncharacteristic mood of self-pity that Sarah descended at last to the inn's public dining room. She had been unable to shake out all the travel creases from her black dress, and she was miserably conscious of presenting less than her usual neat appearance. She had not taken her hair down the previous night and had found her scalp so tender this morning that she couldn't bear the repeated discomforts of dragging a brush through the tangled length. Her solution had been to sweep the untidy mass up under the cap she had tucked into the top of the cloak bag at the last moment when she discovered that Lottie, who refused to concede that her nurseling had reached the age of wearing a spinster's cap, had failed to pack any. It was a pretty, embroidered lace cap but did nothing to relieve her pallor. The only color in her face was provided by silky brown brows and golden-brown eyes set in a thicket of dark lashes.

All too conscious of her defects, Sarah had no inkling of the effect her slender graceful person and perfect madonnalike features had on others. Had she been told that there was about her an air of beautiful fragility, she would have retorted that in general she was as strong as a horse and a capable individual to boot. Honesty would have compelled the reluctant qualification that the strength was in abeyance of late, however. Indeed, Sarah was conscious of an annoying weakness in her knees as she gratefully accepted the chair an attentive waiter held out to her.

It was well past the hour for breakfast, and in any case Sarah felt hollow to her toes, so she was easily persuaded to order a sustaining meal. In the end she discovered she was prevented from doing justice to the chef's offerings by a slight queasiness left over from her traveling ordeal, but she was able to swallow enough to put some stiffness back into her legs. If she lingered somewhat longer than was strictly justified by the amount of food she consumed, it was no doubt due to a natural reluctance to embark on the crucial stage of her mission until she had replaced a sadly depleted store of courage. She sat quietly in a corner, equally indifferent to the comings and goings in the busy hostelry and the interested looks directed her way by the predominantly masculine patrons of the dining room. Had her absorption in her thoughts been one degree less absolute, she might have noticed that her protective waiter had deflected several abortive attempts on the part of other diners to attract her attention. As it was, he felt well-repaid by the sweetness of her valedictory smile when at last she gathered up her belongings and prepared to leave the shelter of the inn.

The final stage of her journey must be accomplished by post chaise, of course. Sarah set off from the coaching inn toward the nearest post house, emerging into the sunshine on the main street of Marshfield with her shield of courage buckled on once more. If there was not actually a spring in her step, at least she proceeded with more confidence than she could have summoned up only an hour before.

Marshfield was something of a surprise in daylight, boasting as it did an exceedingly long main street: at least Sarah could see no end of buildings in either direction. The innkeeper had told her there were over a dozen such establishments in the town and she could well believe it, judging from the bustle of traffic around her. The street was lined with tall houses built almost exclusively of the local brownstone, but as each was individual, the result was surprisingly attractive, she thought as she walked briskly in the direction of the posting house.

It was very late in the afternoon when Sarah drove up to Beech Hill in a "yellow bounder," as the post chaises were known because of their distinctive paintwork. She had managed to hang on to her precarious courage while waiting for a vehicle to hire, but the closer she came to her destination, the more precarious her grip. Her head, though free of yesterday's shooting pains, felt stuffed and unfamiliar, almost too heavy for her neck and shoulders to support. Obviously the sunshine and brisk late winter air had done nothing to put color in her face because the postilion had paused when assisting her into the chaise to ask if she felt quite well.

Her thoughts made the same monotonous revolutions as the wheels. What would she do if her grandfather denied himself to her? But he would not do that; no person with the slightest claim to humanity could be so hard. Perhaps she should have gone to an inn in the closest village to the estate and sent a note to him advising him of her proximity and requesting an interview. Barring the fact that she didn't know the area and had no idea if there was a suitable place to wait for a response, it all came back to the ever-present dread that her grandfather would simply refuse to answer this as he had every past attempt at communication over the years. Then she would quite literally have no further recourse. She *must* gain entrance to Beech Hill!

Sarah was not prepared to have her first sight of her family home bring such a shock of recognition with it. She had not quite reached her twelfth birthday when her father had brought her to see her grandfather on the eve of their departure for America, but even as a child she had been struck by the grandeur and beauty of the entrance front of the house coming into view at the end of a long drive lined with lovely old copper beeches. She gave a slight gasp now. It was almost as if she had carried a pictorial map in her head all these years, so complete was her memory, even to the warm honey color of the stone. The imposing facade of nearly two hundred feet in length had struck awe in the imagination of the untraveled child and was no whit less imposing in the eyes of the adult Sarah, who still had seen

no private home to equal it on either side of the Atlantic. Her
father had told her the house was erected in the last decade of
the seventeenth century, and its design was old-fashioned and
inconvenient even in his youth. As far as she was concerned,
no practical considerations could diminish the overall effect of
the majestic symmetry of the central portion of the facade with
its triangular pediment flanked as it was by twin apartments,
whose more important rooms at the ends were emphasized by
being projected forward a bit under less elaborate pediments
of their own. The raised entrance level above a rusticated ground
level was reached by a rather daunting double flight of steps
to a massive central doorway.

Daunting was the *mot juste*, Sarah admitted with an inward
shudder she could barely contain as the hired chaise drew to
a halt at the bottom of the stairs. Now that the moment she had
driven herself toward was upon her, she found her spirit had
retreated fourteen years into the past and her body was curiously
resistant to direction—or perhaps it was that her mind was
simply incapable of exercising purposeful direction over her
limbs. She was forced to alight from the chaise under the
compelling eye of the postilion or she might have sat there in
trembling indecision indefinitely.

Refusing his offer to knock and directing him to wait, Sarah
lifted her skirts and began the steep ascent on leaden legs, never
taking her eyes from the massive front door, which seemed to
her terrified fancy to be growing larger and more forbidding
as she approached. She had been excited and expectant on that
other occasion, one that her childish understanding had regarded
in the light of an adventure. Now she wondered with a
retroactive stab of pity if her father's feelings on that day had
been as turbulent as hers were today. Her head felt double its
usual size, and her mind echoed with a vast ringing emptiness,
incapable of forming coherent thought. She moistened dry lips
with the tip of her tongue, prayed that she would be able to
produce some sound when necessary, and lifted the ornate door
knocker and let it fall. The sound didn't register, her painful
attention was on the beautifully grained wooden door, willing
it to open, recalling with a sudden return of nausea that it had

opened the last time—and shut soon after with a resounding finality that had turned her father's ruddy face ashen. *That must not happen!*

"Good afternoon, madam. You'll be the new housekeeper, I expect?"

"I . . . I beg your pardon?" Sarah had to try twice before she could produce a voice in reply to the bewigged and liveried servant who opened the door.

"I asked if you were the housekeeper Lord Eversley arranged to send to us." The man's eyes ran over her black costume and past her to where the post chaise waited.

Never afterward was Sarah able to adequately account for her next action, though desperation and light-headedness certainly played a major role. Her lips parted and a much stronger voice than before said, "Yes. My name is Sarah . . . Sarah Boston."

3

S arah regretted the lie the second the words left her lips; she even tried to deny them, but though she opened her mouth, she was unable to frame a sentence. She was seized with an uncontrollable trembling that prompted the alarmed footman to lower her to a chair and call out to another servant who was approaching the area.

The next half-hour forever remained a blur in Sarah's memory. At the end of it, her chaise was paid off and dismissed and she found herself established in the housekeeper's room on the lowest level, clutching a cup of tea in her shaking hand while her dazed eyes followed the motions of a pleasant-faced maid, who was unpacking her portmanteau. The woman, whose age appeared to be somewhere in the middle thirties, glanced up and met Sarah's look. Her firm generous mouth smiled widely, and there was both kindness and understanding in the fine gray eyes that appraised the newcomer.

"A poor traveler, are you? Well, never mind, you'll feel much more yourself when you get that tea inside you, Mrs. Boston," she said, giving Sarah the courtesy title commonly accorded housekeepers. "We weren't expecting you until Friday, or a carriage would have been sent to Marshfield to meet you. Did you come all the way from London?"

"I . . . Yes, I found I could come a bit earlier." Sarah was floundering, and she raised the cup to her lips and drank thankfully of the hot revivifying liquid while thoughts, regrets, and fears jostled one another for position and precedence in her mind.

What on earth had she done? What had possessed her to hide her identity—worse, to claim a false identity, which would surely be found out in three days when the expected housekeeper appeared? Not that the time signified. Long before then she would have to make her explanations, of course, but to whom? She closed her eyes and swallowed against rising hysteria. At least she was inside Beech Hill. An hour ago her paralyzing fear had been that she would be denied admittance sight unseen. She had put that out of her grandfather's power now. Surely there would be opportunity enough in the next three days to arrange an audience with him. If she lacked the ingenuity to arrange a face-to-face meeting, then she did not deserve to succeed in her mission.

While Sarah was trying to bolster herself into a more confident posture, the maid had been efficiently removing articles of clothing from the portmanteau, which she then stowed away in a chest of drawers. Now she gave an exclamation of admiration that brought Sarah's eyes around in time to see her tenderly remove the last wad of tissue paper that had been stuffed into the bronze-green bonnet, which she now held up. "What a beautiful bonnet!"

"Oh, Lottie, how could you?" Sarah groaned inwardly. If the wretched hat was inappropriate for a poor relation, it was inconceivable for a housekeeper. She smiled weakly, noting a gleam of curiosity in the maid's eyes. "It is lovely, isn't it? It was a present from my last mistress, totally inappropriate, of cousre, but I could not wound her by refusing to accept it."

"No," the maid agreed, but the interest in her eyes sharpened. "Why did you leave your last position, if you do not mind my asking?"

"My . . . my employer died suddenly, and his widow closed up the house to return home to take care of her elderly parents."

"I see. Is this all the baggage you have with you, Mrs. Boston?"

"My trunk will be here in a day or two," Sarah said, still improvising and uneasily aware that those intelligent eyes were studying her openly. There was a bristling pause, then the maid seemed to come to a decision. There was no impertinence in her manner, but she came right to the point.

"You seem very young to have a position of such responsibility, Mrs. Boston, and your accent is that of the gentry."

"Yes, well, my circumstances are a bit unusual," Sarah began, choosing her words with care. "As you have obviously guessed, my family has been established on the land, but we have been growing poorer over the years, and when my father died unexpectedly, what was left of the property went to a distant cousin. My mother was already gone and there was not enough money for me to maintain an independent establishment. I might have gone to live with distant relatives and resigned myself to a life of unpaid drudgery among near strangers, who would have done their duty but who did not welcome my presence," she went on, getting into her stride, "but I opted to work for a salary in the houses of complete strangers instead."

"But a housekeeper is still only an upper servant." The maid's eyes were wide with shock.

"True, and it is perhaps a trifle awkward being neither fish nor fowl, so to speak, but to my way of thinking it was more demeaning to live among the gentry and try to maintain the fiction that I was still one of them when it was obvious that my circumstances belied the claim."

"Could you not have married? Even looking as ill as you did a few moments ago, it's plain to see that you are quite lovely, prettier even than Sir Hector's granddaughter, who, I am told, was considered one of last Season's beauties."

"I never met anyone I wished to marry." Sarah produced the automatic lie while her mind headed down another path. This was a most extraordinary conversation to be having with a servant, but the well-spoken woman facing her was evidently no ordinary servant. "I do not even know your name," she said abruptly.

"My name is Grace Medlark." The maid smiled and her quiet-featured face came alive, rendering her most attractive with her soft brown curls and neat figure.

"Why was it necessary to send to London for a housekeeper, Grace?" Sarah asked, her curiosity as great now as the other woman's had been earlier. "Surely you could have filled the position admirably."

"I could, but the housekeeper must live in. I am married and live in the village with my family. I come in two or three days a week to help out, though it has been every day just lately since the last housekeeper left."

"Why did she go?"

Grace's lips twisted wryly. "Why do any of them go? The general, Sir Hector, is not an easy man to work for; in fact," she added with the air of someone coming to a sudden understanding of a universal truth, "that about sums him up: the general is not an easy man. Things were different in the old days when my mother worked here. That was when Lady Ridgemont was still alive. He loved her very much, as did most everyone who knew her. She had a softening effect on her husband and generally acted as a mediator between him and the servants, and the locals, and even their children. From the time she died—it must have been all of five-and-twenty years ago—the general began to grow more and more difficult to get along with. He had already disowned one of his children, and the others only come here when they want something. He has alienated all of his neighbors except Lord Eversley, and of late there has been a steady procession of servants coming and going."

"I am astonished that you bothered to unpack for me," Sarah said dryly, and noted the gleam of amused understanding that appeared in Grace's eyes. She would have liked to pump the maid for information about her father but prudently refrained. She did inquire, "How is it that this Lord Eversley has remained friendly enough to assist in hiring a housekeeper?"

"Lord Eversley's father and the general were fast friends in the old days, and the son seems to feel almost a filial duty toward his old neighbor. The estates adjoin and share the woodland between them. Except for the family's rare visits, Lord Eversley has been the only caller to be welcomed at Beech Hill for several years. Before Sir Hector became so poorly, Lord Eversley was used to stop in three or four times a week to play a game of chess with him."

"Sir Hector is ill?"

"He has long suffered from a painful arthritic complaint and the gout, but of late his heart has weakened. He has not left his room in nearly a month, and the doctor is quite concerned, I believe. I know that he spoke to Lord Eversley last week when he chanced to call during one of Doctor Rydell's visits. You look distressed, Mrs. Boston."

"Sarah. Please call me Sarah."

"Very well, then, Sarah. You need not concern yourself personally with Sir Hector's health except insofar as it imposes on the housekeeping. Any personal care he requires is performed by his valet. Somers has been with the general for thirty years or more; indeed, he is the only servant in residence who has been here for any length of time. Even the estate steward has taken over only in the past year when his father, who filled the position before him, died. The maids and indoor servants come and go, and we find it nearly impossible to keep a cook, the general being notoriously hard to please and prone to complain about his food. If I mistake not, the last housekeeper never laid eyes on Sir Hector during her entire stay. She said it was like working for a phantom, but she found out otherwise when her supervision of the laundry became slack. Sir Hector likes his sheets soft and scented with bayberry. It is unlikely that you need have any contact with him at all."

Sarah smiled faintly, thinking all the while that Grace could not know how far from the mark her attempts at offering reassurance were falling.

When Sarah had recovered her composure and freshened her appearance, Grace brought her along to the steward's room, where she was introduced to Millbank, Sir Hector's butler, and Tom Gridley, the young estate steward. Presently the maid left her to return to her home, promising to act as her guide the following day, when it would be time enough to initiate the new housekeeper into her duties. Sarah watched her go with the same desperation with which a child being deposited at school for the first time must regard his parents' disappearing carriage.

Sarah had cause to be grateful later that evening to the unnatural pallor that had lingered even after the migraine had largely departed. She dined with the upper servants, an occasion fraught with danger for someone attempting a desperate masquerade. She had never spent any time in a large country house and certainly could not be expected to know anything of the rigid protocol existing belowstairs. For once she had no qualms about taking advantage of the fact that men found her misleading appearance of fragility appealing. She said very little at table, but her brain was functioning at a feverish rate as she tried to assimilate the nuances of the relationships existing among those who would be her associates for the next day or two. She liked ruddy-faced Tom Gridley, who seemed to be an honest, easygoing fellow who took people at face value. In contrast, the butler took pains to impress upon her his superiority over the local servants by virtue of having worked for a time as under-butler in an earl's London establishment. Her instincts told her he was also the type to take as many liberties as a female permitted. She didn't care for the predatory look in his blue-gray eyes and kept her own on her plate when she sensed his attention swinging her way.

The other two persons at table the first night were Somers, Sir Hector's valet, and Mrs. Hadley, the cook. The latter eased her considerable bulk onto a chair with a gusty sigh of relief and, after briefly acknowledging Sarah's presence with a friendly greeting, launched herself into a litany of complaints concerning the deteriorating condition of her feet, knees, and back as a result of long hours of working in the stone-floored kitchen. She directed her remarks mainly toward the newcomer, who contrived to look properly sympathetic, while conscious that all present went on unconcernedly with their meals. It seemed safe to assume that Mrs. Hadley's complaints were a regular part of the program at supper. The cook dominated the conversation, being as garrulous as she was wide, but though she could be counted on for a contribution—and many of them tart—on any subject raised, there seemed to be no real malice in the woman's makeup. She kept a sharp eye on the kitchen maid who waited on them, correcting her once or twice, but then dismissing her in good time to return to the more lively society of the servants' hall.

The general's valet stood in striking contrast to the over-stuffed, voluble cook. Somers was a thin desiccated little man with a pointed nose, a thin mouth, clawlike fingers, and a fringe of gray hair framing a bald pate. He was sparing of speech, initiating none and only replying to the questions of the others when he chose to exert himself. By the end of the meal Sarah had concluded that he was held in healthy respect by all the others, even the self-important Millbank deferring to him on occasion. Surprisingly, he had the appetite of a vulture, and Mrs. Hadley called his attention to the choicest bits offered. The food was plentiful and of a good quality. Though Sarah had no standard of comparison, she was quick to note that the servants at Beech Hill, at least the upper servants, did well for themselves.

Finding herself ravenous after two days of near fasting, she made a excellent meal under the approving eye of Mrs. Hadley, who forthrightly declared that the new housekeeper looked "peaky" and promised to "fill her out" with good wholesome food. Won over by the woman's genuine goodwill, Sarah dropped her guard and smiled warmly back, an action she had cause to regret as she felt the quickening of interest around the table in her person. Her face flamed and she avoided the butler's eye, but she hadn't missed the peacocky gesture of adjusting the folds of his cravat. Even Somers, who had barely glanced at her upon introduction, was now regarding her with an intentness that rendered her uncomfortable. Her smile faltered and she missed the first question in the kindly inquisition now conducted by Mrs. Hadley, who repeated her question patiently. Sarah recited the fabrication she had concocted for Grace Medlark that afternoon. She was beginning to doubt her creative ingenuity and ability to satisfy the cook's more pressing inquiries when Tom Gridley unknowingly came to her rescue.

"How was the general today, Somers? Any better?"

To Sarah's palpitating relief, the casual question sparked a discussion of her grandfather's symptoms that allowed her to fade into the background once more, where she was determined to remain. Pleading travel fatigue, she excused herself shortly thereafter, retiring to the more-than-adequate bedchamber that was assigned to the housekeeper. As she removed her clothing and prepared for bed, she could not prevent the ironic reflection that Sir Hector Ridgemont's servants were considerably better-housed and -fed than his grandchildren.

Though perhaps undeserved, Sarah's sleep was that of the just that night, and she didn't stir the next morning until a diminutive maidservant appeared with a cup of chocolate, an unlooked-for luxury that opened her eyes wide. Despite the auspicious beginning to her stay at Beech Hill, Sarah's nerves were vibrating as she took stock of her appearance. The black dress with its delicate white bib and collar, recently pressed by another little maid, was neat and sober enough, but the charmingly frivolous cap did not, to her critical eye, bespeak the housekeeper. It would have to do, however, since she possessed no other and could scarcely ask Mrs. Hadley or one of the maids for the loan of a mobcap. She had never had her hair cut according to the dictates of fashion because her father had cherished a prejudice in favor of long hair. The worried lines smoothed out of her face as she concluded, mistakenly, that by pulling back the customary soft waves over her temples into the bun at the nape of her neck she had added years and dignity befitting her assumed position. Anyway, it was the best she could do.

Grace Medlark conducted Sarah all over the large house after introducing her to the laundress and the eight housemaids and two laundry-room maids who would all be under her direction. Long before the tour was completed Sarah had arrived at a sober appreciation that the position of housekeeper in a house the size of Beech Hill was no sinecure, even when the resident family consisted of a solitary invalid.

The two-story great hall probably had not been used except sporadically for large ceremonial occasions for generations, but its location as the center of the house demanded that it be perfectly maintained at all times. The saloon behind it had been used for family dining when a family indeed resided on the estate, and was still kept in readiness to perform this function no matter how seldom required. Around this central core were four symmetrical apartments and between the apartments were two front staircases and two other good-sized chambers, a chapel on one side of the great hall and a library on the other. Each corner apartment contained an antechamber or withdrawing room, a bedchamber and two small rooms behind this, taking up the length of the bedchamber. The larger of these had originally functioned as a servant's bedroom and the other served variously as a cabinet or dressing room or private sanctum. Each corner apartment also had a back staircase leading down to the rusticated basement level for the use of the servants.

A first-floor room above the dining saloon had been designed for a family living room, Grace explained, but like all the other apartments on that level, it was rarely needed of late. A second floor contained nurseries and bedrooms for female servants. The indoor male servants were billeted in the rusticated level while the outdoor servants slept in the stable wing. Sarah learned that the one modern innovation in the house had been the wiring of the main apartments a few years before so that a numbered bell board outside the servants' hall could record from which room a summons had come and the appropriate servant could be sent off to answer it. Since no one was in residence save the general, Sarah could not work up much enthusiasm for this ingenious invention. She would have infinitely preferred the convenience of running water above the lowest level of the house. She reminded herself that the problem of toting water all over the house for cleaning purposes would belong to the real housekeeper in two days. To this paragon also would belong the domain of the stillroom with its stoves for preparing tea and coffee and the making of items from biscuits to preserves and medicaments to be stored on its shelves. While she was here, she would enjoy taking a shelf-by-shelf tour of the fascinating place, though Grace said the previous housekeeper had shirked her responsibility in this area also and had let the supplies dwindle without replacement.

Sarah thoroughly enjoyed her introduction to her father's childhood home, but by the time Grace left her to catch up on some duties of her own, she had discovered that it was going to be no simple matter to secure an audience with her grandfather. His personal apartment was the one in the southwestern corner of the house next to the chapel. Grace was the only maid he would tolerate in his rooms to do the cleaning, but even she had been excluded from his bedchamber these past weeks. When showing Sarah the withdrawing room that was part of this apartment, she had nodded toward a closed door in the far wall and confided in a whisper that poor Somers scarcely ever got to leave the apartment these days as he had had to take over the cleaning chores in the bedchamber also.

At the time Sarah had experienced a little thrill of excitement at actually standing in the next room to her grandfather at last, but by late afternoon of a busy day she had come to realize that in order to make sure of seeing him before the arrival of the real housekeeper, it might be necessary to walk boldly into his bedchamber uninvited. She dreaded the necessity, which would set her at even more of a disadvantage than she already was, but she could see no alternative if her grandfather had no immediate intention of even meeting his new housekeeper.

Sarah was in the kitchen chatting with Mrs. Hadley before the servants' meal when Somers came in carrying a tray, his air faintly apologetic. "The general didn't fancy the custard, after all, Cook. He said it didn't taste like the old-fashioned sort."

The cook's huge curled knuckles went to her hips, elbows aggressively sticking out as she retorted, "That receipt has been in my family for generations. If that don't make it old-fashioned, I dunno what would."

"Somers, I have a receipt for custard that my father was used to say came from his mother," Sarah said eagerly, but it was the cook who replied, "Well, it can't hurt to try it, though I doubt anything would please the general these days, poor man, he's that finicky. You tell it to me tomorrow, dearie, and I'll make some for him."

"Mrs. Hadley, I know you need to get off your poor feet for a spell at this time of day," Sarah said, smiling coaxingly at the puffing cook. "Why not let me mix up some custard now, then it can bake while we have our meal, and Somers will be able to take some up to Sir Hector before he goes to sleep tonight.'' Before the cook could voice the doubt spreading over her globular countenance, Sarah turned to the valet and continued, ''The only thing is, Somers, that the custard receipt calls for brandy, so will you please find some for me—the good brandy, please?'' Her smile became mischievous as the doubt spread to the spare features of the valet, and she held up her right hand. ''I solemnly promise not to sample a drop, Somers; it will all go in the custard.''

Sarah held her breath, but her smile had done the trick. The cook gave a comfortable chuckle and Somers relaxed the sternness of his features minimally. ''Very good, miss,'' he said, handing her the tray he still carried. ''I'll fetch the brandy.''

Sarah was less attentive to the conversation at table that evening. Her thoughts were with her custard baking gently in an oven. It had to be perfect, it just had to be! That custard could be her ticket to her grandfather's presence. Not that she would not get to see him eventually, she reassured herself, but infinitely better to be summoned than to burst in uninvited. It was all she could do to keep her eyes off the clock on the sideboard while the meal dragged on. Only another ten minutes or so now before the custard would be done. It wouldn't do to overcook it.

It was a salutory lesson in self-discipline to sit quietly at the table, answering when spoken to, when the success of her mission might be hanging in the balance. She glanced at the clock. Fifty minutes since she had placed the custard in the oven. Her glance winged to the cook, willing her to cease her conversation with Millbank. She would give Mrs. Hadley five minutes longer to act on her own, then she would have to slip in a casual reminder. It would never do to let the cook suspect that a simple custard was of paramount importance to the housekeeper.

It lacked one minute to the time limit Sarah had set when Mrs. Hadley heaved herself out of her chair with a sigh. ''I've to check something in the oven,'' she explained, edging her bulky frame away from the table.

Sarah forced herself to remain in her place over the next fifteen minutes, though her contributions to the conversation were uninspired at best. At the end of that time, Mrs. Hadley stuck her head back into the room to tell Somers that the custard was ready whenever he should care to take it up to the general. At that point Sarah excused herself to go to her own room. Her nerves were on the stretch and she feared she would give herself away. Impossible to sit decorously at a table participating in mindless small talk when her brother's future was at stake.

In her room, she felt too keyed up to remain stationary. There was no real cause to expect a summons at all, she told herself dampingly as she opened one of the linen presses that lined half of the room. Even if her grandfather, in his weakened state, sampled and liked the custard, it did not necessarily follow that he would recognize his wife's receipt, or that he would have any interest in learning where it came from. She had assumed too much, she thought as she began to inventory the household linens. She had better resign herself to the necessity of shamelessly invading her grandfather's privacy tomorrow if she were to put her case to him during this grace period.

She was closing one of the linen presses, too dispirited to continue the task, when a knock sounded at the door. Her heartbeat, which had slowed down over the last half-hour, began a rapid tattoo in her breast again as she crossed the floor to open the door.

Somers stood there, his thin features inscrutable. "The general presents his compliments, miss, and desires you to wait upon him in his room."

"R—right now, Somers?"

"Yes, miss, if it should be convenient."

Sarah recognized the polite rider as the mere concession to form that it was. The summons had come. There was not even time to glance into a mirror to check her appearance.

"Very well, Somers." She stepped across the threshold, closing the door quietly behind her, and meekly followed the small lean figure toward the main staircase. It would have been quicker to use the backstairs that led out of the cabinet behind her grandfather's bedchamber, but this was evidently to be a rather formal visit.

During that long walk, Somers did not so much as utter a syllable that would give her a clue as to what to expect, and

Sarah was too frightened to ask any of the questions crowding into her head. She entered the withdrawing room on his heels and was led over to the door that Grace had pointed out earlier. It was still closed, but the valet gave a discreet tap and opened it for Sarah to step through.

"Mrs. Boston, sir."

She sensed rather than saw that Somers had remained in the antechamber when he closed the door. Her eyes did a quick circuit of the room and located the tester bed against the shorter wall to the right of where she had entered from the middle of one of the long walls. She was vaguely aware of heavily draped windows on the walls to her left and a fireplace containing a merrily burning fire across from where she had entered, but her eyes had instinctively sought the figure propped up against the pillows of the huge bed. He was probably having a much better look at her than she was at him, she realized, standing quietly in the glow of a candelabrum on a nearby table while her eyes adjusted to the semigloom of the area by the bed.

Sarah's first impression of her grandfather was one of immense stillness; in fact, it passed through her mind that he might be asleep, until she became conscious of a gleam of light that must be reflecting from his eyes. She received a fleeting impression that the rigid figure was in the grip of a strong emotion before the white hand on the coverlet relaxed its tight grip on the fabric. A voice that startled her with its unexpected strength snapped, "Well, do not stand there like a stick, woman, come in. You say your name is Boston?"

"Yes—that is, I—" In the act of charting her way safely around the obstacles of a table and an oddly placed footstool, Sarah realized she had mechanically repeated the lie that had gained her entrance to Beech Hill.

But before she could correct herself, that whiplash voice demanded, "What is the first part?"

"The first part?"

"Of your name, of course. Are you hard-of-hearing or just slow-witted?"

"I . . . Neither," she managed, aware of his snort of disdain before she swallowed and said with determined civility as she stopped about three feet from the side of the bed, "My name is Sarah, Sir Hector."

"A good plain name, Sarah; it was my wife's name."

"Yes, I know," Sarah murmured, intent on studying the gaunt-featured face glaring at her from his nest of pillows. This then was the man who had played such a vital though invisible role in her life. Somehow she had never gone beyond her childish picture of her grandfather as a stone-faced giant, domineering, unyielding, loud-voiced, and harsh, whereas . . .

He was speaking again, roaring actually, and she stared at him blankly. "I . . . I beg your pardon?"

"Don't bother telling me your wits don't wander, girl, because I wouldn't believe you. I asked you how you knew my wife's name was Sarah?"

"I heard it mentioned, Sir Hector. I—"

"In the servants' hall, I collect. That's all servants know how to do these days: gossip about their betters. So you are the prize housekeeper Eversley found in London, are you?"

"Well, I—"

"Did he interview you personally?"

"No." Sarah stopped, scenting a trap. "Actually, Sir—"

"I thought not. He'd have seen you were much too young for the position. What did you do, girl, smile at the agent and flirt with your eyelashes?"

"No, I did not," Sarah said firmly, feeling that she had wandered into Bedlam and determined to clear matters up if her grandfather would ever allow her to complete a sentence. "Sir Hector—" she began.

"Well, you must have used some kind of female trickery on him because anyone but a fool can see you're nothing but a chit of a girl. Still, that custard you made was very tolerable indeed. Reminded me of the way the kitchen made it years ago. I'll think it over and talk to you tomorrow." Sir Hector's voice had diminished considerably by the end of this speech. Though beginning to be concerned that he might have overtaxed his strength, Sarah was desperate to make her explanations while she had his ear.

"Sir Hector, I must tell—"

"Not now, girl, tomorrow. Send Somers to me when you leave." The general waved a dismissing hand. The piercing eyes that had followed her progress into the room closed abruptly.

Sarah stared into the shuttered face of the old war-horse for an undecided moment and conceded defeat. She turned, taking her frustration with her, and soberly delivered Sir Hector's message to the waiting Somers before heading back to her own quarters at a much slower pace than when she had come this way fifteen minutes earlier.

Her brow creased in frowning concentration, Sarah went over the strange interview just concluded. She had been mentally prepared for an acrimonious scene with her grandfather, though she had rather expected cold uncaring formality from him. What she had not expected after such an epoch-making event was this flat feeling of anticlimax. Nothing had been settled. She would have to stoke up her courage all over again tomorrow to present Richard's case to her grandfather.

The face of the man she had just left stayed with Sarah long after she had attained the comparative privacy of the house-keeper's room. One thing the abortive meeting had accomplished was to remove forever the image of a gigantic ogre that had shadowed her childhood. It had not been possible to assess accurately the size of the man lying in his bed, but whatever stature the general may have maintained in his prime, at eighty-six he was a gaunt old man whose flesh was inadequate to cover a once substantial frame. She'd still have known him anywhere by the thin beaky nose and large nostrils that her father had also possessed. Even Richard at eleven was developing a restrained version of the same distinctive profile. Sir Hector also had a full head of silky white hair at his advanced age, perhaps another family trait that might be considered to offset the hawkish nose.

Sarah recalled her first impression that the man staring at her with piercing dark eyes had been rigid with some strong emotion. By the time she had come close enough to see his features clearly, that impression had been banished by the cold calculating expression that was no doubt natural to him. That at least accorded with the picture she had carried around in her head all these years—that and the parade-ground voice, which in timbre and strength would do credit to an active sergeant major. She had never pictured her grandfather as mortal, or even old, however, and the man she had just met was obviously both.

As Sarah slowly prepared for bed on her second night at Beech Hill, she reflected soberly that she might well have been too late had she allowed herself to be swayed by Lottie's arguments urging a postponement of this meeting until the weather should have improved.

4

The man frowning over a letter he was reading was too engrossed to hear the opening of the breakfast-room door. He did look up as a light footstep sounded on the parquet floor, and his dark-browed, dark-skinned face lightened into an affectionate smile.

"Good morning, Mama. You are looking very pretty and bobbish today."

"Why, thank you, dearest. Can't you simply taste the hint of spring in the air today? Good morning, Timpkins. Thank you." This last was addressed to the butler, who pulled out a chair for the viscountess with a flourish and as broad a smile as a well-trained butler ever permits himself.

"How many times must I remind you not to encourage Timpkins to flirt with you, Mama?" The teasing drawl was pitched softly as the butler left the room.

But Lady Eversley said, "Hush, Mark, he might hear you. I will not have you making sport of our faithful Timpkins." The smile trembling on her pursed lips negated the severity of the scolding words. "I must say, though, I am relieved to see you can joke this morning. You were scowling so fiercely when I entered that I feared you'd had bad news."

"You mean this?" Lord Eversley tapped the paper he had laid down on his mother's entrance as he pushed the cream pitcher closer to her. "Not bad news, just puzzling. It's a note from the general asking me to call in at Beech Hill so he might thank me for finding him a gem of a housekeeper."

"What's puzzling about that?" Lady Eversley set her straight

46

white teeth into a slice of toast with a satisfying crunch and put up a dainty fingertip to catch a dribble of butter at the corner of her lips, which she then proceeded to lick clean.

"Better not let Aunt Abernathy catch you at that trick. She'd be mortified."

Lady Eversley looked up quickly and blushed, deepening the amusement in her son's eyes.

"Don't look so guilty, Mama. You escaped your elder sister's censorious eye forever when you married Papa. She cannot pursue you into your own home with her prissy notions of proper conduct for a lady."

"No, but Elmira was nearly always in the right of it, you know. I fear I was a sad trial to her."

"Not for long. Papa snapped you up within a month of your come-out, happily for Anthea and me. Just imagine if he had preferred a pattern card of propriety like Aunt Abernathy. It's too horrible to contemplate." Lord Eversley delivered himself of a theatrical shudder, which brought a dimple out of hiding at the corner of his mother's mouth.

"Now you are being ridiculous," she scolded, "and you didn't answer my question. What is so puzzling about the general wanting to thank you for finding him a new housekeeper?"

"The fact that unless I have totally misunderstood my latest communication from Coke, the woman he engaged for Beech Hill is not due to arrive there until tomorrow."

"Probably she was able to get away earlier, after all." Lady Eversley returned her attention to her interrupted breakfast.

Lord Eversley pushed back his chair and rose. "Most likely, that is the story. Anyway, it is time I was looking in on the general again. His condition seems to have worsened rapidly of late. Rydell is worried about him and so am I—enough that I thought it my duty to write to Horace Ridgemont last week. I received a reply from him yesterday. It seems the whole family is about to descend on Beech Hill."

"Like a pack of jackals!"

"As you say, Mama, but the general did not exactly encourage the affections of his children over the years."

"I know. I have not forgotten how harshly he treated poor

Gerald. It broke Lady Ridgemont's heart in the end, but for all his faults, I cannot think he deserves the ingratitude I always sense in Horace and Adelaide. He has been more than generous to them and their children, but they never visit him except when they want something. There is a pettiness and hypocrisy about them that they never learned from either of their parents.''

The viscount put comforting hands on his mother's shoulders and bent down to kiss her soft cheek. ''They are his family, such as they are, and they have a right to be apprised of his deteriorating health. If I had not written, Rydell would have.''

His mother turned slightly to smile into concerned dark eyes as she patted one of his hands. ''Of course, dearest. Now, you had best go warn the general about what is in store for him. And perhaps the new housekeeper too, poor soul,'' she added feelingly. ''I do not envy her the next few days.''

The new housekeeper at Beech Hill awoke that morning with no inkling that her state was pitiable, but only a firm resolution to make the explanation to her grandfather that she had been unable to make during their first meeting. Time was running out on her. It would be so much less embarrassing for all concerned if she could make her request and secure her grandfather's answer today so that she might remove herself from the house before the real housekeeper arrived. She was considering when might be the best time to beard the lion in his den when another summons was delivered by Somers. This time, however, she kept him waiting for a moment while she washed her dusty hands and neatened her hair. She needed the assurance that she looked presentable when she made her confession to her grandfather and put forth her request.

As he had the evening before, Somers opened the door into the general's bedchamber for her and announced, ''Mrs. Boston,'' before closing it behind her. This time, however, the draperies were pulled back from the three long windows, letting sunlight flood the room, illuminating the snapping dark eyes of the man in the bed and glinting off the gold fob and tiepin worn by a second gentleman with equally dark and even more forbidding eyes.

Sarah was brought up short by the sight of the tall broad-shouldered man rising from a chair near the bed until he fairly loomed over her. Her eyes flew to the watchful old man in the bed. "Oh, I beg your pardon, Sir Hector. Somers must have been mistaken. I was told you wished to see me, but I'll come back later when you are disengaged."

"No, no, Mrs. Boston, stay. I thought you would like to meet the person through whose good offices you were engaged to come to Beech Hill," Sir Hector replied in the most moderate tone of voice Sarah had yet heard from him. "I have just been thanking Lord Eversley for his assistance and was persuaded you would wish to do likewise."

Sarah froze as the sense of her grandfather's words penetrated, and her hands grasped each other tightly in front of her to still their tendency to tremble. She had been tinglingly aware of a controlled menace radiating from the silent spectator but had kept her eyes fixed on the figure sitting up among the pillows. There was nothing for it, of course, except to brazen it out. She gathered her courage about her and turned to meet the black-browed stare that had been trained on her since she had entered the room.

To her credit she did not flinch from the scorching contact, and her voice, though a trifle weaker than she would have preferred, sounded composed in her own ears as she agreed. "Yes, certainly. How do you do, Lord Eversley?" She remembered just in time to drop a demure curtsy.

The viscount's bow was sketchy at best. "Your servant, ma'am . . . Mrs., er, Boston?"

"Yes, that's correct," Sarah replied, her chin tilting as she heard and resented the questioning inflection.

"My agent, Mr. Maxwell, did not mention that the person he had engaged was so young," Lord Eversley continued in an abrupt manner.

"Perhaps because he did not consider me too young for the position, sir."

"In view of your long years of experience at housekeeping on a large estate?"

Sarah's resentment grew that he should play cat-and-mouse

with her, and she cast all caution to the winds, replying coolly, "In view of my satisfactory performance over a moderate span of time in a bustling country house on a slightly lesser scale than Beech Hill."

"May one ask why you found it necessary to leave so satisfactory a position?"

"My employer died suddenly and his widow closed up the house to return to her old home to support her elderly parents, who were in failing health." She tacked on a hasty "sir" at the end and turned again to her grandfather, who appeared to be following the quick exchange with an expression she might almost term sly amusement on his hollow-cheeked face. "You must be wishing to get on with your visit, Sir Hector. If you will excuse me, I—"

"The general and I had finished our little talk before you came in, Mrs. . . . Boston," Lord Eversley intervened smoothly. "As there are one or two questions I would like to ask you about my agent, and as I see our host in growing tired, may I suggest we both retire and allow him to rest."

Sarah would have said her grandfather was looking remarkably alert, but even as her eyes sought his, a look of exhaustion crept over his features and he waved a dismissing hand. "Yes, yes, I must rest now. I'll see you in the next day or so, Eversley."

"After you, Mrs. Boston." The viscount was holding open the door almost before Sarah realized he had moved over to it with the quickness of a cat, cutting off her escape. Wordlessly she passed through, looking straight ahead.

Seeing Somers making a show of tidying up some ornaments on a tabletop in the antechamber, Lord Eversley took her elbow in a light grip and said, "We'll go into the library, Mrs. Boston. We won't be disturbed there."

Sarah followed him straight across the width of the great hall and into the antechamber corresponding to her grandfather's for the suite in the southeastern corner of the house. He opened a door in its long inner wall and she found herself in the corridor behind the great hall, certainly the shortest route to the library, though not the most public. It was no comfort to Sarah to note the gentleman's familiarity with the layout of his neighbor's house.

He pushed open the library door and stood back. She had no option but to enter, though she took only a step or two before turning to confront the domineering and antagonistic figure of Lord Eversley. Strangely, her initial terror of discovery had faded, leaving a residue of resentment against the man who had aroused the uncomfortable emotion. After all, she intended to make herself known to her grandfather at the earliest opportunity. Though she would naturally prefer that the situation not become known in the neighborhood, she considered herself capable of dealing with this rough, uncivil man.

Brave words, but she felt her color rise under his searching regard, and she was unable to carry out a short-lived resolution to make him speak first, though she held her ground in the teeth of a great desire to put more distance between herself and this man. "You said you had questions you wished to ask, sir?" she began, furious that her voice should sound so breathless.

"Yes, your name for a start."

"You heard my name," she said with a fair assumption of surprise.

"I heard the name you gave General Ridgemont, but I doubt it is your real name."

"I'm afraid I cannot help your doubts, sir."

"Do not be pert with me, young woman. I know you are not the person hired for this position and I intend to discover who you are. There is a fortune in portable treasures in this house."

For the moment she ignored the implication in his last statement. "How can you possibly know I am not the housekeeper hired by your agent? You did not personally conduct the interviews."

"You gave yourself away earlier when you did not correct me when I said my agent's name was Maxwell. It isn't. Can you supply the correct name?"

Sarah bit her lip. "The name has slipped my mind for the moment. I had interviews for several positions and cannot be expected to recall—"

"Stubble it! The name of the woman my agent hired for this

post was Glamorgan.'' The tight control Lord Eversley had
imposed on his simmering temper showed definite signs of
cracking. ''I intend to find out who you are if I have to shake
it out of you,'' he said very softly, taking a step forward as
if to put this threat into action.

Sarah's puny defenses crumbled. ''How fortunate to be born
masculine and thus be always able to bring brute strength to
bear in any contest with a female,'' she cried with some
bitterness.

For a second there was a flicker of something that might have
been regret in his eyes, and his voice lost some of its former
hardness as he said with a faint touch of humor, ''You women
have your weapons too. Do not begrudge us our brute strength.''

''But I do,'' she said forlornly. ''It makes life so unfair.''

Lord Eversley's hand lifted in an involuntary gesture toward
her cheek, but he checked it before she noticed the movement
as she was staring rather blindly at the shelves beyond his
shoulder. His lips tightened. ''Who are you?''

''My name is Sarah Ridgemont,'' she said simply, holding
his gaze while he registered incredulity.

''Sarah . . . Ridgemont? Gerald Ridgemont's daughter?''

''Yes. Did you know my father?''

Lord Eversley shook his head. ''I was too young when he
left to remember him,'' he said rather absently, obviously busy
dealing with the implications of her disclosure. ''Do you have
some proof of your identity? I assume the general is not yet
aware of who you claim to be. And why should you conceal
your identity in the first place and attempt to pass yourself off
as a housekeeper?'' His gaze had sharpened again by the time
he rapped out his last question.

''What would constitute proof of identity?'' Sarah asked,
anxiously fastening on to the vital word. ''I have some of my
father's papers and my mother's marriage lines, but not with
me.'' Somehow she had never considered that her grandfather
might choose not to believe in her existence when confronted
with it.

''You speak of your father's papers. Where is your father?''

"He died over a year ago, just about a year after we returned from America."

"Does your grandfather know this?" Those straight black brows drew together.

"I wrote to him at the time, but he never acknowledged my letter, just as he never acknowledged any other communication over the years." A shade of weariness had crept into the soft voice, and Lord Eversley put a hand under her arm again.

"Come, sit over here and tell me the whole story of how you came to be here today in such unlikely circumstances."

Sarah did as requested, touching lightly on their years in America, her brother's birth and her mother's death, coming at last to her recent illness with its aftermath of doubt that she and Lottie could provide a secure future for Richard. He heard her out in silence, his aspect growing steadily grimmer as her tale unfolded, until she spoke of their initial hopes and subsequent disappointment in the hat shop, whereupon he uttered an explosive, "My God" that caused her to falter and look up at him with stricken eyes.

"Is it so very bad?" she whispered. "I know that in England people of the upper class do not engage in trade, but it is not so in America, and we have to live," she finished defensively. "There is not much point in starving to death for the sake of remaining true to one's origins."

"No, no, forgive me. I meant no criticism. What about your mother's family?"

"My mother was the only child of elderly parents. We did not go to America until after my grandparents died. Mother had a small annuity, which came to me, but it is barely adequate to feed and house us."

"I see. So you came very recently to a decision to ask your grandfather for help. Have I that correctly?"

"Yes, but only for Richard's education, so that he will have a trade or profession in which to support himself."

"Then, why the masquerade? Having taken the decision to appeal to your grandfather, why are you in this house under an assumed name, pretending to be a housekeeper?"

Sarah hung her head. "I don't know if I can make you understand what went into such an impulsive and—I see now—foolish decision. I'm not entirely certain I perfectly understand myself, but I was dreadfully afraid that I would be turned away at the door when I gave my name, like the last time. That thought had been with me, torturing me throughout the long ride on the stagecoach. Also, I was still feeling very unwell from the migraine and . . . Well, when the servant opened the door and assumed I was the new housekeeper, I seized on this as a way in. Of course, I wish now that I had not done it but . . ." Her words trailed off and she lifted a hand and let it fall in a little gesture of helplessness.

"You must tell your grandfather the truth without delay."

"You need not look so sternly at me. I have every intention of doing so. I tried to tell him at our first meeting last night, but he did not give me a chance. I shall certainly tell him today because the real housekeeper is expected tomorrow."

"She's not the only person arriving tomorrow," Lord Eversley said grimly. "Thanks to a newly developed talent for meddling, I took it upon myself to write to your Uncle Horace advising him of his father's poor state of health, with the result that he is coming for a visit with his entire family, a wife and two sons. Not only that," he continued in the face of her appalled exclamation, "but he tells me it is more than likely that his sister, your Aunt Adelaide, Lady Townsend, will also descend on Beech Hill with offspring in tow."

"Oh, dear," gasped Sarah, "how disconcerting!"

He smiled without mirth. "To say the least. This is going to be a very well-attended deathbed scene."

"Is my grandfather dying?"

Her expression was serious but not unduly concerned, and Eversley had to remind himself that the young woman facing him across the length of a fireside sofa had no cause to mourn the passing of the man who had denied her and her brother their birthright. "His doctor and I feared so last week, but I must say that I thought him somewhat improved today. Unless your little surprise should give him a relapse," he added dryly.

The color drained out of Sarah's face and she stared at him

in mounting horror. "Do you mean that it will be my fault if
he dies? That I should not, after all, tell him who I am?"

"No, no," he said hastily. "That was a poor attempt at a
joke. The general survived my announcement of his children's
pending visit; in fact, he seemed pleased in a strange sort of
way. He even made a ghoulish remark about a flock of vultures
coming in for the kill."

A shiver passed through Sarah's delicate frame. "Of which
I am another," she said on a sigh. Her chin firmed and she
looked him straight in the eye. "I may not be very proud of
myself, Lord Eversley, but I intend that my brother shall have
a fair chance in life and I shall do everything in my power to
see that he gets it." She stood up, indicating that the meeting
was at an end. "Are you satisfied that I am telling the truth,
Lord Eversley?"

"I'll soon find out if you're not," he replied ungallantly,
noting the spark of anger in soft amber eyes, though she made
no retort. As he got to his feet, she bethought herself of something. He could see the indecision in her face, and her hands
had clasped each other again. "Yes?" he asked in
unencouraging accents.

"I know I have no right to beg a favor from a stranger, sir,
but I wonder if you would be so kind as to frank a letter for
me. Lottie and Richard will be expecting me back today or
tomorrow at the latest, and I do not wish them to worry. May
I—?"

"Of course," he said gruffly. "Write it now. I'll take it with
me."

Lord Eversley never took his eyes off Sarah's lithe figure as
she spun about and headed toward the large desk in search of
paper. His thoughts defied description as he watched her
accomplish her task without self-consciousness or wasted effort.
To himself he owned to a rare disinclination to leave a woman's
company. To Miss Ridgemont he made a stiff bow as part of
a spare and formal leavetaking some few minutes later.

Lord Eversley's mind was occupied with the events of his
visit to Beech Hill all the way home, and each and every thought
originated in the person of Sarah Ridgemont or arrived at her

shortly thereafter. There was work to be done that he had postponed in order to obey the general's request. He spent a busy afternoon going about estate business, but Sarah's pale face intruded between his eyes and whatever he was reading more often than was acceptable to his peace of mind.

That the situation brewing at Beech Hill was piquant went without saying, and he had the satisfaction of seeing his mother rendered nearly speechless with astonishment as he gave her the bare bones of the story when they were at last alone in the family parlor after dinner.

"Gerald's daughter at Beech Hill as a housekeeper—I cannot believe it!"

"That never should have happened. As best I can understand, she simply funked the telling of her name—too afraid of being turned away. Did you know that when she was twelve years old Gerald brought her to meet her grandfather before taking his family to America, and the general refused to see them?"

"No, I never even knew Gerald went to America or that there was a son. Did the general not tell you of Gerald's death? You have grown closer to him than anyone these past few years."

"Not a word."

"Then it is possible that Horace and Adelaide are also unaware that they no longer have a brother. How very sad, to be sure."

"From what Sarah told me, I don't believe Gerald ever had any further communication with either of them after his father disowned him."

Lady Eversley shook her head at the folly and sadness of it all. "Tell me about Sarah," she begged eagerly. "I knew of her existence because Lady Ridgemont told me Gerald had written to his parents of the child's birth. She found the letter quite by accident. The general actually intended to keep the news from her. I was very fond of Lady Ridgemont. My own mother being dead, she had been like a substitute mother to me from the time I arrived at Eversley as a bride. I have always felt that that final cruelty took away her will to live. She was dead within the year, and any chance at a reconciliation between father and son died with her. That was about twenty-five years ago, so Sarah must be six-and-twenty by now.''

"She looks younger despite her disguise."

"Does she favor the Ridgemonts?"

"She certainly doesn't have the Ridgemont nose. She is of moderate height with a light and graceful figure, though she's too thin. She has a creamy complexion, a little too pale, but that may be because she has been ill lately. Her features have the serene classical perfection of a Renaissance madonna except for an incongruous dimple in the center of her chin. She was wearing a cap of some sort, but her hair, which is an incredible variety of colors—basically bronze, but overlaid with gold and copper—is not styled in today's fashion. She wore it bundled up in a knot at the back of her head."

Seeing that her son had apparently gone off in a reverie, Lady Eversley prompted, "Her eyes?"

"Large and solemn and again of a golden brown spectrum."

"She sounds quite lovely. Is she a lady?"

"Of course she's a lady!" The viscount looked slightly affronted.

His mother hastened to add, "Well, dearest, after the life she has led, going off to America and running a hat shop in London, it is a natural question. I do not know a thing about her mother's family except that the general had had another bride lined up for Gerald and refused to accept the marriage."

"Was that the cause of the estrangement? I was under the impression that the general disowned his son because Gerald left the army. Did he leave under a cloud?"

"I have never known the details," Lady Eversley said vaguely. "The runaway marriage was the last straw. Gerald actually jilted the girl his father picked, you know. The marriage had been arranged and the notices sent to all the newspapers. It was a terrible scandal at the time."

"Gerald Ridgemont is beginning to sound more like the proverbial black sheep every moment. The fault wasn't all on the general's side."

"Oh, by no means. Gerald was a weak son of a strong

father—the worst possible combination—but I don't hold with disowning one's children and never will. And so I told the general once, which was why I was never his favorite person."

"You relieve my mind, anyway, Mama." She looked up expectantly at the oversolemn tone. "I mean about not being in favor of disowning one's own flesh and blood."

Lady Eversley's still-pretty face broke up into laughter. "As if that worry had ever crossed your mind!"

"Well, I also have the dubious distinction of bringing scandal upon my family," her son said, all humor dying out of his face.

"Don't, Mark! None of that business was your fault. It's time you put it behind you and married again. I am longing to cuddle some grandchildren."

"You know you may cuddle Anthea's brood whenever you choose to visit her in Kent or invite them here, Mama."

"Yes, dearest, but I have a particular desire to cuddle a little boy with the Eversley black hair and dark-brown eyes."

Mark gave a shout of laughter. "What a fraud you are, Mama. It's just as likely that my brats would all have red hair and freckles, expecially if I weakened and married the Calderby girl you have been oh-so-subtly thrusting across my path of late."

"But her hair is really quite pretty and she is a charming girl, do you not agree, Mark?"

"Yes, my dear. I agree she is a charming girl, but I am thirty-five years old and I am not interested in charming young girls of eighteen or nineteen."

Mark's voice was very gentle, but his mother, recalling snippets of gossip she had heard concerning a dazzling female in Marshfield who was a good deal older than eighteen and had no need to consider a reputation long since lost, was not comforted by his patience with her attempts at matchmaking. She sighed and allowed him to change the subject.

5

Sarah had every intention of making her explanations to her grandfather as soon as Lord Eversley departed, but she had scarcely left the library when she came upon Grace Medlark in the corridor. The generally calm Grace was in a state bordering on agitation as she stopped short in front of Sarah.

"I've been looking everywhere for you. Sir Hector has just sent word by Somers that his son, Mr. Horace Ridgemont, and his whole family are coming for a visit tomorrow; and Lady Townsend—that's his daughter—is due shortly also, with her son and daughter. The cook is having a spasm in the kitchen— Lady Townsend is nearly impossible to please, she finds fault with almost every dish—and we have to get all the bedchambers ready, and it's almost noon already."

"Stop and get your breath, Grace; you are looking nearly distracted. I've begun an inventory of the linens, so I have a fair notion of which are most presentable. We'll light a fire in one of the bedchambers and air them for a few hours today and then make up the beds later. The maids can do all the necessary sweeping and polishing first."

Grace scarcely seemed to be listening. "Lady Townsend likes her sheets changed daily, and that toplofty dresser of hers always causes ructions in the servants' hall. Cook says she'll be blowed if she'll take orders from someone with the appetite of a hummingbird and—"

"We'll come back to Cook directly, Grace. What I would like to know at the moment is which bedrooms customarily get assigned to whom. You are probably the person who would remember best." Sarah smiled encouragingly.

After a moment Grace smiled back and continued in a calmer vein, "Mr. and Mrs. Horace Ridgemont always have the southeastern suite. We make up a bed in the servant's room there for Mr. Horace. Their servants are housed in the main servants' quarters. Lady Townsend prefers the northeastern apartment adjacent to the dining saloon, and her dresser always sleeps in the small room there."

"That's fine. Now, what about the grandchildren? Tell me about them—names, ages, and so forth. Are any still children? Should we prepare the nursery?"

"Oh, no. I believe Miss Arabella is the youngest. She must be nearly twenty now. She has already had a London Season. Master Vincent is the oldest—Lord Townsend, I should say. The baron, his father, died two years ago. Let me think now. He is about three years older than his cousin William, Master William must be seven-and-twenty now and Master Cecil is two-and-twenty," she finished, pleased with her feat of memory.

"Shall we put all the young people in the first-floor apartments, then?"

"Yes, that will be fine. If we put Miss Arabella in the apartment above her mother she'll be able to use the back staircase when she wishes to run down and speak to Lady Townsend."

"Will they all have servants with them?"

"Yes, but none save Lady Townsend's dresser will sleep in the guest apartments. We'll just distribute the others in the regular servants' quarters. And the coachman and grooms will be housed in the stable wing, of course."

"How fortunate that this house is large enough to accommodate such an invasion," Sarah said with a gleaming smile, which brought an answering twitch to Grace's lips for a time.

"You have chosen a fitting word, more fitting than is quite comfortable," she said with serious intent. "I do not like to gossip about my betters, but yours is the responsibility for this enlarged household and you should be warned that the whole family has not been together under this roof in a number of years. There are personality differences and . . . and—"

"You mean they don't all like one another even though they are closely related?" Sarah had no qualms about stating plainly what loyalty or delicacy forbade Grace to utter, but she did not pursue this interesting topic for lack of time.

They had been walking back toward the servants' hall as they discussed the housing arrangements. Sarah stopped about twenty feet from the kitchen entrance. "Are we likely to find Mrs. Hadley in hysterics?" she whispered, placing an urgent hand on Grace's arm.

The maid laughed. "No, no," she said soothingly. "Cook is a somewhat temperamental personality, but she likes an audience when she creates. I had to leave to seek you. She will have calmed down by now and will already have set several plans in motion. I'm afraid Sir Hector will not be of much help in selecting menus. He doesn't take much interest in food these days, though he'll not begrudge the cost of setting a hospitable table. Most of the planning will fall on your shoulders—and Cook's, naturally—but Mrs. Hadley doesn't like to have to deal with the family," she added in warning tones. "You will have to do that."

There was a rather frightening list of things that she was going to have to do, Sarah thought worriedly as she got ready for bed that night, and the most important item on the list, disclosing her identity to her grandfather, was yet to be accomplished. She had confidently assured Lord Eversley that she would end the intolerable situation immediately, but this intention had been placed beyond her power to fulfill. The urgent necessity to initiate the preparations for houseguests had occupied her hands and attention for several hours, and when at last she had felt able to turn her attention to her own problem, she had run into the stone wall of her grandfather's refusal to see her. The general was resting, she was told by Somers, guarding his master's door on the first occasion when she had applied for admission. She had gone away, leaving a message that she wished to speak with Sir Hector at his earliest convenience. There had been no convenient moment evidently by the time the servants had retired for the night. She had made one last attempt to gain admittance to her grandfather's room a half-hour earlier, to be told by his faithful Cerberus that the general was asleep. She really had no option but to continue the masquerade.

Resolutely she closed her mind to the embarrassing possibilities inherent in the situation tomorrow should she still not have met with her grandfather before the descent of the family upon the house, or the advent of the real housekeeper. There was no way of knowing what time this vital personage would arrive. If the woman were not to run off in screaming hysterics at the unexpectedly increased responsibility into which she was to be unceremoniously pitchforked, then she herself must continue to supervise the monumental task of getting the household in full readiness for guests to ensure a smooth transfer of the housekeeping reins.

Sarah got into bed with her head stuffed full of the chores to be done on the morrow, but as her tired muscles relaxed at last into the comfort of the mattress, a picture of Lord Eversley rose before her eyes, complete from the shining abundance of raven hair to the equally refulgent top boots he had worn. This same mental picture had reappeared repeatedly during the harrowing day just completed, but on each occasion she had banished it to go about her vital business. This time she allowed herself the luxury of dwelling upon the surprising person of her grandfather's only friend. The surprise was because, on first learning of his existence, she had assumed he would be of her father's generation, since his father had been her grandfather's friend originally.

From the instant she had crossed over the threshold of the general's room today, she had been engulfed in the aura of power and dominance the visitor emanated. At first this aura had been distinctly threatening, evoking a corresponding mustering of defenses on her part, but by the time she had finished telling him her story, she had felt the initial hostility had been replaced by something perhaps a degree warmer than neutrality. Her resentment had also vanished, to be replaced by—what?

Sarah considered the question carefully and admitted at length that she envied the man his natural assurance, and what was odder yet, she envied even more the woman who had this confident strength at her disposal like a shield. How comforting it must be to be married to such a man, to have him always there to protect one from the buffets of fortune. "The slings and arrows of outrageous fortune" came unbidden into her head, and she laughed at her own dramatic nonsense, calling herself a craven coward. This unflattering self-assessment had no power to disturb her rest that night, however, for she drifted off to sleep on the thought.

Considering the ominous portents of disaster for the day, Sarah awoke with a positive feeling of well-being to the third morning of sunshine in a row. Taking this for a good omen, she hopped out of bed and completed her simple toilette in an expeditious fashion, suppressing a spurt of distaste as she donned the same black-and-white gown again. Thanks to the inordinate amount of space required for the bronze-green bonnet and matching spencer in the portmanteau, Lottie had been able to include only two lightweight dresses, neither of which was suitable garb for a housekeeper. She gobbled a hasty breakfast, set the maids to the various cleaning tasks still to be done, and spent an hour conferring separately with Mrs. Hadley and Millbank about a dinner menu that would contain enough flexibility to accommodate all or some of the expected guests at a time to be determined eventually by the hour of their arrival. This was no easy accomplishment, but Sarah had already grasped that, for all her unending complaints and displays of temperament, the Beech Hill cook had a tremendous capacity for hard work, and the strength of character to keep her minions productively occupied in the kitchen and scullery.

The masculine staff had diminished over the last few years as Sir Hector had become increasingly reclusive, but Joseph, the young footman who had opened the door to her, was very reliable and quick to learn. It was probable that they would have to bring in some extra help temporarily, but thankfully, that was Millbank's problem, not hers.

Sarah had barely had an opportunity to set her foot outdoors since she had arrived. She had not been near the stable area or the orchards or seen what the gardens or succession houses had to offer at this fallow time of year. She intended to quiz

Grace on the availability of flowering plants to brighten up the
guest apartments as soon as she had spoken with her grandfather—that is, if she did not find herself packing her bag for
immediate departure afterward, she reminded herself soberly,
trying to ignore the queasy sensation in her stomach as she set
off for her crucial talk with Sir Hector.

Well, at least she wasn't packing, she thought ten minutes
later as she went in search of Grace, but she could not derive
a substantial measure of comfort from that bare fact. Her step
had lost something of its spring as she relived the scene in Sir
Hector's antechamber. Short of physically overpowering his
faithful attendant—a wild idea that actually crossed her mind
at one point—she had been able to discover no way to gain access
to her grandfather. Somers' frozen courtesy had never faltered
under her increasingly pressing demands to be admitted for five
minutes only, but he had been as unmovable as Gibraltar.

"Those are my orders, Mrs. Boston. The general does not
wish to see anyone at present," he repeated in the face of her
increasingly vehement assurances of the vital nature of her
business with Sir Hector and her sincere belief that he would
wish to see her if he knew. Not a flicker of emotion had passed
across the inscrutable facade presented by the valet, and she
had been forced to give up for the time being, swamped by
panic-ridden visions of herself forced to greet her unknown
relatives under a false identity. Almost as disconcerting was
the idea of meeting the new housekeeper with a declaration that
she was the housekeeper. She closed her eyes against a still-
more-agonizing vision of herself trapped forever in Sarah
Boston's identity, condemned to remain indefinitely in her role
as housekeeper, and bumped into Grace in one of the corridors.

In the end the only indignity Sarah was spared that day was
a meeting with the rival housekeeper, who did not put in an
appearance, after all. Sarah would have been duly grateful for
this small blessing had she been given the tiniest breathing space
in which to contemplate a blessing, but such was not the case.

By midafternoon the guest rooms were prepared, a supply
of towels was warming, and appetizing smells were issuing from
the kitchen wing. Sarah had even snatched a half-hour to mix

up some gingerbread against a delayed dinner when the first sounds of an arrival were reported. None of her importunities to Somers having been effective in gaining the crucial audience with her grandfather, she had no choice but to meet her father's family in the guise of a housekeeper. It took several repetitions of Lottie's maxim that the Almighty never sends us trials without also supplying the strength and courage to overcome them before she could quiet her racing pulse and assume a suitable composure for greeting Mr. Horace Ridgemont and his family.

Sarah stood inside the great hall with a clear view of the party ascending the steps as their shoulders appeared in turn. First to come into sight was an elegantly groomed man of middle years who bore a striking resemblance to her father on a smaller, more finely drawn scale. Unprepared for the rush of emotion that caught her by the throat, Sarah swallowed against dryness. For the past year she had shied away from any dwelling on their lack of family connections. She had never consciously speculated about the personality or appearance of members of her father's family, but now, seeing her Uncle Horace for the first time, she had to put forth a stern effort to keep the polite little smile suitable for a housekeeper from spreading all over her face.

Her uncle had no such problem. He was gazing at her with a slight pucker between straight black brows, a look of mingled curiosity and suspicion in his eyes as he removed a handsome brown beaver hat. Sarah hastened forward, dipped a nominal curtsy. "Good afternoon, Mr. Ridgemont. I hope you had a comfortable journey."

"As comfortable as traveling can be at this time of year. I don't believe I've seen you here before."

"No, sir. I am Sarah Boston, the new housekeeper."

This information failed to remove the mistrust from his searching eyes, but he nodded and turned his head to speak to the woman standing just outside the entrance doors peering back down the steps with an anxious air. "Madeleine, this is my father's new housekeeper, Mrs. Boston."

The woman coming reluctantly into the hall was an unlikely match for her husband's trim, distinguished person. Her figure was frankly matronly, and Sarah could think of no better

description for her brown pelisse and hat then "serviceable."
Graying mouse-colored hair was tightly crimped about a face
distinguished mainly by its apple-cheeked roundness. The round
blue eyes that briefly met Sarah's held none of the reservation
that had been in her husband's, and little interest. Her faintly
anxious look was explained in the next moment as Sarah
followed her gaze to the entrance where two young men had
just appeared, one—the younger, Sarah judged—helping the
other to ascend the last few steps.

Mrs. Ridgemont broke away from her husband and Sarah to
hover over her son, who, having reached the flat surface, had
let go his brother's arm and was now leaning heavily on a cane,
his breath coming a little fast. "Are you all right, my dear?
Are you in much pain?" his mother asked.

"I'm fine now, mama, really. It's just that stairs are still a
bit difficult."

Sarah was struck by the sweetness of the young man's
expression as he smiled at his worried mother. She had been
doing some rapid thinking as the situation became clear to her,
and now she said, addressing herself to her elder cousin, "We
had allotted the first-floor apartments to the younger generation,
but it will only take a few moments to prepare the suite in the
northeast corner of this floor for you, sir. It would spare you
the awkwardness of the stairs."

"Oh, yes, William do sleep here on the ground floor," urged
Mrs. Ridgemont before her son could reply. "Your ankle will
never get stronger if you abuse it climbing stairs."

"Thank you, I will be glad to stay on this floor." Mr. William
Ridgemont smiled gratefully at Sarah, who then turned to his
father, who was looking a bit impatient by now.

"We have prepared your usual suite, sir. If you and Mrs.
Ridgemont will follow me, I will—"

"Perhaps I had better go along with William to his rooms
in case he needs any help," Mrs. Ridgemont suggested, hanging
back.

"Cecil can do anything his brother requires," Mr. Ridgemont said. "Come along, Madeleine." He proceeded toward
his usual apartment without further delay, and Sarah was

relieved to see his wife set off in his wake after her son echoed his father's sentiments in soothing tones.

It was apparent that Mrs. Ridgemont would have preferred to be with her injured son, but she said everything that was proper, commenting favorably on the appearance of the rooms and expressing appreciation for the flowering plants Grace had located. She accepted Sarah's invitation to have refreshments sent up to the withdrawing room immediately and went into the bedchamber to put off her hat and pelisse. Promising to send up the abigail as soon as the men servants should have brought up the baggage, Sarah took her leave to begin preparation of the northeast apartment for its unexpected guest.

To her surprise, her uncle accompanied her to the door that led to the back stairs. "I am going in to see my father in a moment. How is his condition, Mrs. Boston?"

Sarah hesitated. "I have only been at Beech Hill for three days, Mr. Ridgemont, and have only seen Sir Hector briefly on two occasions, both times in his bed. Lord Eversley told me on the second occasion that he and the doctor had been very concerned that his condition had worsened greatly of late, but that he thought him somewhat improved yesterday. Not knowing when last you saw your father, I fear I cannot guess how much of a change for the worse you will discover."

"He was not bedridden when I was here eight months ago," her uncle answered abruptly. "Thank you, Mrs. Boston, I'll go and see for myself if Eversley has cause for this urgent summons." He nodded dismissal, and Sarah proceeded downstairs to see about linens for her cousin's bed and set tea preparations going forward.

As she entered the northeast bedchamber a few moments later, accompanied by a maid carrying sheets, she thanked providence that this apartment had received a thorough dusting and polishing the day before. She poked her head into the antechamber to see that both her cousins had removed their outer clothing and were comfortably established, Cecil in a green velvet wingback chair near the fireplace, and William on the sofa, his injured foot resting on a footstool that had been dragged over to the sofa. He started to rise on spotting her in the doorway.

"Please don't get up, Mr. William. You'll need to rest that foot after a long carriage trip," she cautioned, noting a drawn look about his mouth though his blue eyes were eager and friendly. She glanced to Cecil, whose dark eyes held a familiar gleam, and her manner stiffened a little despite her efforts to keep her voice pleasant. "Annie will light the fire in the grate as soon as we finish in the bedchamber, and I'll show you to your suite, Mr. Cecil. There will be refreshments in your parents' apartment when you are ready."

"Cecil will take care of the fire in here. I've already made a lot of extra work for the staff, I fear," said Mr. William Ridgemont apologetically. "I'm sorry, but I don't believe I heard your name earlier."

"I am Sarah Boston," Sarah replied, struggling to keep the increasing abhorrence she felt for the name she had saddled herself with out of her voice.

"I'll be happy to light Mrs. Boston's fire," drawled Cecil Ridgemont, rising from his lounging position, his wiry grace and slim straight carriage giving promise of development along the lines of his father's mature elegance when he had outgrown a youthful penchant for the less-restrained styles of fashion. Sarah met his amused male glance with the blank civility she had perfected over the past year and excused herself to help Annie in the next room.

Never in her life had she been more grateful to call an end to a day, Sarah acknowledged some six or seven hours later as she all but fell into her bed. She had been on the move since early morning, but physical exertion alone could not account for the almost pathological weariness that dragged at her limbs and set a supply of silly tears behind her eyelids that threatened to spill over at intervals. It would not be so upsetting if she could only think of the seven people whose acquaintance had been thrust on her today as passing strangers, but that was proving impossible. These people were her family, and the deception under which she had been forced to meet them would forever stand in the way of normal relations. When she was unmasked, as was inevitable unless she abandoned her quest and disappeared from their lives, they would all suffer some degree of embarrassment and resentment over the position her duplicity had placed them in, and this would remain a barrier to the development of amicable relations.

It was not that she even desired to feel close to any member of her father's family; she had not been drawn immediately to any of them with the exception of William, the person closest to her in age and the one with the least share of what she now recognized as Ridgemont family traits, but she would never cease to regret that they could not have all met on equal terms, free to like or dislike each other as personal preference alone decreed. She was being well and truly punished for the original lie, she thought on a hiccoughing sigh, but lying here wallowing in regrets would change nothing.

Although Sir Hector had admitted his son into his presence briefly, he had not left his apartment for dinner or seen any others of his family, including his daughter, who had unsuccessfully sought admittance to his room before dinner. Somers had impressed this upon Sarah when she had brought up more custard and proposed taking it in to Sir Hector herself. The custard had gone in with Somers, and she had been sent away with an impersonal injunction to "try again tomorrow."

Sarah was not looking forward to tomorrow. Her position *vis-à-vis* her uncle's family had been difficult enough, but at least they had been prepared to accept her at face value and cooperate with Sarah Boston, housekeeper. Her Aunt Adelaide had been another matter entirely. She and her daughter had arrived about two hours after her brother and his family, with, according to Joseph, the footman, as much baggage as the entire Ridgemont contingent combined. Not that Sarah had needed this information to form an accurate idea of her aunt. One look at the beautifully groomed and richly dressed woman being escorted into the hall by an obsequious Millbank told Sarah that here was what was meant by the term "a lady of fashion." And her aunt's first sentence, pronounced in carefully cultivated, imperious tones, was sufficient warning of difficulties ahead.

Sarah had come forward to relieve Lady Townsend of a huge sable muff. Her quiet introduction of herself as the housekeeper had sent two arched brows soaring upward and two disdainful dark eyes roaming her person with every evidence of displeasure in what they found.

"Nonsense," stated Lady Townsend, looking down a feminine version of the Ridgemont nose from her superior height. "You are obviously too young and inexperienced for such responsibility. Where is Grace Medlark? She knows how I like things done."

Sarah had explained that Grace returned home to her family each evening, a consideration that Lady Townsend clearly found unacceptable and that she proposed to suspend during her stay at Beech Hill.

"I'm afraid that won't be possible, Lady Townsend, but Grace has personally supervised the preparation of your favorite rooms, and the maids have been instructed in the way you like your bed dressed. We shall all try to make you comfortable."

Sarah's speech was so pleasant and conciliatory that the sense of her words didn't sink in at first. When Lady Townsend realized that her wishes were being denied, albeit politely, her dark eyes froze and her lips thinned. "I'll speak with Grace myself," she declared.

At that point her ladyship's daughter, who had been wearing a bored expression on her pretty face throughout this dialogue, intervened. "Yes, Mama, but that can wait till tomorrow. Let's not stand in this drafty hall arguing about servants while our baggage is being brought in. I wish to supervise Elsie when she unpacks for me or she'll have all my gowns creased."

Without another word to Sarah, Lady Townsend had turned on her heel and headed for the suite reserved for her use. Sarah had trailed along after her just long enough to see her in the rooms and promise that her abigail would be sent up immediately. The words has scarcely left her lips when a thin, redheaded female with an expression that outdid her mistress in superciliousness appeared in the bedchamber doorway and announced that they would require another lamp for the dressing table. Sarah could only hope she had concealed her surprise as she promised to rectify the omission and send refreshments to the apartment at once.

"Tea only," Lady Townsend had ordered, "unless you wish something to eat, Arabella?"

Eager to be on her way, Miss Townsend had denied any interest in food. She had offered no other remarks while being shown to her rooms on the first floor. When Sarah had asked tentatively if they were not to have the pleasure of Lord Townsend's company, after all, she had replied shortly that her brother always drove himself. To a further question about when they might expect Lord Townsend, she said airily that it was anybody's guess when Vincent would turn up.

The first dinner, Sarah had concluded, held the promise of disaster. After conferring with Mrs. Hadley, she had decided to put it back a half-hour to give her absent cousin a bit of leeway. Her uncle had merely grunted when she explained it to him. She had sent a maid to the other guests with the message.

It was by the merest chance that Sarah had caught a glimpse of her eldest cousin when he arrived. She had been crossing the great hall after delivering this message to her uncle with some idea that she might catch her grandfather in a receptive mood when she saw Millbank escorting a tall dark man toward the east staircase. Unmistakably a Ridgemont in coloring and features, on Vincent the family nose was a dashing aquiline model that enhanced virile, slightly dangerous good looks.

In her bed, turning restlessly despite her fatigue, Sarah admitted that her aunt's children were definitely more physically impressive than her Ridgemont cousins, though she had been both attracted and repelled by an assurance in their demeanor that bordered on arrogance. Of course it would not do to judge hastily, first impressions could be misleading. One thing she hoped she had misjudged was the potential for discord among such strong personalities. Millbank had reported that the atmosphere at dinner had been constrained though not actively hostile. Lady Townsend, as expected, had reviewed most of the culinary offerings unfavorably, but all the others had done ample justice to Mrs. Hadley's beautiful roast of beef and well-presented side dishes, for which Sarah was heartily thankful.

But she could not look forward to tomorrow with any lessening of apprehension as she finally drifted into an uneasy slumber.

6

Mark Trebeque, sixth Viscount Eversley, made his way through the fine stand of trees that separated his estate from Beech Hill, more or less setting his horse a walking pace on a brisk late-winter morning with more than a hint of spring in the air. He breathed in deeply of the cool pine-scented air, enjoying the earthy undertones of decomposing vegetation, and glanced around for signs of budding life, determined to rein in an eagerness he was reluctant to acknowledge, though why this should be so was puzzling in itself. Surely there was ample reason to be curious, even concerned with what was going on at Beech Hill. It was he who had set the wheels in motion, so to speak, with his letter to Horace Ridgemont; therefore, it was not surprising that he should feel some concern for how that unfortunate girl was faring at the hands of a family long noted for its internecine tendencies.

There was no denying he had experienced a stab of compunction the other day on leaving Sarah Ridgemont to the doubtful charity of her relatives. She had faced him so valiantly, but those beautiful somber eyes had betrayed her self-doubts. Indeed, she had all but confessed her shame at even approaching her estranged grandfather for assistance. If she had been an able-bodied male, he might have agreed with her scruples, but the simple truth was that she was bearing a burden too great for even the most valiant-hearted female to shoulder. He had found himself wishing to offer his support when she confronted her grandfather, but of course he had no rights where she was concerned.

He had sent off a letter to his man in London that same afternoon directing him to investigate the truth of what she had told him. He owed this much to the general, though he would take his oath that the girl was genuine. If eyes like hers could lie, then there was indeed little hope for humanity.

Yesterday had seemed a thousand hours long while he forced himself to stay away from Beech Hill. The household would be at sixes and sevens, frantically preparing to house more guests at one time than had come under the general's roof all told in the past half-dozen years. Still, he would not have been surprised to receive a peremptory summons from Sir Hector demanding an accounting of his behavior in not challenging the identity of the alleged housekeeper the other day.

A disturbing thought caused the viscount to slacken his control on the reins, and the big black bounded forward, eager to stretch his legs. Mark let Heracles have his head while he examined and rejected the idea that Sir Hector might have sent his granddaughter packing. Adamantine though his nature assuredly was, the general had lived his entire life by a rigid code of honor; that was really at the core of his harsh treatment of his son. Gerald's failure to adhere to his father's standards had tarnished the Ridgemont name in Sir Hector's view. He was not an ungenerous man, however, nor one to permit innocent children to suffer for the sins of their elders. If Mark understood the general's sense of duty at all, he could be assured that the old man would make provision for his son's children, even if he declined to associate with them personally.

Having worked his way to this conclusion, Mark gradually slowed Heracles to the decorous trot he deemed appropriate for a neighbor arriving to pay a morning call as he approached the Beech Hill stables. He had deliberately timed his arrival for an hour when the men might be expected to be out riding, since his main concern was to see how the Ridgemont women were treating Sarah. Simple human kindness was not a commodity in great supply among the Ridgemonts at any time. If the general really were dying, the fortuitous appearance of two more heirs was not an event calculated to tap the wellspring of human kindness that the charitably inclined might expect to locate deep within Lady Townsend. The knighthood died with Sir Hector, and Beech Hill was unentailed. He could leave his fortune and property wherever he liked.

The viscount banged the knocker, a little smile tugging at the corners of his firm mouth at this last thought. How he would have liked to have been present when the Ridgemont clan had been apprised of the existence of two additional members.

The footman's ready smile appeared in response to the remnants of Lord Eversley's as he pulled back the door. "Good morning, sir. A nice day for a ride."

" 'Morning, Joseph. Yes, it's beginning to smell like spring. How is the general today?"

"Not too chipper, sir. At least he's seeing no one this morning."

Mark paused in the act of handing hat and gloves to Joseph. "Oh? I'm sorry to hear that. Is Mr. Ridgemont in?"

"No, sir. He and Mr. Cecil and Lord Townsend are out riding. The ladies and Mr. William are in the drawing room if you'd care to step upstairs, sir."

"Thank you, I'll do that." Mark ran a smoothing hand over his black hair and followed Joseph down the length of the great hall to the west staircase on the left. He had his rather stern features composed into a mask of social affability by the time the footman announced him.

The mask nearly slipped when a swift sweep of the elegantly appointed room showed him that Sarah was not among those present. Consciously he smoothed back an incipient frown and pasted on his best imitation of a courtly smile as Lady Townsend crossed the few feet of floor between her chair and the door to greet him enthusiastically. In London last Season she had done her best to drag him into her net for her daughter, failing a bigger fish, but her best had not been good enough. The girl was a dazzler, he admitted readily as he bowed first to Mrs. Ridgemont and then gratified Miss Townsend by bringing the hand she extended up near his mouth, but he'd seen the dazzlers of more Seasons than he cared to admit degenerate into shrill and shrewish wives after a year or two of marriage. His eyebrows rose as William Ridgemont limped across the room to shake his hand.

"What is all this? A martyr to gout at your age?"

William grinned good-naturedly. "Not yet, thank goodness. I twisted the cursed ankle while boxing last week. It's taking its own good time to heal."

"The gout," exclaimed Mrs. Ridgemont indignantly. "Oh, I see. You are funning, Lord Eversley. I am happy to be able to say that in the ordinary way William enjoys superb health, but he was ever prone to accidents even as a child. Why, I recall once when he was only ten—"

"Mama, I hope you don't plan to disclose all the foolish peccadilloes of my childhood," her son said with a teasing smile. "Lord Eversley must already think me a clumsy oaf on the evidence of his eyes."

"Of course he does not," stated the fond parent unequivocally, her mild blue eyes daring the viscount to contradict her.

"Of course not, ma'am," he agreed with composure, avoiding the mocking amusement in Miss Townsend's sparkling dark eyes.

"Come and sit here by me, Lord Eversley," that young lady invited with a flirtatious sweep of curling black eyelashes. "Your arrival must have been divinely designed to rescue me from terminal boredom. There's never anything to do at Beech Hill," she continued, treating him to a delectable pout of rosy lips as he seated himself beside her on one of the pink damask settees placed facing each other at right angles to the fireplace. "Grandfather is such a hermit these days that no one ever comes to visit and—"

"Speaking of your grandfather," Mark said, ruthlessly interrupting her complaints, "Joseph told me he is seeing no one today. Is his condition worse?" He directed the question to Lady Townsend, who shrugged pettishly.

"I am not the one to answer you, Eversley, not having been admitted to his presence since our arrival."

"You've not seen him yet, ma'am, none of you?" Mark asked, startled.

"Horace saw him yesterday, but Somers has taken it upon himself to deny him to everyone this morning. He said Father had a bad night and was sleeping this morning."

"What did Mr. Ridgemont think after seeing him yesterday?"

"Horace said he looked much weaker than the last time he'd been here but remarkably alert for all that. His voice had lost none of its power, and my brother noticed nothing of the shortness of breath you described in your letter."

Mark's dark-complexioned face wore a look of attention that was deceptive, for he was actually cudgeling his brain for an inspiration that would shed some light on Sarah's situation, though by now he'd been in the room long enough to find the silence on the subject of a long-lost granddaughter ominous. In the next moment he was saved further fruitless cogitation by a light tap on the door, followed by the entrance of Sarah herself.

There was a flash of panic in the soft eyes that flew to his before Sarah got her expression under control. Lady Townsend had just finished speaking, and the loudest silence he'd ever heard outside of a classroom where no one knew the answer descended on the group in the drawing room as all eyes fastened on the young woman in the sober black-and-white gown standing just inside the door.

Sarah straightened her shoulders and gripped her hands together. "You sent for me, Lady Townsend?"

"Yes. You will be good enough to explain why Grace Medlark has not been to see me this morning."

"But I thought you knew, ma'am." Sarah's eyes widened. "I gave your abigail the message that Grace sent. One of her children is ill, so she was not able to come today."

"I received the message. I then sent a maid to the village to Grace's house to stay with the child while Grace reported to me. That was over an hour ago."

"I knew nothing of this, Lady Townsend. Which maid did you send?"

"Do you expect me to know the name of every maid in this house?" Lady Townsend's face assumed a haughty mien. "If you were competent at your job, you would know where your staff was at all times.''

Sarah's eyes dropped. "If you will excuse me, I shall check with the maids to find out who went to Grace's house and what the situation is.''

"Other than walking into the village myself, I suppose I have no choice. Very well, you may go.''

Mark had sat embalmed in shock during the first part of Lady Townsend's tirade, but rising anger soon thawed his muscles and he stood up as Sarah slipped out of the door. His face an urbane mask, he bowed to the ladies and apologized. "I must beg you to excuse me too, ladies, for the moment. I must see Mrs. Boston about something . . . something I brought for the general.''

After an all-encompassing glance around a stunned circle, he took himself out of the room, giving no sign of the urgency that propelled him. His rudeness would be talked about, but he couldn't help that. As he set off in pursuit of Sarah, his mind remained for a second on the scene he had just witnessed. William Ridgemont, he was pleased to note, had looked as embarrassed as he had felt at the public chastisement that arrogant harpy had handed the person she still obviously thought of as her father's housekeeper. Mrs. Ridgemont's face had worn a vaguely sympathetic expression, and Arabella Townsend had been frankly bored by the incident.

"Sarah," he called in low tones as the young woman ahead of him was about to start down the stairs. He caught up with her when she halted in surprise, and taking her arm in a firm clasp, he pulled her along after him into the room above the library, which functioned as a picture gallery. Once inside, he released her and stood with his back against the door, his arms folded in front of his chest.

"Now, my girl, you may tell me why this hideous masquerade is still going on. Why have you put yourself in a position to be abused by that termagant? You promised me to tell your grandfather the truth two days ago.''

Sarah considered objecting to the familiar form of address

employed by Lord Eversley, but one look at the set furious face of the man looming over her decided her on the more prudent course of restraint. "Do you think I have not tried?" she cried, frustration ringing in her voice. "I have tried to speak to my grandfather at least a dozen times in the last two days. He won't see me."

"Why not?" Mark's features took on a puzzled cast. "He was not so dangerously ill two days ago that a short conversation should prostrate him—at least not an ordinary conversation," he amended, shooting her a look that spoke volumes. "Lady Townsend told me he saw his son briefly but has refused as yet to see her. Well, he won't refuse to see me. Come along!"

Sarah found herself being rushed down the staircase and across the great hall at a pace that required an undignified skip on her part to maintain, and she decided it was high time she asserted her independence.

"I'll be black and blue for weeks," she declared waspishly, jerking her elbow out of his grasp.

Some of the sternness died out of the dark-brown eyes that gazed down into her mutinous face, to be replaced by a trace of sympathetic amusement. "I'm sorry. I do seem to tow you about a good deal, don't I?" He slowed his pace to allow her to catch her breath. "Tell me, what is Mrs. Glamorgan's part in this charade?"

"The new housekeeper? She hasn't one. She has not yet arrived."

His eyebrows shot up. "So she could pop up at any moment to round out the cast of this merry little farce. I had Coke, my London agent"—he laid stress on the name and grinned boyishly at this reference to their earlier set to—"give her enough money to hire a post chaise from Marshfield, so her arrival will be unannounced."

Sarah sighed. "I feel as though I am traveling through a bad dream. No matter how I struggle to escape, my feet keep taking me deeper into a dreamworld."

"Now, do not, I beg of you, become fanciful. We are about to call a halt to this deception."

Lord Eversley's confident expectations received a rude

setback at the door to Sir Hector's apartment. The ubiquitous Somers was at his post, and he was not in the least intimidated or influenced by the viscount's insistence on disturbing the general "for five minutes only."

"I'm that sorry to refuse you, sir, but the general had a bad night and he's sleeping now. I cannot disturb him. Indeed, you wouldn't want to destroy his first real rest in days, would you, sir?"

Lord Eversley knew when he was defeated. He smiled ruefully at Sarah, who accepted the situation with a philosophical little shrug. "We can scarcely barge in on an eighty-six-year-old man enjoying his first repose in days," he agreed, but the thoughtful stare he bent on the implacable Somers would have wilted a lesser man.

"The general said as how he'd be available to visitors after lunch, sir," the valet offered as they prepared to leave the suite.

"Then you may expect us directly after lunch, Somers," Lord Eversley said.

As he and Sarah left Sir Hector's drawing room, he smiled into her grave countenance and pleaded in the tones of a conspirator, "Do you think you could arrange to be lurking somewhere in the shadows when I knock this afternoon? I'd prefer not to run the gamut of your relatives if at all possible. I can imagine what they thought when I followed the housekeeper out of the room a few moments ago." He watched the parade of emotions passing across his companion's features ranging from slight surprise to a mischievous comprehension that dissolved into apprehension at his last remark.

"Now, do not start worrying again. This strange situation will resolve itself very soon now."

"It is most generous of you to wish to support me in my meeting with my grandfather, sir. I have no right to expect anything of the sort."

"I involved myself by frightening you at our first meeting at your grandfather's bedside. Had I been less threatening, we might have succeeded in straightening out the tangle of mixed identities then and there."

As they were now in the great hall near Joseph's chair, and

the footman was coming forward to see Lord Eversley out, Sarah was unable to do more than give him a low-voiced confirmation of their next meeting after lunch.

The men of Beech Hill returned from their morning ride a few minutes before lunchtime, and Horace Ridgemont was not pleased upon entering his apartment to find waiting for him a message from his sister desiring him to wait upon her at his earliest convenience, with the word "earliest" underlined twice. An exclamation of annoyance forced its way between his lips, but he did not consider for more than a second postponing the confrontation until they should meet at table. It never was any good to try to avoid Adelaide when she was on one of her rampages—she had the devil's own persistence—but his mood was anything but conciliatory as he entered her antechamber a few minutes later. His sister was pacing the length of the room wearing a look of aroused fury that boded no good for anyone crossing her path. He decided to go on the attack first.

"It's of no use, Adelaide, to rail at me because Father has refused to see you. He wouldn't see me this morning either. Somers said to try again after lunch."

"That isn't why I sent for you, Horace." Lady Townsend stopped in front of her brother and demanded, "What do you know about this person who calls herself a housekeeper?"

"Mrs. Boston? I don't know anything about her. What is there to know? She seems very young for the position, but Father says she's the best housekeeper he's had in years. She's only been here a few days, but she organized the staff to prepare for our arrival on very short notice, and it went quite smoothly."

"Bah, that woman is no more a housekeeper than I am!"

"What are you raving on about?"

"Does she look like any housekeeper you've ever seen?"

Horace stirred uneasily. "Just because a woman is young and attractive, it does not follow that she is incapable of doing the job. Dammit, Adelaide, she *is* doing the job."

"She gives herself away every time she opens her mouth."

"She's perfectly polite and respectful and possesses a quickness of understanding too. She no sooner saw that William was limping than she offered to change him from a suite upstairs to one on this floor, and all done with no fuss or—''

''Idiot! I'm talking about her speech. No servant ever spoke without a trace of some accent that betrayed their origins, even Grace Medlark, whose mother was Mama's dresser for years. I knew there was something phony about that Boston creature the instant I clapped eyes on her, and now I have proof that she is not what she claims to be.''

''What do you mean? What kind of proof?''

Lady Townsend walked over to a large ornately carved table under a Venetian pier glass and returned holding a small object that she thrust into her brother's unwilling hand with an exclamation of triumph. ''This!''

Horace Ridgemont looked from his sister's face, alight with vindictive satisfaction, to the tiny gold brooch in his hand. It was in the form of a lover's knot, he saw, completely made of delicate filigree work, except for one pale opal in the center that glowed with soft color as he turned the pin over in his fingers. ''This is your proof that Mrs. Boston is not what she claims to be, a brooch?'' His eyes questioned his sister, whose angular features assumed an even more offensive degree of superiority.

''Well, all I can say, Horace, is that if you have forgotten the brooch our mother wore for years, which was given to her by our father, I have not. This is that brooch.''

There was a short silence, then Horace asked almost reluctantly, ''How did you come by this, Adelaide?''

''As I said, I suspected that woman from the beginning. Today I had Dawkins, my abigail, search her room for some evidence of her real identity. She found this,'' Lady Townsend replied with an assumption of nonchalance that did not quite ring true. She went on quickly as an expression of distaste spread over her brother's hawkish features. ''The question that you should be asking is how did this Boston creature come by our mother's brooch?''

''And do you have an answer to that question too?'' he asked, dropping the pin into her hand as if contact with it burned his fingers.

"I should think it would be as plain as the nose on your face. No one could have taken that pin but Gerald. Somehow, Gerald has learned of Father's illness and he has insinuated into this house that woman with her misleading meekness and the sort of insipid good looks that might be expressly designed to impress a sick old man. It would not be the first time a rich old man has been charmed out of his money by a clever young woman with a honeyed voice and a gentle manner. The woman is an adventuress, I tell you. We've got to get her out of this house."

"How do you plan to accomplish this?"

"I tried to see Father after Dawkins brought me the brooch, but Somers said he was sleeping. He promised Father would be receiving visitors after lunch, however. That is probably all to the good. I am persuaded it will be better for us to confront him with this together."

"But I am not at all sure I wish to be with you when you break this news to Father," her brother said mildly. "Tell me, Adelaide, does it not trouble your conscience at all that you violated someone's privacy by searching her belongings?"

"A servant? Don't talk rubbish, Horace. What would our position be now without this brooch? We cannot stay here forever. All that woman would have to do is wait out our visit until the house was clear again so that she would be free to employ whatever arts of fascination she chose on a doddering old man with no one to impede her. Would you like to wake up one morning to find Father dead and Gerald and this woman in possession of our inheritance and that of our children?"

He did not answer her at once. There was a puzzled frown on his face and he said as if musing to himself, "How could Gerald have found out about Father's illness? The last I heard of him was that he had gone to America many years ago. And how could he get the woman in here in the second place? Father told me Eversley found Mrs. Boston for him, or at least his agent in London did."

"Eversley! Horace, Eversley was here this morning and his behavior was most peculiar. We were all sitting in the drawing room when Mrs. Boston came in to speak to me. When she left, Eversley excused himself to go after her with some trumped-up excuse about a package he'd brought for Father. Eversley must be working with Gerald in this."

"Now you are letting your imagination run away with you, Adelaide. Eversley was only a child when Gerald went away, and he is a good friend to Father. To accuse him of trying to harm Father would be a grave error on your part, believe me."

"I'm not so stupid as to accuse him of anything," Lady Townsend retorted, firming her already decided chin, "but I shall certainly discover how he came to send that Boston woman here before the day is much older. Are you going to come with me to see Father or not?"

Mr. Horace Ridgemont stared into his sister's challenging eyes for a long moment, his own troubled. Then he said quietly, "Very well, I shall go with you after lunch."

7

J oseph had barely relieved Lord Eversley of his hat and gloves in the hall of Beech Hill after lunch when Sarah glided through the archway leading to the west staircase and came down the great room toward them.

"I'll take Lord Eversley in to see Sir Hector, Joseph," she said with a tiny smile.

"Very good, ma'am."

Mark examined her pale face as they headed silently across the hall. "Is anything wrong, or are you simply suffering from nervous anticipation?"

She raised amber eyes full of distress to his. "Someone searched through my belongings this morning. I don't believe anything is missing, but I cannot be certain because I neither packed nor unpacked for myself this time. Lottie packed for me in London, and Grace Medlark unpacked for me and put my things away that first day while I was feeling too ill to pay much attention. I've not been able to wear anything but this wretched gown since I came here, so I haven't been through the drawers thoroughly, until I noticed just before lunch that some of my things had been disturbed."

"You are quite sure these items were disturbed by other hands?"

"Oh, yes," she replied with a little shudder. "It's a horrid feeling to know that someone has been snooping among one's personal possessions."

They had reached the door into Sir Hector's drawing room by now and were greeted by Somers as usual, but not the usual

Somers. The thin little man's unencouraging aspect of this morning—indeed, of the last few days—had been transformed into a semblance of a benevolent smile.

"You may go right in Lord Eversley, Miss Sarah. The general is expecting you."

With his foot halfway over the threshold, the viscount pulled up mentally. *Miss* Sarah? As he took in the scene in the bedchamber, his hand went out in an unconsciously protective gesture toward Sarah, then dropped to his side. By habit his eyes winged to the big bed, which today was devoid of its recent occupant and made up smoothly with a colorful quilt. He felt the girl beside him stiffen and gently nudged her a step or two forward with a hand at her waist.

Sir Hector was sitting up in a maroon velvet wing chair by the fireplace clad in a gorgeous dressing gown of a bright-blue brocade frogged in black. A white silk scarf was folded neatly at his throat, and his abundant white hair, rivaling it in brightness, was carefully brushed. He was wearing the breeches and silk stockings of an earlier day, and his feet, resting on an ottoman that matched the chair, were shod in soft house shoes.

"Come in, come in," he invited with a beckoning wave of his hand.

Benevolence here too, Mark marveled, until he checked the expressions of the other two people in the room.

Sir Hector's children were seated side by side in a pair of armless walnut chairs of the Queen Anne period, and their faces were anything but welcoming. Horace Ridgemont had the embarrassed mien of a man caught stealing sheep, and Lady Townsend's expression was so eloquent of malicious satisfaction that, without actually moving, Mark aligned his body closer to Sarah's. He noted with interest that Sir Hector's benevolence had vanished and his face, as he glanced at his daughter, mirrored the expression on hers as she glared at Sarah and burst into speech.

"Your entrance is well-timed, Mrs. Boston. Perhaps you will be good enough to tell your employer just who sent you here and how you came to have in your possession a gold brooch that belonged to my mother."

Sarah stared at her aunt, appalled. "*You* searched through my belongings?"

"Don't be impertinent! Of course I did not search your—"

"You merely ordered the search, Adelaide?" Sir Hector asked in a deceptively genial tone, but with a look of disgust quivering about his thin lips that sent a tide of red surging up from his daughter's throat.

She shot back defensively, "You will be grateful that I did when you discover who this adventuress is and who sent her here."

"No one sent me here—" Sarah began, only to be drowned out by the general's best military roar.

"I know exactly who this young woman is. Come here, child," he ordered much more softly, holding out a compelling hand to the white-faced girl, who obeyed him mechanically, though the eyes that flashed to his face were terrified. The general took her trembling fingers into a decidedly strong clasp of his thin gnarled hand, but his eyes were on the others in the room as he waited for their reactions to his suave announcement. "Horace, Adelaide, Eversley, I have the honor to present my granddaughter, Sarah Ridgemont."

The reception that greeted Sir Hector's little bomb was almost everything he could have wished.

Sarah gasped and clutched at the arm of his chair for support.

"So that accounts for it," exclaimed Horace Ridgemont, his eyes devouring his niece.

"You knew?" whispered Sarah, her eyes all for her grandfather.

The general chose to ignore the girl by his side for the moment. "Accounts for what?" he asked his son in tones of deep interest.

"Something . . . some elusive something about her that bothered me, teased at my memory, though I was sure I'd never met her before."

Adelaide Townsend had not uttered a sound in her consternation, though shock, disbelief, and fury all warred for prominence on her countenance for a time. Now she challenged hoarsely, "How can you possibly be sure she isn't tricking you? You have no proof."

Her father gave a snort of laughter. "Oh, she tried to trick me, all right, into believing she was a housekeeper."

"I didn't . . . that is, I did not intend—" blurted Sarah, to be ruthlessly overridden.

"But all it took was one look at her standing in the candle-light that first night to see that, except for the silly hole in her chin and somewhat lighter-colored eyes, she is her grandmother to the life. I can tell you it gave me quite a turn."

"It is probably no more than a romantic fancy," protested Lady Townsend. "The girl appeared at your bedside at a time when you were thinking of Mama, and you invested her with a resemblance that exists only in your mind."

"You think I dreamed it up, do you?" the general snapped, reaching into a drawer in the table beside his chair. "Perhaps you also think I am heading into my dotage. Did I dream this up too?"

He held out a small framed painting, and after a slight hesitation, Horace Ridgemont leaned forward and took it from him. Silently Lord Eversley came forward to study the likeness of a young woman that Horace was holding for his sister's frowning inspection. The young woman pictured wore the elaborately coiffed hair of the middle years of the eighteenth century, but the unsmiling face was uncannily like Sarah's as the latter stood wide-eyed and tense, enduring the measuring looks of the others as they glanced from the portrait to her and back again.

"I do not really remember Mama like that," Horace said half-apologetically. "In my memory she was older, still lovely, of course, but more smiling, at least for most of the time that I lived at home."

"There is a resemblance," Adelaide admitted grudgingly, "but that doesn't constitute proof that she is Gerald's legitimate child, and what part does Gerald play in all this anyway?"

"No part. He's dead," snapped her father.

In the silence that greeted this terse pronouncement, Sarah, who had been gradually coming out of a state of shock, turned to her grandfather and pleaded, "If you knew who I was all the time, Sir Hector, why did you permit this . . . this . . ." She hesitated, and he finished for her.

"Is 'farce' the word you are seeking? Why did I allow your pretense of being a housekeeper to continue?"

"Yes," she said humbly.

"I do not intend to answer until Eversley does some explaining. What was your role in all this charade, Eversley? And don't think to gammon me that you did not know more than you told because I watched your face when I dropped my bombshell, and you were not in the least surprised either to learn who Sarah was or that I also knew who she was."

The viscount withstood the general's intimidating stare with commendable aplomb. "I wondered when it would be my turn, sir," he said with a grin. "I realized at our first meeting the other day that Miss Ridgemont was not the person hired by my agent, and I charged her with it immediately afterward. I said nothing to you at the time for fear of disturbing you. I thought only to spare you aggravation if she turned out to be the adventuress Lady Townsend has suggested." Mark's face was carefully expressionless as he permitted his eyes to run over the avidly listening face of that lady.

"When Sarah told me who she was, I exacted a promise that she would make an opportunity to tell you the truth as soon as possible and went merrily on my way. It was not until this morning that I learned that she had been unable to see you to tell you her story despite numerous attempts to do so. At that point, General, I might say that my curiosity was aroused as to why it was suddenly so difficult to secure an interview with you. Do not credit me with any unusual prescience, however. It wasn't until Somers said just now that you were expecting *Miss* Sarah and me that curiosity turned to suspicion and, shortly thereafter, suspicion to conviction."

"I see." The general nodded and directed a calculating stare at his friend. "So Sarah Boston told you she was Sarah Ridgemont. And you believed her without any proof, did you?"

"I did, sir." Behind the urbane mask, Mark's teeth went tight in annoyance. The old war-horse had him nicely boxed and was preparing to enjoy his discomfiture.

"The young are so credulous," murmured Sir Hector, rubbing salt into the wound. "So you left me to my fate and went merrily on your way—to use your own words."

Though not phrased as a question, Mark was aware that he was not alone in hearing the question in the statement. He hesitated, knowing the cost already, but reluctantly told the truth. "I did write to Coke in London to . . . to check on Sarah's story," he said evenly. "I felt I must do that for you, sir." He could sense that Sarah flinched at this report, and something in her face closed up against him as she avoided his glance.

"I see," the general repeated. "And what was Sarah's story? And has Coke confirmed it, for the sake of her aunt's peace of mind?"

Lady Townsend's lips pressed together angrily at this piece of sarcasm, and Sarah shrank further into herself.

Mark said, somewhat more aggressively than was quite polite, "Perhaps you will first tell me, sir, why you refused to let Sarah confess the simple truth, that she had been so afraid you would turn her away that she seized on Joseph's error in thinking her the new housekeeper in order to gain access to you. She tried to explain right from the beginning, did she not?"

"Yes," admitted the general readily.

"Did you not realize what a false position all the members of your family would be placed in if you allowed Sarah to meet them in the guise of a servant?" Mark persisted, trying to phrase the question as gently as he could.

"Oh, yes, I realized it," said the general, refusing to accept any mitigation of his offense. "It was too rare an opportunity to miss," he explained simply when Sarah turned disbelieving eyes on him.

The viscount disciplined a smile as Lady Townsend's bosom swelled in anger at the Turkish treatment her father had meted out to his family so knowingly.

"Well, Father, you've had your little joke at our expense," Horace Ridgemont said. "What next?"

"Next I wish to hear Sarah's story. Eversley is ahead of us

there. Yes, do sit down, child, before you fall down," he urged as the viscount brought a chair forward for the drooping girl. "Where is your mother? Did she send you here?"

"My mother?" Sarah gaped at Sir Hector in amazement. "Mother died in Boston nine years ago. Father wrote to you when it happened."

For the first time the general looked discomposed. "I never received that communication, Sarah," he said gruffly. "You may think what you please about my treatment of your father— that was between him and me—but I hope you will believe that I would not have ignored you and your brother this past year had I known you were alone in the world."

"A brother too?" This from Lady Townsend.

Mark noted that some silent understanding was reached between the general and his granddaughter before Sarah removed her gaze from his regretful face to explain for the benefit of her uncle and aunt, "I have an eleven-year-old brother, Richard."

"How have you been living since your father died?"

Sarah swallowed with difficulty and her eyes fell before the demand in the shrewd old eyes commanding hers. Lady Townsend leaned forward, hoping no doubt to hear something discreditable, Mark thought savagely as he dashed to the rescue. His voice was cheerful as he declared, "Sarah is afraid you will consider she has abased the fair name of Ridgemont by operating a hat shop in London to augment the inadequate annuity that is all she and Richard have to live on, but I am persuaded you will applaud her courage and tenacity instead."

The viscount felt a strong rush of sympathy as he watched the general absorb this additional blow to his pride, and he was moved to admiration by the old man's quick recovery. Ignoring his daughter's scandalized repetition of "*A hat shop*," Sir Hector gave Sarah's clenched hand a pat in her lap and said stoutly, "I have nothing but respect for such evidence of enterprise in one of my blood, but all that must end now. I won't have my grandson reared in a hat shop," he added, then moderated his voice, which was again escalating toward a military bark. "I presume your presence here means you have come to me for assistance?"

Sarah nodded. "I cannot afford to give Richard the kind of education that will prepare him to earn a good living."

"You may drop that care from your mind as of today. And what of yourself, Sarah? What future do you envision for yourself? Have you never had the opportunity to marry?"

"I was betrothed at seventeen to a young man in Massachusetts, but my mother became ill and died quite suddenly before my marriage could take place. I could not leave Richard then—he was only two years old—so I ended my engagement. As for the future, once we are assured that Richard's is provided for, Lottie and I will be able to manage. Without the hat shop," she added with the first real smile Mark had ever seen. It was full of promise like sunshine after rain, and he wished suddenly and with an unnerving hunger that it were directed at him instead of an old man of eighty-six.

"Who is this Lottie?" asked her grandfather sharply.

"She was my mother's abigail before she married, then my nurse and Richard's, and always and forever our dearest friend," replied Sarah, a hint of steel in her musical voice, as if she sensed an undefined threat.

"Harrumph!" The general cleared his throat and began again. "You have been fortunate to have had such a faithful friend, but I want you all here now. My grandson shall grow up in the home of his ancestors."

"Here? But, Father, you cannot possibly accept the charge of a child at your time of life," protested Horace. "Madeleine and I will be happy to—"

"Fustian! Oh, I know you mean well, Horace, but I've decided not to die quite yet, after all," Sir Hector announced casually to his stunned audience. "In fact, that is partly why I have denied myself to everyone these past few days. I've been in that damn bed so long I'm weak as a kitten, and I needed to practice walking about a bit if I was ever to get out of this room again and confound that know-it-all doctor of mine."

"Poor Somers," the viscount remarked out of the blue.

"Actually, Somers enjoyed himself immensely, except that he had a tender conscience about Sarah," said the general with a malevolent grin.

"Did Somers recognize me too?"

"That miniature of your grandmother has stood on my bed-side table for close on a half-century. Like Horace, Somers had a disturbing impression that he should know you, and when you left this room after our first meeting, he noticed my mental state and put two and two together."

At that moment Somers appeared in person at the door. "I am very sorry to interrupt, Sir Hector, but Mrs. Medlark insists on seeing Miss Sarah—Mrs. Boston, I mean. Says it's quite an urgent matter."

As Grace herself could be seen behind his shoulder, hovering anxiously, both Sarah and Lady Townsend rose.

"It is I Grace wishes to see, I believe, Somers. I sent for her earlier," said Lady Townsend.

"Is it your little girl, Grace? Is she worse?" Sarah's face mirrored Grace's concern.

"No, no, Sa—Mrs. Boston; she's some better. It's not that, but I must speak with you."

"Well, come in, woman, and get it off your chest. A crisis in the kitchen?" boomed the general.

"I must speak privately with Mrs. Boston, Sir Hector," Grace insisted.

"What, secrets from the master of the house?" roared the general with a heavy-handed playfulness so out of character that all save Sarah gaped at him goggle-eyed.

"It's all right, Grace," Sarah said soothingly. "I'll come with you now, if you will excuse me, sir?"

"Not yet. Out with it, woman, What has happened?"

Grace looked at Sarah in alarm. When that young woman only repeated Sir Hector's question, she swallowed and stammered, "There is a woman at the door who claims to be the new house-keeper. I've told her she is mistaken, but she says she won't leave until she sees Sir Hector."

"Mrs. Glamorgan," cried Sarah and Lord Eversley in unison.

The general seemed to comprehend this situation immediately. He turned to Sarah. "Well, you brought this on yourself, my girl, so as your last official act as my housekeeper, you may exercise whatever store of diplomacy you possess in dealing with this person, and then see about transferring yourself to one of the family apartments. There is one still free, is there not?"

"Yes, sir, the one above this," Sarah said, sounding like a person in a daze, which was no more than the truth.

Grace was in no better state than Sarah as her puzzled eyes darted from person to person in search of enlightenment. Sir Hector waved the two women off. "Go about your housekeeping business now. You may as well tell Grace what just happened here. If you talk fast, you may be allowed to finish the telling before the news drifts up from below to meet you, complete in all details."

"I beg your pardon, sir?" Sarah was growing more confused by the moment.

The gentlemen wore broad smiles now, and even Lady Townsend looked wryly amused as Sir Hector explained, "It is one of the eternal mysteries of the universe how the servants always know everything that happens in the family almost as soon as it transpires."

As Sarah and Grace prepared to leave the room, the general dismissed his son and daughter and requested that Lord Eversley remain for a few moments as he had a favor to beg of him. Sarah glanced back once to see Lord Eversley watching her with a pensive look. On catching her eye he gave her a farewell smile, but she could not seem to make her lips curve upward and she turned hastily to catch up with Grace.

He hadn't really believed her despite his comforting support through her recent ordeal. He had written to his agent in London directing him to "check" her story. Somehow, despite all she had gained today, there was a cold little sensation of loss in the region of her heart, which was quite nonsensical, she told herself bracingly. He would be married, of course, with a quiverful of children in his nursery. How could it be otherwise for such an attractive man? At a guess she would put his age in the middle thirties, though he looked much younger when he smiled. Ah, well, Lord Eversley was not her business. With her grandfather being such a recluse, it was unlikely that she would be on calling terms with the neighboring families.

Sarah was unaware of Grace's silent scrutiny while they

walked through the antechamber behind Lady Townsend and
her brother, but when the other two headed across the great
hall toward the Ridgemont's suite, Grace halted Sarah before
she could follow them through the door.

"I left that woman waiting in the hall to see Sir Hector,"
she said in low tones. "Come into the chapel for a moment so
you can tell me what is going on before we have to meet her."

Obediently Sarah changed course and the two women left the
antechamber by the door that opened into the corridor leading
past the chapel to the west staircase. As soon as they slipped
into the empty chapel, Grace turned to her companion. "What
is going on, Sarah? Do you know who this Mrs.—Mrs.—"

"Mrs. Glamorgan."

"Who this Mrs. Glamorgan is?"

"She is the housekeeper Lord Eversley's agent engaged for
Beech Hill." Grace's eyes flickered, but she stood in silent
expectation while Sarah hesitated, seeking the least hurtful words
for her explanation. She took a deep breath and plunged. "I
am Gerald Ridgemont's daughter, Grace. I am truly sorry that
I lied to you that first day. It was a cowardly thing to do, but
I was so afraid my grandfather would refuse to see me that I
jumped at the chance Joseph's mistake in thinking me the new
housekeeper gave me to get inside Beech Hill. You were so
helpful and friendly that I hated myself for piling lie upon lie,
but once started, there seemed no way to end the deception,
at least not until I had told my grandfather the truth. And he
wouldn't see me after that first brief interview when I couldn't
quite find the right words.

"Actually, he recognized me immediately from my
resemblance to my grandmother, but for some reason, perhaps
to punish everyone a little, he preferred to let the deception
continue until today. I hope you will forgive me, Grace. I would
not like to lose my first friend at Beech Hill."

Grace's fine gray eyes had studied Sarah's contrite face during
this difficult confession, and now her generous mouth widened
into an unforced smile. "I was fairly certain you had never been
a housekeeper before, but you seemed so . . . so troubled that
I wished to help you. Is your name really Sarah?"

Sarah nodded. "After my grandmother. And Mother had Sarah for one of her names too." Sensing the curiosity that Grace was too well-mannered to attempt to gratify, she amplified her remarks to clarify the situation. "My father was used to say that I was a combination of his mother and mine. Both my parents are gone now. My mother died while we were living in America and my father last year after we had been back in England about a year. There is just my brother and myself now and our good friend Lottie Miller, who has taken care of us since we were born. Richard is only eleven, and my grandfather has just decreed that we are to come here to stay. Richard will love living in this beautiful country, but I am not entirely certain it is a wise move. My aunt and uncle . . ." Her voice trailed off.

Grace finished briskly, "Your aunt and uncle will learn to accept the situation in time. It will be wonderful to have young people at Beech Hill once again. Was that what Sir Hector was talking about when he referred to the empty suite?"

"Yes. My goodness, we've forgotten about Mrs. Glamorgan cooling her heels in the hall all this while. Come help me pacify her, Grace. Perhaps for now we might simply say I have been acting as housekeeper pending her arrival. She'll hear the whole story soon enough, in any case."

As the women left the chapel and headed for the great hall and the understandably irate Mrs. Glamorgan, Sarah said hesitantly, her voice pleading, "Grace, I hope I'll always be just Sarah to you—please?"

Grace smiled gently. "When there is no one around to hear or criticize, you'll be Sarah. Will that do?"

"Thank you, Grace."

And for the second time that day Sarah's rare smile illuminated her face.

8

With Sarah's departure all the general's vitality seemed to drain away, the viscount noted with distinct unease as his eyes returned from following her graceful figure through the door. Her grandfather maintained his upright position in the chair by sheer force of will, but the hands resting on the chair arms were shaking, and Mark did not care for the rapid rise and fall of his chest in shallow breathing.

"Why not let Somers put you to bed for a while now, sir?" he suggested, concealing his concern under a matter-of-fact air. "It's obvious you've been conducting yourself these last few days in a manner not prescribed by your doctor. If you wish to enjoy your family's visit, you'd be wise to slow the pace a bit. I'll come by tomorrow for a talk."

He made to rise, but the general removed one hand from the arm of his chair in a brief staying gesture all the more compelling because of the effort involved, an effort that was costing him strength. Mark subsided, wishing Somers would return.

"Must talk now, then I'll rest this damned disobliging body. I won't allow it to deprive me of my triumph."

The viscount was silent as the general paused to recoup his strength after this defiant speech. Better perhaps to let him get whatever it was off his chest. It would only disturb his rest to have it worrying him.

"I want that boy brought here immediately, before that independent miss"—by which description Mark had no difficulty in recognizing Sarah—"takes a long look at her loving relatives and gets cold feet and tries to cut and run."

His lips twitched once at the general's dispassionate summing-up of his family. Before the proud old man should have to frame a request, he said, "I shall write to Coke at once directing him to make travel arrangements for the boy and their old nurse."

"And have him close that damned hat shop for good and all!" Sir Hector's voice rang with some of its old authority for a moment. He chuckled wickedly, adding, "Though it was worth it to see Adelaide nearly go off in an apoplexy at the thought of her stiff-rumped friends learning that a niece of Lady Townsend was a shopkeeper." He wheezed to a stop and started coughing.

Really alarmed now, Mark was pouring a glass of water from a pitcher on the bedside table when Somers, soft-footed and competent, came into the room and took it from his hand with a reproachful look.

"Time you was back in bed, Sir Hector," he said in the tone of a father speaking to a recalcitrant child. "Give you an inch and you take an ell as usual." He held the glass to the general's mouth and waited patiently until the paroxysm quieted before repeating, "Bed for you for the rest of the day, sir, unless you wish me to send for Doctor Rydell."

Sir Hector waved away the glass. His head fell back against the chair back now, a look of exhaustion on his spare features, but his voice still held a trace of its former truculence. "Rydell is an old woman, and so are you, Somers. I'll rest now, but I am going to dine with the family tonight."

"We'll see about that," said Somers, beginning to loosen the scarf about his employer's neck.

The viscount deemed it a good time to make his escape and did so, calling a brief good-bye from the doorway.

Sir Hector's iron will was betrayed by his aging body and he did not, in the end, dine with his family that evening.

By the time Sarah had met and placated Mrs. Glamorgan and enlisted Grace's assistance in acquainting the wiry, birdlike little woman with her new domain, two hours had passed. The housekeeper was understandably surprised to find so many more people in residence at Beech Hill than she had been led to believe, but she accepted the situation, as tactfully represented to her by Sarah, with scarcely a blink and was ready to set to with a will after refreshing herself with a cup of tea and gingerbread in the room that was shortly to be hers. Any curiosity she might feel as to why a granddaughter of the house had been occupying the housekeeper's suite she kept to herself. She did wish to know, also understandably, to whom she was to report.

In the blank silence that greeted this reasonable inquiry, Grace said firmly that Miss Ridgemont was that person. Sarah was too nonplussed to protest at the time, but when she and Grace were alone later, she tried to explain that she could not possibly usurp such power when every other person resident at the moment had a better right by virtue of long acquaintance with Beech Hill.

"With the exception of Sir Hector, every other person in residence at the moment is merely visiting," Grace rebutted calmly. "You are to be living here; therefore, you will naturally be Sir Hector's hostess."

But this Sarah would not hear of. "For the moment, because I am acquainted with the preparations that have been made for this visitation, I'll make myself available to Mrs. Glamorgan, but if one of the other ladies demurs, I shall step aside at once." She stated her position firmly and refused to consider herself in any way her grandfather's hostess. "That honor belongs to his daughter until or unless he says otherwise."

Grace held her peace, and with Mrs. Glamorgan overseeing the move, Sarah's few belongings were transferred to the apartment above her grandfather's, which had been readied earlier for William's occupation.

Strange uneasy emotions were churning in Sarah's breast as she approached her grandfather's rooms late in the afternoon when the necessary housekeeping arrangements and preliminary dinner preparations had been effected. She had the sense of being a stone caught up in an avalanche as it rolled downhill. Events had overtaken her and moved her along without her connivance or permission. She felt she should take a hand in her own destiny before she found her life and Richard's completely in the control of others, but she no longer knew what she wanted. Her path had seemed clear back in London. Was it only four days ago that she had embarked on her fateful journey?

It had never once crossed Sarah's mind that her grandfather might expect his long-unacknowledged grandchildren to come live under his roof. One part of her wished to yield to the blissful sensation of security that had enveloped her when Sir Hector had ordered her to cast off all worry about Richard's future, but there was another side of her nature that rebelled against being taken over almost as a possession, perhaps even as a weapon in what had all the appearance of continuing hostilities with his children. Or if that was too strongly expressed, she thought, trying to be fair, at least she was conscious of a strong desire to retain some of the autonomy of action she had enjoyed by virtue of the very poverty she had desperately sought to escape. It was true that no benefit came without a price attached, she decided soberly, and she was terribly unsure what price was going to be demanded of her in exchange for financial security, and if she would be willing to pay it wholeheartedly without resentment.

The main difficulty was that she did not know her grandfather at all well yet, and what little she did know of him she had been taught to despise. In a way it could be considered almost disloyal to her father to place their lives in his father's keeping, but she must have known that when she made her original decision to seek help. Richard must be her first concern.

Her brow was furrowed as she knocked on the hall door to the antechamber, but this much she had accepted. She must not let loyalty to her father blind her to her grandfather's virtues.

Somers opened the door to her, and it was clear to her seeking eyes that the benevolence of the early afternoon had been replaced by worry.

"What is it, Somers? Has anything happened?"

"Sir Hector is not so well, Miss Sarah. The events of the past few days have been too much for him. The doctor is with him now."

Guilt rose unbidden in Sarah's heart at the severity of the valet's expression. "I am very sorry, Somers," she said quietly.

"I'm afraid I never considered my grandfather's possible state of health when I came here, and . . . and events seemed to slip out of control shortly thereafter."

"It's not your fault, Miss Sarah," Somers said, his features softening at her sincere distress. "Sir Hector is that pleased to have you here, I know, but what with all his plotting and planning, he overdid, and now he's paying for it. He won't leave his bed again today, nor yet tomorrow, no matter what nonsense he talks about dining at table."

"I should say not! We'll see that he does not attempt it." Sarah's vehemence seemed to appease the valet, who nodded in agreement before turning his head as a man came out of the bedchamber. "Excuse me, Miss Sarah; here's the doctor now."

Sarah stood undecided as the doctor and Somers held a low-voiced conversation, after which the valet accepted a vial from the other's hand and disappeared into the bedchamber. She felt an intruder, but the doctor was closing his bag and coming toward her now, so she held her ground.

"I am Sarah Ridgemont, Sir Hector's granddaughter, Doctor—?"

"Rydell, Simon Rydell at your service, Miss Ridgemont."

As the doctor bowed politely, Sarah blinked and tried to keep her surprise from showing on her face. Her grandfather's doctor was quite young, under thirty, she guessed, and quite frankly the handsomest man she had ever laid eyes on. Her Ridgemont cousins were all attractive, and Lord Eversley was more than that, though his features were a bit too strong and his jaw too rocky for the epithet handsome to spring to mind. This man was an Adonis. As tall as Cousin Vincent and Lord Eversley, he was slimmer than either and without the muscular development of the natural athlete. From his wavy chestnut hair to his well-shaped chin with its hint of a cleft, however, all was perfection. Large clear eyes with a light-gray iris rimmed in black were fringed with thick dark lashes any female would covet, his nose and mouth were examples of the classical ideal, and the bone structure of his head would inspire any sculptor worth the name to heroic efforts at duplication.

Sarah blinked again, realizing with something of a start that

Doctor Rydell had spoken to her. "I beg your pardon, Doctor?"

"I said there is no immediate cause for concern about your grandfather, Miss Ridgemont. He will overcome this latest setback with a few days of rest." His voice was pleasantly pitched with an intonation of gravity. "That is not to say, however, that he will ever make a complete recovery. You must not expect this. Sir Hector is an old man, and his heart is wearing out. Every time he has one of these little attacks, brought on by physical or emotional upset, it puts additional strain on the heart. He improves, but never to quite the place he was before."

"I see. You have dissuaded him from attempting to dine with the family, I trust?"

A little smile lightened Doctor Rydell's countenance. "He is feeling too weak at the moment to wish to do anything but lie in his bed. The problem will arise in a day or two when he's feeling more himself again."

"Must he be considered permanently bedfast, Doctor?"

"Not entirely. If he has spent a quiet day and wishes to dine with the family, I would encourage him to do so. On days when he has been more active or entertained visitors perhaps, I would recommend a tray in his room. Use your common sense and try to keep upsets to a minimum."

The doctor smiled again. "Sir Hector tells me you are the granddaughter who resided in America until recently, so you may not be well-acquainted with his, shall I say, peppery nature. He does not like to be crossed in anything and doesn't suffer fools with even nominal patience. This has been the attitude of a lifetime, I would assume, but now he is applying it to his malfunctioning body, which tends to bring on just those emotional upsets that are most dangerous to a weakened heart. In a way it is like dealing with a sick child. He must be humored, cajoled, and kept from doing harm to himself."

Sarah smiled at him quite suddenly, liking his understanding and humanity. She could have no idea that the rest of his warning was driven straight out of his mind by the radiant quality of that smile as she pursued her own train of thought. "Are you acquainted with my uncle, Mr. Horace Ridgemont, Doctor Rydell?"

"No, ma'am, I am fairly new to this locality and have not had the honor of meeting any of the general's family with the exception of yourself."

"Then please may I make you known to him now? I am persuaded he will be anxious to hear your professional opinion of his father's condition."

On receiving the doctor's assurance that he would be pleased to meet Mr. Ridgemont, Sarah personally conducted him to her uncle's apartment and performed the necessary introductions. She did not see her aunt, nor did she remain during the men's conversation.

That evening, Sarah took as much time to dress for her first dinner with her newly met family as she would have needed for a court presentation. Considering that she had only one gown suitable for evening with her—and that one over two years old— this might be considered excessive even without the assistance of an abigail to speed the process.

She was scared witless, she admitted to herself, staring at her image in a long mirror in her luxurious new quarters. There was no escaping the knowledge that she would rather by far submit to having a tooth drawn than face that circle of hostile faces, or, at best, blank faces concealing hostility.

When she had looked in on her grandfather after leaving Doctor Rydell with her uncle, she had been moved to pity by a frailty about his person that had not been so apparent at their other meetings. He had apologized for "throwing her to the wolves" without the protection of his presence at her first social meeting with her relatives. She had seen that this bothered him a great deal, though the unworthy thought had crossed her mind that part of his perturbation was probably attributable to disappointment at being forced to miss the drama personally. She had applied her best efforts to convincing him that she had no fears on that head and had no intention of allowing herself to be intimidated or put in her place by any of her relatives, should that be their intention, which she doubted. Her voice and eyes had been steady and calm while making this vainglorious claim, but she could not long meet his eyes filled with amused derision. Fortunately, Somers had rescued her from having to haul down her flag by popping up to remind her sternly that her visit had gone beyond the five minutes agreed upon when he had admitted her in defiance of the doctor's ban on visitors. She had given her grandfather's hand a gentle squeeze and fled in relief.

Alone in the bedchamber, Sarah could not, to her shame, summon up even a vestige of the confidence she had boasted of to Sir Hector. She scowled at her image in the mirror. If beauty and suitable attire were a woman's armor, she might as well be going into battle in her shift! She stared with displeasure at the plain skirt of her soft coffee-colored muslin gown with its darker brown ribbon at the waist. She did not possess a dress with so much as a single flounce at the hemline, and flounces were all the crack in England, she had discovered. Well, it couldn't be helped; they would have to take her as they found her. She pinned her grandmother's brooch, which had been returned to her by one of the housemaids—not Dawkins— onto the bodice of the dress and turned away from the glass.

Something about the way her hair had gone back caught her frowning attention and Sarah spent the next ten minutes unpinning and rebrushing the thick, slightly wavy mane. She had dispensed with the cap out of defiance, knowing Arabella's shining dark ringlets would be displayed to advantage in a fashionable coiffure. Her father had thought her hair beautiful with its variegated colors, and he would not permit her to cover it or cut it short. Basic bronze with gleaming gold and copper overlays was how he had described it, and the thought of her father's pride in her appearance stiffened her spine as she headed toward the saloon on reluctant feet.

The double doors of the saloon stood open, and she regretted the time she had taken to redo her hair when a swift glance informed her that all members of her father's family were present. She stopped just inside the doorway, her chin automatically elevating and her face muscles going quite still as she braced for the impact of seven pairs of eyes studying her person with attitudes that ran the gamut from polite noninterest on the part of her uncle's wife to the undisguised animosity dwelling in her Aunt Adelaide's dark eyes.

Seeing that this lady had no intention of performing her social duty, Horace Ridgemont came forward with his hand out-stretched and ended the awkward silence. "Well, my dear Sarah, may I be the first to welcome you officially into your family at long last?" His voice was a trifle overhearty in the manner of a conscientious host, but Sarah appreciated the gesture and she smiled warmly at him as she gave him her hand.

"Thank you, Uncle Horace."

"I believe you have at least met everyone—" he began, to be interrupted by a suave voice saying, "Then you are mistaken, Uncle, for I have not yet had the felicity of being presented to my new cousin, an omission I trust you will now repair?"

Horace Ridgemont's geniality dropped away like a discarded cloak as he eyed his nephew with patent dislike, a gaze the younger man returned with bland assurance.

"Sarah, this is Vincent, Lord Townsend," he said shortly.

"How do you do, Lord Townsend," Sarah murmured.

"You cut me to the quick, Cousin Sarah," Vincent said, bowing low over her hand, then looking up directly into her eyes, his own alight with exaggerated reproach. "Surely we can dispense with titles, being so nearly related."

Sarah retrieved her hand gently. "Of course, if you wish it, Cousin Vincent."

"Oh, indeed I do wish it. You are obviously the best thing that has happened in this family in years, and we must celebrate the event," Vincent declared, showing her an expression of almost theatrical admiration.

"You are too kind, Cousin." Sarah kept her own expression demure, but there was a dancing light in her changeable eyes that caused Vincent's to gleam in self-mockery, to her mind the first real emotion he had displayed.

"Hush your nonsense, Vincent," his mother advised tartly. "You'll have the girl believing you."

"I am thankful to reflect that no son of mine would indulge in such an exaggerated, one might almost say offensive, form of gallantry," put in Mrs. Ridgemont in flat tones.

Her sister-in-law bridled, but Vincent said gently, "Is that a comforting reflection, Aunt? I am so glad."

"Cecil would indulge at another time and place," Arabella said with sweet provocation. "In fact, I would take it as a favor if you would let him practice on you for a change, Cousin Sarah." She threw a saucy glance at her younger male cousin, who went beet-red and might have retorted ungallantly had not his brother turned to Sarah at that moment with his delightful smile.

"Do I understand that we have yet another member of the family to meet, Cousin Sarah? You have a young brother?"

Sarah smiled at him in relief, a shining smile that caused the two Townsend ladies to examine her in narrow-eyed speculation as she replied, "Yes, Richard is only eleven, but he is well-grown for his age and possesses, I believe, a quickness of understanding and a cleverness beyond the average for boys of his age, though you may say this is just a fond sister's partiality," she added with an apologetic air.

"Even as young as eleven, William gave evidence of his superior mental abilities," Mrs. Ridgemont chimed in. She was prepared to go into greater detail, Sarah feared, but at that moment Millbank appeared in the doorway to announce dinner.

They trooped down the west staircase to the dining saloon, Lady Townsend complaining all the time about the inconvenience of a house with its drawing room and dining room on different levels.

The family usually arranged itself in two camps for meals, Sarah noted, one at each end of the long table. She saw that her place was to be between the two, with Vincent and Cecil flanking her. Across the table, William Ridgemont occupied the same middle position between his mother and Arabella.

Sarah was very glad to be seated after the awkward few minutes in the drawing room. At least at table there was something to do with her hands and a natural place upon which to fix her gaze when the conversation took an embarrassing or difficult turn. Not that conversation was general except for a few sporadic bursts. Horace Ridgemont addressed himself wholeheartedly to the food on his plate. Between mouthfuls he spoke mainly to his sons and, more rarely, to his wife. For most of the time Sarah parried Lord Townsend's practiced gallantry

with determined affability, all too aware that he kept it up mainly
to annoy the two elder ladies. Not a particularly sweet nature
Vincent's, she decided, wondering if he ever did or said anything that was not studied, not for effect. A little of Vincent's
company would go a long way, but Sarah's attempts to engage
Cecil in conversation in the intervals when her aunt had
commanded her son's attention were not entirely successful.
He seemed shy of her, and recalling the almost-insulting male
appraisal yesterday when he had thought her a housekeeper,
she wondered if it was embarrassment or if he was uncomfortable around females of his own class—at least those older
than he, she amended, intercepting a teasing glance flung at him
by Arabella.

Noting that she was being observed by the newcomer, Arabella tossed her dark curls and asked with assumed artlessness,
"Tell me, Cousin Sarah, what is it like to run a hat shop?"

Sarah smiled nicely. "Like the rest of life, I would imagine:
sometimes interesting, often dull and tedious."

"Was it a successful business?"

"That will do, Arabella," said Lady Townsend. "The less
said about a business, the better. It is too utterly appalling to
contemplate the name of Ridgemont being splashed across a
shop window." She shuddered feelingly.

"But the name of Ridgemont was never mentioned, ma'am,"
explained Sarah. "The shop is called simply Sarah of Boston."

"Aha," cried Arabella, with the air of one solving a mystery.
"So that is the origin of the Boston alias."

Sarah bit her lip but remained silent, determined not to be
drawn into any arguments or explanations with any of these
people. She was again grateful to William, who rescued the
situation with an innocuous question to Arabella.

The uncomfortable meal dragged on with Sarah forcing
herself to eat enough to avoid drawing attention to herself. It
was not the fault of the food, which was of a uniformly high
quality, the newly developed housekeeper side of Sarah was
pleased to note, despite the occasional disparaging comment
from Lady Townsend. She found it a bit unnerving to dine with
the family under Millbank's eye after sharing a table with him

for the previous days, but she would just have to accustom herself to doing so. She would also, she thought with a sinking heart, have to get used to what seemed to be a family habit of sniping at one another, trying to draw fire as it were—that is, she would have to get used to it unless the family reverted to its former pattern of short, widely spaced and noncoinciding visits.

Sarah, speaking only when directly addressed, was well-placed to note that it was William Ridgemont who unobtrusively smoothed over a number of bristling pauses before the individual under attack at the moment could retaliate in kind. By the time dinner was finally over, she had discovered he was indeed a rarity among those of Ridgemont blood, a person who did not derive enjoyment by pricking the sensitive places of others with barbed comments.

The day's events had left Sarah emotionally exhausted, an increasingly familiar condition she could only hope was not to become her permanent reaction to her relatives' proximity. She longed for privacy but had not the courage to beg to be excused from the after-dinner gathering of the females in the main drawing room upstairs.

The elder ladies exchanged forced small talk, mainly, Sarah felt, because her Aunt Townsend wished to make her dislike of the interloper plain. It was left to the younger element to entertain one another. Sarah eyed her female cousin warily, but Arabella, bored without male society, abandoned her affected manner in favor of satisfying a natural curiosity about this odd specimen in their midst.

"You never did say, Cousin Sarah, whether your hat shop was successful. Was it?"

"That depends upon one's definition of success. Our hats enjoyed a mild vogue that was personally gratifying, but we were not very successful in the more mundane business skills, such as getting people to pay their accounts."

Arabella digested this. "So you were an artistic but not a financial success," she summed up with devastating accuracy.

"Admirably put," Sarah observed dryly.

Miss Townsend had barely started on what Sarah was

convinced would be a minute investigation into the details of daily life of a handy specimen of a class of persons her own privileged rank barred her from encountering when the gentlemen returned from drinking their port. Cecil headed for his young cousin with the light of retaliation in his eyes, and William beat Lord Townsend to the seat beside Sarah on the pink settee.

The next hour was not the ordeal Sarah had feared. For the first time that evening she was able to relax in William's undemanding company. He told her something of his life, alternating between the small country estate in Hampshire that his mother preferred, as it had been her childhood home, and the Ridgemont town house in London that belonged to his grandfather. She was content to listen to these light renderings without much need to comment, but she was sincerely touched when he turned sympathetic blue eyes to hold her glance and said simply, "I am most sorry about your father's death, Sarah. I never knew my uncle, of course, but I do know it must be a great sadness to find oneself alone in the world without any family. I am glad that you and Richard are no longer in that position."

The ready tears that had plagued Sarah all week crowded behind her eyelids once more, but she held them back determinedly as she essayed a trembling little smile eloquent of gratitude for this one truly kind member of her family.

"Thank you, William. You are the only person who has spoken of my father at all, and I am grateful. He may not have been a satisfactory son or brother, but he loved his family, and we miss him very much."

"I am sure you do."

William and Sarah, forging tentative bonds of friendship in an emotionally charged moment, were unaware that at least two pairs of eyes were avidly following the progress of their quiet conversation. Horace Ridgemont's expression was thoughtful as he studied the pair, and his wife's characteristic attitude of polite uninvolvement had been jolted into sudden defensive alertness.

9

It took a moment or two for Sarah to orientate herself after her slowly opening eyes lighted on a curly maned beast, fortunately more fanciful than ferocious. She blinked, and other strange objects in a stranger forest alive with flowers and vines came into focus. The underside of the canopy over the huge tester bed was lined with a gloriously printed fabric that could provide hours of visual enchantment. Her eyes moved with languid fascination from tawny beasts to riotously colored flowers of outlandish proportions nestling among the jungle vines, barely aware that the even gray light coming in the windows she had not covered the previous evening meant the end of the pleasant succession of sunlit days they had been enjoying in Gloucestershire.

Conscious of that precious rarity in her busy life, a day with no pressing demands on her time and energy, Sarah stretched her arms in lazy contentment while her eyes made a slow tour of the appointments of the most luxurious setting she had ever called her own, even temporarily. Yesterday she had been too distracted by anticipatory fears of her first social meeting with her father's family to appreciate the lovely old mahogany furnishings, which included a beautifully grained wardrobe on the wall to the left of the bed. Except for her amusing beast-and-floral canopy fabric, which was repeated in the overdrapes of the three windows, this was actually one of the plainest rooms in Beech Hill, with its light-green walls and ceiling adorned with a fairly simple plasterwork trim that was painted ivory. To her admittedly inexpert eye, all the furnishings seemed to date from the early seventeenth century and had been lovingly cared for over the years, judging by the beautiful sheen on the polished wood surfaces.

Sliding out of the bed, Sarah padded over to the wardrobe, her bare toes caressing the soft wool of the pale Aubusson carpet. Her few clothes looked lost in the wardrobe's vast interior, and she chewed on her bottom lip, some of her former contentment evaporating as she contemplated the one daytime dress she had brought with her other than the unspeakable black gown that she silently vowed never to put on her back again. Though not in the latest style, the plain long-sleeved cotton dress was a pretty peach color that lifted her spirits after a year of unrelieved black.

A knock on the hall door caught her with her hand on the peach cotton, which she instantly dropped, taking herself in her skimpy light night rail back to the safety of the bed on a dead run. Hands on the bedclothes pulled up to her chin, she called permission to enter.

Two young maids, goggle-eyed with curiosity despite their correctly prim demeanor, came in carrying hot water and hot chocolate.

"Good morning, Miss Ridgemont," they chorused.

"Good morning, Clara. Oh, thank you, Maria, that smells heavenly. You may put it here." Sarah made room for the chocolate on the bedside table and hoisted herself up into a sitting position against the pillows. She sipped the chocolate, trying not to appear self-conscious in the face of shy darting looks from the maids as they went about their early-morning routine.

"Mrs. Glamorgan presents her compliments and wishes to know if you'd like one of the maids to act as your dresser, Miss Ridgemont," Clara, the bolder of the pair, put in eagerly.

"No, that won't be necessary," Sarah began, then seeing the deflated expressions of the two girls, she went on to soften the blow with a smile and a cheerful explanation. "As you can see," indicating the open armoire with a wave of her hand as Maria bent to pick up the fallen dress, "I have almost no clothing to take care of at present, and when my young brother arrives with our . . . my companion, I am persuaded she will expect to do all that I require. But you will thank Mrs. Glamorgan for me, will you not?''

"Yes, miss," they responded dutifully, but disappointment still hung heavily and Sarah was seized with an inspiration.

"Are either of you skilled at dressing hair?"

"Maria is," Clara spoke up boldly and generously.

Sarah smiled. "Then perhaps you would be kind enough to do my hair for me tonight before dinner, Maria?"

Maria nodded, too shy to speak, her round face alight with pleasure, while her partner tried gamely to mask her own disappointment.

"We shall be needing someone to wait upon the nursery suite when my brother arrives, though he is not a little boy to require a nursemaid." Sarah casually tossed another ball into the air and was rewarded by the straightening of Clara's drooping figure.

"I have four younger brothers, miss," she volunteered eagerly, "and my mother says I keep them in line better than she does."

"Well, that is a splendid recommendation. If Mrs. Glamorgan agrees, you shall be in charge of the nursery, Clara. Tell her I shall be down presently to discuss the arrangements for my brother and Miss Miller."

Sarah smiled dismissal, and the two girls departed, bursting with new importance.

Left alone once more, Sarah finished the chocolate and completed her modest toilette, debating whether or not to wear the lace cap during the day. She finally decided against the spinsterish addition and found justification in her grandfather's approval when she slipped down the back stairs to seek news of him from Somers before going in to breakfast with those members of the family who came to the table in the morning.

"Go right in, Miss Sarah," the valet invited in response to her inquiry into her grandfather's condition. "Sir Hector's feeling more comfortable this morning, though he's fretting himself to flinders over how you're getting on with the family. He'll be pleased to see you looking so bonny," he added to Sarah's astonishment, but this departure from his usual severity was negated by an immediate warning to her not to encourage the invalid in any ridiculous notions about joining the family for lunch or dinner.

Sarah promised faithfully and went into the bedchamber.

Sir Hector was sitting up in bed this morning, freshly brushed and shaved and wearing a fine wool shawl over his shoulders, though a fire burned in the fireplace. Despite his alert manner, there were lines of fatigue in his gaunt face that had not been apparent the previous day. The doctor was correct: any unusual exertion or upset took its toll on his remaining strength.

Sarah banished gloomy thoughts and came forward with a smile that grew a little quizzical under his measuring gaze.

"Well, I am relieved to see the end of that black gown. My mother wore nothing but black the last thirty years of her life. I never could abide the idea of women running around dressed all in black like a bunch of noisy crows. I won't have it on my account."

Sarah let this speech pass without comment, contenting herself with giving her grandfather's hand a brief squeeze before seating herself in the chair by the bedside. "How are you feeling this morning, Grandfather?"

"Can't anyone around here come up with another topic of conversation than my health? Personally, I find the subject a dead bore."

Sarah smiled into his irascible countenance and asked, "Is there a topic of conversation you would prefer, then?"

"Several. First, tell me how dinner went last night. I can see by your sunny look that that bunch of backbiters didn't cow you, though I'll be bound that they tried."

"Everyone was most civil, Grandfather. They cannot really be expected to like having a complete stranger thrust into intimate contact with them of a sudden, with the promise of another yet to come."

"You have as much right to be here as they have."

"In a sense, of course, but there are also the claims of long acquaintance and the ties of affection that Richard and I cannot have."

"You all have just whatever claims I choose to allow you, no more, nor less," snapped the general.

Sarah did not reply to this piece of arrogance, but her troubled gaze did not waver under his, and in a moment Sir Hector continued in a challenging vein.

"Do you mean to try to gammon me that you noticed any so called ties of affection in that group of sharks?"

"Not so much between families, perhaps, but within the families, certainly," Sarah replied, selecting her words with care.

"Hah, so much for your powers of observation, young woman," her grandfather scoffed. "Adelaide don't give a tinker's damn for any soul on this earth. All she cares about is her social position. Insofar as the girl's looks and Vincent's modish air and athletic feats add to her consequence, she is proud of them. Let either fail to form an advantageous connection, however, and you'll soon see how much real affection exists in that ménage."

"That is a harsh judgment," Sarah said, then added hastily, "not that I am in any position to dispute it or agree with you. Uncle Horace's family seems a united group, however."

"I don't deny Horace is fond enough of his sons, but he totally dominates that nonentity he married. For her part, any affection she feels is poured all over William indiscriminately. It's a wonder the fool hasn't been the ruination of that boy."

"I find William an exceptionally kind and agreeable person," Sarah said, and withstood the sharpening of her grandfather's gaze in the short silence that followed this positive statement.

"He's the best of the lot. Got a good head on his shoulders. Vincent's a worthless fribble, and Cecil—"

"Cecil is very young yet. I daresay they will all improve on acquaintance."

"You are to be commended more on your optimism than on your perception," was her grandfather's dry rejoinder.

Sarah was determined to refrain from adding to the dissension in the family. "As you can see, Grandfather, I survived my introduction nicely."

''I see you buried the cap with the black dress,'' the general said unexpectedly. ''Good. It's a crime to cover hair like yours. My wife's hair was just like that, all colors blended.'' He cleared his throat noisily and went on in a stiffer voice, ''What is the boy like?''

Sarah laughed, though she was feeling much heartened by her grandfather's implied approval. ''Now that I have met the whole family, I can say with confidence that Richard is a typical Ridgemont. His hair and eyes are dark, and he already has the beginnings of the nose. William and I seem to be the only ones who don't favor you at all, sir.''

''You need not look so smug about it,'' grumbled Sir Hector. ''You could do worse, nose and all.''

Sarah burst out laughing, her pearly teeth gleaming between parted lips. ''I should not minister to your vanity by telling you that I find the Ridgemont look quite intriguing and attractive.''

''Do not try to mollify me, girl,'' her grandfather warned, elevating one eyebrow in a devil-may-care expression that inadvertently dealt Sarah a blow. Her father had exhibited that same mannerism on a number of occasions. For a second her grandfather's features slipped out of focus as she struggled against a rush of sentimental tears, but he restored her equilibrium with a timely change of subject.

''I wanted to tell you that Eversley is arranging transportation for the boy and your old nurse through his agent in London. They should be here in a day or two.''

''That is very kind of Lord Eversley.''

''I told him to close down that shop too,'' Sir Hector added, sending her a sideways glance that managed to be both arrogant and unsure at the same time.

Sarah said nothing for a moment, her face reflecting her uncertainty, then honest, gold-flecked eyes met piercing dark ones. ''The insecurity of our existence in London was very worrisome because of Richard, but there was often a sense of accomplishment too in conducting a business enterprise that was very satisfying personally. I shall miss that.'' There was a faraway look in the lovely eyes as her faintly mournful voice trailed off.

It might have been fear at the thought of losing her that sharpened Sir Hector's tones as he declared, "There are plenty of challenges right here. It's no sinecure to run a house this size and manage a discordant group of relatives."

"Goodness, you are not suggesting that I could manage this family in any sense, are you, Grandfather?" Alarm rang in her voice.

This time it was he who patted her hand. "No, no, of course not, though your grandmother could do it."

"But that was long ago, before my . . . before there were grandchildren; at least they were only babies," she finished lamely in an attempt to cover up what would have been an ill-advised mention of her father's banishment.

"Yes, yes, now it is I who am becoming fanciful. It must be your resemblance to your grandmother. Even your voice has the same soft cadence as Sarah's. I sometimes forget you are a mere slip of a girl."

"Arabella is a girl, Grandfather. I am six-and-twenty and have lived a varied existence on two continents, sometimes even a precarious existence. My girlhood seems lost in the distant past."

"Then it's more than time you had some enjoyment in your life. The boy will be going off to school shortly—you know that?" he probed, testing her reaction.

"Yes. It is what I have wished for him," Sarah said with composure, "though I shall greatly miss his bright presence. Of necessity I have been more a mother than a sister to Richard."

"It's high time you were thinking of children of your own. And you need not treat me to that patronizing little smile, girl. No female with your looks and my money behind her will languish long on the shelf. As soon as the word gets out, you will have your pick of the eligibles in the area. I haven't had time to work it all out yet, but I am persuaded Lady Eversley will take you about. She's got a good heart and she was fond of your grandmother."

"I would say you have been powerfully busy inside your head, Grandfather," Sarah said dryly as she rose to her feet. "I must run or I'll be late for breakfast. I'll come back later.''

Sarah made her escape with as much dignity as she could call to her aid, conscious of her grandfather's eyes on her straight back. She was battling an urgent desire to protest that she had no intention of being bartered on the marriage mart, but there was no point in upsetting him at this stage of his machinations. They existed only in his imagination at present, and it was up to her to see that they stayed there. Perhaps, she concluded optimistically, he would be so content with her company that these grandiose designs for her future would fade from his mind. For one thing, he should learn that Lord Eversley was not the only person available who could give him a game of chess or piquet.

After the active and emotionally wrenching period just passed, Sarah's first full day as an official member of the Ridgemont family was quiet and relatively serene. Neither of her aunts having evinced any interest in the housekeeping arrangements now that Mrs. Glamorgan was installed, Sarah was left by default to deal with that lady, which she did in an amicable fashion, thanks to the thorough understanding she had gained of the inner workings of the household during her stint as housekeeper. Mrs. Glamorgan was an efficient individual who preferred to deal with persons of equal competence.

The large sunny day nursery with its exciting array of books and games was being readied for Richard. Sarah had initially intended to put her brother in the servant's room in her own apartment until he should become accustomed to the immensity of Beech Hill, but her grandfather had vetoed this plan as "coddling." Knowing that Lottie would not be far away in any case, she had not disputed the general's arguments that the boy needed to "harden up" before going off to school. In consequence, two adjoining bedchambers near the nursery were prepared for Richard and Lottie.

It occurred to Sarah that her grandfather habored some fears that a boy reared primarily by women would be too soft, but she did not raise the issue with the old soldier. He would soon discover that two years of attending day school and negotiating the streets of London on his own had contributed to developing

an independence and a quiet competence in his youngest grandson. Buoyed up by her intimate knowledge of her brother's
sturdy nature, Sarah went about the house with a light heart
in happy anticipation of an imminent reunion with the two
persons she loved best in the world. There was a spring in her
step and a glow in her eyes that was not even dimmed by her
Aunt Townsend's disparaging glance at her simple gown when
she passed her on the staircase midway through the morning.

Sarah popped in to see her grandfather again before lunch
and met Doctor Rydell, who had just finished examining his
patient. She smiled at him warmly as he stood up at her entrance
into the general's bedchamber.

"I trust you find my grandfather much improved from
yesterday, Doctor?"

"I do indeed, Miss Ridgemont," he replied, returning her
smile with interest. "In fact, I was about to suggest to Sir Hector
that I would have no objection to his joining the family for lunch
tomorrow if he feels up to making the effort."

"Don't talk about me as if I were absent or senile," growled
his ungrateful patient.

"I'm sorry, Grandfather," Sarah said soothingly. "Somers
is on his way in with your luncheon tray now. Do you think
it might be a good idea for Doctor Rydell to meet the rest of
the family?"

"Now, there's a high treat for him," Sir Hector replied with
a snide twist of his lips. He waved his hand dismissively. "Why
bother to ask my permission? Females always do whatever they
like no matter what a mere male thinks."

Sarah glanced at him in consternation. "Of course I shall not
if you do not wish it, Grandfather, but I believe Aunt Townsend
would be relieved to hear of your improvement from the doctor
himself."

"Oh, do whatever you wish, girl." Sir Hector's permission
was grudging, but Sarah took immediate advantage of the valet's
appearance in the doorway to usher the doctor out, promising
to look in on her grandfather again after his rest.

The Ridgemont ladies were ensconced in the drawing room
along with William, who still could not get a boot on his injured

foot though he had dispensed with the cane and was walking with more ease. The other men had not yet returned from their morning ride, apparently.

Sarah performed the necessary introductions in her quiet manner, observing as she did so that Mrs. Ridgemont responded with absentminded civility and William with his customary friendliness. Lady Townsend took over the conversation instantly, directing Doctor Rydell to a chair near hers while she embarked on an intensive interrogation into her father's condition.

Sarah took a chair and became, like the others, redundant to the interview being carried on by her aunt and the doctor. He had answered a bit hesitantly at first, but Sarah, who had been observing the scene closely, was not fooled into believing him intimidated by his noble inquisitor's peremptory manner. The young doctor dealt competently with his even more intimidating patient, and he had appeared quite at ease with Horace Ridgemont the previous day. Having noted the stunned expression on his face just now when he had been presented to Arabella, rather like a man who has nearly stepped off a cliff, Sarah would have ventured a more intriguing explanation for his initial inability to satisfy Lady Townsend's demand for coherent information. Fortunately, he regained his composure within seconds, and she was able to release the breath she had been holding.

Sarah glanced at Arabella to see if her cousin was preening herself on this latest conquest, but that young lady was sitting uncharacteristically still, her eyes demurely fixed on the work in her lap. In Sarah's limited observance of her coquettish cousin, this was unusual behavior indeed in the presence of a personable young man. She might have been led into the error of accepting that a mere doctor was outside Arabella's sphere of interest, had she not made the additional discovery that the younger girl's hands were utterly motionless on her embroidery and her bent head was angled just enough to permit a covert study of Simon Rydell from the corner of her eye. Sarah's own features grew still as she reflected that it was a mercy Lady Townsend was too engrossed in her interrogation to suspect her daughter's interest in a man she would undoubtedly consider ineligible as a suitor. They could do without that complication at Beech Hill. She took some comfort in the knowledge that the two young people would have almost no opportunity to meet again in the ordinary course of events.

Doctor Rydell was dismissed with conscious graciousness by Lady Townsend after she had extracted all available information from him. While waiting for Joseph to appear to show the doctor out, William engaged him in easy conversation. No words were exchanged between Arabella and Doctor Rydell, though Sarah was on tenterhooks that one or the other would betray the mutual attraction she was now convinced existed between them. She did not really relax until she saw the doctor's back disappearing through the door.

Lunch was an uneventful meal. Arabella was somewhat more subdued than usual, Vincent persevered with his gallantry toward Sarah when he remembered that it provoked his female relatives, and Cecil unbent enough to address one or two innocuous remarks to his new cousin. Sarah came away with the hopeful feeling that some minor progress had been made in the process of gaining acceptance within her family.

The women retired to their private quarters after lunch, though Sarah accepted a diffidently expressed invitation to go around the picture gallery with William in an hour's time so that she might become acquainted with some of her ancestors.

True to his word, William proved to be a competent guide to the modest collection of paintings assembled over the years. They were mostly portraits, she saw at once, with a smattering of military scenes and paintings of battles. After an hour's tour she had gained a much better understanding of the strong military tradition in her family.

"Poor Father," she said on a sigh, gazing up at a portrait of her grandfather in young middle age, strong and erect in the uniform of a colonel of hussars. "He was not at all suited to a military career, but it must have been nearly impossible to go against generations of family tradition. Was your father ever in the army?"

William shook his head. "No. It was generally the eldest son who went into the military, and my father was already married and settled by the time Uncle Gerald left the army. Had he been younger, my grandfather might have insisted on buying him a commission, though he was even less suited to the life than your father, I would imagine.''

"Neither you nor Cecil . . .?" Sarah hesitated, fearing to intrude.

"Not so far. I was considered too sickly after a bout of rheumatic fever in my boyhood. Cecil has toyed with the idea at times and may yet ask Grandfather to buy him a pair of colors.''

Sarah enjoyed her tour of the gallery until she learned, on entering the drawing room, where tea was being served, that Lord Eversley had called during the interval she had spent looking at pictures with William. Though she was determined not to acknowledge any disappointment at this piece of news, her earlier pleasure dissipated to the point that it required a real effort to produce the enthusiasm she owed William when Mrs. Ridgemont inquired how she enjoyed the tour. She must have been convincing because her aunt settled back in her corner of the settee with an air of satisfaction.

Arabella was in high spirits again, and the cause became clear when she announced that Lord Eversley had been the bearer of a note from Lady Eversley inviting everyone at Beech Hill to drink tea at Eversley the following afternoon.

Sarah experienced a confusing rush of contradictory emotions as pleasure at the thought of seeing Lord Eversley again was instantly swamped by a riptide of reluctance to meet his wife. She was shaken by the unexpected violence of her feelings on the subject and sat unmoving until her heart slowed its pounding and she could finally trust her voice to sound only mildly interested.

"Are you acquainted with Lady Eversley, cousin? What is she like?"

Arabella shrugged. "Pleasant enough, and she is still quite good-looking for her age. How old would you say Lady Eversley is, Mama?"

"She is five-and-fifty if she's a day," Lady Townsend replied, "but she has always taken very good care of that complexion of hers. Expense is no object with Marguerite Trebeque."

"Five-and-fifty? Is Lady Eversley not Lord Eversley's wife, then?" Sarah was looking at her aunt, but it was Arabella who answered casually.

"Lady Eversley is his mother. He doesn't have a wife any longer."

"But he did have once? What happened to her?" Sarah persisted, hoping she had succeeded in keeping her tones tepid.

"She died a long time ago," Lady Townsend said, "five or six years at least."

"It was a terrible scandal," Arabella put in with relish.

"Arabella!"

The dark-haired girl ignored her mother's warning and continued with a rush, "His wife ran away with another man while he was fighting with the army in Portugal."

Sarah's eyes widened and she glanced at her aunt for confirmation, but Lady Townsend was glaring at her daughter. "That will do, Arabella," she said repressively. "It is most unbecoming in a young girl to repeat scandal, especially when Eversley has paid you conspicuous attention and you are about to accept his hospitality."

"But it is nothing to do with Lord Eversley really, Mama. No one could hold him to blame for his wife's indiscretions."

"How did she die?" Sarah made no attempt to disguise her interest at this point.

"In childbirth, a twelvemonth after Lord Eversley—though he was only Major Trebeque then because his father was still alive—left for the war."

Mrs. Ridgemont clucked her tongue in disapproval.

"How came you by that piece of information?" demanded Lady Townsend angrily.

"Vincent told me." Arabella was the picture of injured innocence.

"Well, Vincent had no right to sully his sister's ears with such stuff, and so I shall tell him."

Mrs. Ridgemont made some remark about the license permitted to young people these days, but Sarah allowed the ensuing discussion to wash over her head unheeded as she stared into her cooling cup of tea. Compassion for Lord Eversley had ousted any other emotion for the moment.

How he must have suffered at the hands of an unprincipled woman. Even though he was abroad when the actual elopement and subsequent death took place, the ripples from the scandal would certainly have reached him, and he must have been a prey to searing doubts about the contribution that his own enforced absence might have made to the tragic situation. The blow to his pride would have been sufficient to scar him without even taking into account the probable heartbreak if he had loved his wife deeply and believed in her love for him. It must be a degrading experience to lavish love on a worthless individual, an experience that would tend to warp the soul.

Sarah sat lost in her melancholy reflections, only dimly aware of the talk swirling around her, but that awareness included gratitude to William, who gently led the conversation into amusing trivialities that called for no more than an occasional smile or nod from the newest member of the family.

10

Sarah's eagerness to meet Lord Eversley again, this time on his home ground, was somewhat tempered by a natural feminine disinclination to appear at a disadvantage in the company of other females. Of course, she would always be at a disadvantage in her cousin's company, she allowed, staring gloomily at the peach dress in the long glass in her room, by virtue of Arabella's youthful sparkle and dramatic coloring. How could any other female not appear washed out and insipid by comparison? Be that as it may, there was no denying it would have given her own flagging confidence a fillip to enter Eversley attired in a modish gown fashioned of some soft luxuriant fabric and featuring no fewer than three flounces on its skirt.

She was caught up in an adolescent but eminently satisfying daydream in which Lord Eversley, oblivious to Arabella's provocative lures, had eyes only for herself, clad in a shimmering cloth-of-gold creation that wrung cries of envy from her cousin, when a knock on the door announced Maria's arrival to dress her hair. Like an iridescent soap bubble, Sarah's mental vision vanished without a trace, and flags of guilty color flew into her cheeks at the folly of indulging in such nonsense.

"My, don't you look pretty in that gown," Maria observed innocently. "It gives you a lovely color."

Sarah smiled her thanks and pointed to the bronze-green bonnet lying on her bed. "I'll be wearing this hat today, Maria, so we'll need to keep my hair pinned a bit lower at the back than I normally wear it."

Maria was captivated by the bonnet and proceeded to place

it on her mistress' head to gauge the effect before she removed the pins anchoring the heavy knot and started brushing Sarah's long hair.

Maria really did possess clever fingers and a good eye for design, Sarah decided some fifteen minutes later as she surveyed the results of the young girl's enthusiastic labor in a hand mirror. She was warm in her praise of the skillfully twisted coil positioned at the nape of the neck below the extravagant bonnet. Maria's eyes shone with pride and pleasure as she blushingly accepted her mistress's compliments, and she exclaimed in genuine admiration as Sarah donned the matching spencer Lottie had made.

"You do look a picture, miss. Isn't it lucky today is sunny and warm enough to do without a pelisse?"

Encouraged by the maid's generous approval, Sarah ran down the backstairs to say good-bye to her grandfather before the Beech Hill party left for Eversley.

Sir Hector, who planned to spend a quiet day in his room in hopes of joining his family for dinner, was reading in the chair by the fireplace, wearing his blue dressing gown, as he had two days before. His face looked more rested today and there was no sign of shakiness in the hands that lowered the book to his lap on his granddaughter's entrance.

Shrewd black eyes in their nest of deep lines skimmed over Sarah from top to toe and came back to her sweetly flushed face. "For whose benefit is this splendor intended? Not mine, I think."

Sarah's lovely color deepened, but she protested laughingly, "Grandfather, I am quite literally wearing the only garments I possess until Lottie and Richard arrive with the rest of my wardrobe."

A frown gathered on the general's brow. "Yes, we'll have to do something about that right away. Can't have you going around looking like a poor relation."

"I . . . I did not mean . . . It is just that I have nothing else with me." Sarah floundered to a stop as determination was added to the arrogant assurance on her grandfather's austere countenance.

"Spare me any squeamish protestations or displays of misplaced independence, I beg you. You are my granddaughter, living under my roof, and you'll dress the part, is that clear?"

"Very clear, Grandfather."

"And you may dispense with the dutiful meekness too. We both know what that's worth," he continued, challenging her to argue.

"Very well, Grandfather." Laughter routed obedience from her clear gaze.

Sir Hector permitted himself, if not an actual smile, at least a little softening of his thin lips. "You'll do," he said gruffly, picking up his book again.

Sarah, accepting this signal that the interview was over, bade him an affectionate good-bye and left through the withdrawing room, where Somers was dusting the jade ornaments on the mantelpiece. They exchanged greetings and a few observations on the beauty of the statuettes before Sarah continued on her way to the great hall, where she found only William and Cecil before her.

"Oh, good. I feared I must be late." Sarah greeted the two men with an impartial smile as they started to get to their feet. "Please, don't get up, cousins. I'll join you on the settee, if I may, Cecil?"

"Of course. By Jove, that's a dashed fine bonnet, Cousin Sarah."

"Yes, you look . . . lovely, Sarah."

William's quiet compliment was all but lost in the simultaneous arrival of his parents from their suite and Vincent from the other end of the huge room. Sarah had no time to do more than give the brothers a brief acknowledging smile before the others were upon them. On the whole she was glad of the reinforcements, for there had been something in William's voice just now, a deep sincerity that had given her a twinge of disquiet.

Unless she had imagined this new element.

In the few minutes that elapsed before they were joined by the Townsend ladies William was his usual placid, friendly self. He made no effort to secure her exclusive attention and applied himself to keeping the conversation general. Sarah relaxed again, to be jolted back to wary alertness by the appearance of Lady Townsend and her daughter.

Despite the warmer temperature, Lady Townsend was wearing a light wool pelisse lavishly trimmed with sable. A matching hat was set at an angle on her dark hair. Arabella looked ravishingly pretty in a daffodil-yellow carriage dress made of a shiny stiff cotton, which she had topped with a soft white cashmere shawl fringed in the same deep yellow that so became her brunette coloring. Sarah's confidence slipped a notch as her eyes lingered on the triple flounce on her cousin's gown. She was aware of a narrow-eyed appraisal from the two women and braced herself mentally.

"Well, Cousin Sarah," Arabella said with a glittering smile, "if that bonnet is a sample of the wares in your hat shop, you have certainly found your calling."

"Thank you, Arabella, for any compliment intended," Sarah replied pleasantly.

To her relief, Horace Ridgemont began to urge everyone toward the open doors, beyond which the sounds of jingling harness advertised the presence of the two carriages that were to convey the party to Eversley.

Lady Eversley's light-brown hair was still unstreaked by gray under its flattering lace-and-muslin cap; she was bent over her embroidery, but the lion's share of her attention was focused, though unobtrusively, on the nearly motionless figure of her son, sitting some eight feet away in the corner of a camelback sofa.

If asked to describe the viscount's present activity, a person who was not well-acquainted with him would certainly reply that he was reading an issue of *The Edinburgh Revue*. Lady Eversley was very well-acquainted with the viscount, however, and her answer would be that he was pretending to read the periodical in his hands. It was a very good pretense, which explained why Lady Eversley's maternal instincts were now fully alerted.

Mark had strolled into the room with the magazine under his arm fifteen minutes ago, at the precise hour at which their guests were expected. He had greeted his mother affectionately and proceeded to barricade himself behind his magazine. Obviously his thoughts were engaged with a subject of considerable interest to him. Equally obvious was that fact that he did not wish to acknowledge or share these thoughts with anyone. As a matter of fact, it was never easy to determine Mark's thoughts or feelings from his controlled facial expression or his manner, which was generally deliberately unrevealing. He had not used to be so guarded, Lady Eversley recalled with a pang of regret. This was a defensive legacy from the scandal that had ended his brief marriage. A very good understanding existed between mother and son, but not even to her did Mark speak of his deepest feelings. She respected his privacy, grieved for his solitude, and longed for his happiness.

Lady Eversley had sensed a difference in her son these past few days, though she was hard-pressed to find words that described the change without going beyond it. "Restless" was the wrong term, "excitement" was too strong, but she felt he was more alive in a way he had not been for years. Watching him as his strong, well-shaped hand turned a page, his mother could not help speculating that one of the young women coming to tea today was responsible for the subtle difference. But which one? She could not say with certainty that the quickened beat in Mark dated from his first meeting with Sarah Ridgemont, and Arabella Townsend had appeared on the scene a few days later. She was counting on this afternoon's gathering to provide the answer.

"Our guests are a bit late. I trust nothing of a serious nature has delayed them."

Mark looked up with a smile. "It cannot be a simple matter to assemble so many ladies at a given time." He paused, listening, then put his magazine aside. "I believe I hear a carriage approaching now."

The viscount reached the driveway just as the two carriages from Beech Hill pulled to a stop. He opened the first and assisted the Townsend ladies to descend after Cecil Ridgemont and Lord Townsend had climbed down. A glance over his shoulder showed him that William Ridgemont was performing the same

service for his cousin Sarah. By the time Mark had welcomed
his guests, helped the footman take the ladies' outer garments,
and ushered the party into the large family sitting room on the
ground floor where his mother awaited them, he had made a
number of discoveries, not all of them welcome.

Arabella Townsend had remained by his side, affecting a
charmingly proprietorial air, but this was her usual tactic in
masculine company and he was capable of dealing with clinging
young ladies. Seeing Sarah for the first time without her black
housekeeper's garb, he had been struck anew by her loveliness.
She had more color today and there was a glow in the beautiful
eyes that had always been somber in his recollection. He noted
that there was a tentative quality about the smile she had given
him on arrival, in contrast to the easy, one might almost say
intimate, smiles that passed between her and William. His sharp
ear also noted that she called him William, though she added
a more formal title when addressing other members of her
family.

None of Mark's thoughts were to be read in his manner as
he performed several introductions—necessary because his
mother had not chanced to meet Cecil Ridgemont or Lord
Townsend since they were children. When it was Sarah's turn
to be presented, Lady Eversley held out both hands in a smiling
gesture of welcome.

"Mark did tell me you were held to favor your grandmother,
Miss Ridgemont, but I was still unprepared to find the resemblance so strong, for Lady Ridgemont must have been over forty
when I came to Gloucestershire as a bride. I was very fond of
her and I am delighted to welcome you to Eversley."

"Thank you, ma'am. I am very happy to be here."

Sarah's smile for his mother was all that Mark could wish.
It was poised shyly on her soft mouth but glowed in her eyes.
If he had not yet been the fortunate recipient of such a favor,
at least it was coming closer to home.

Lady Eversley kept Sarah by her side when the large party
arranged itself about the comfortable room with its French doors
leading into what would be a beautiful terrace garden in a few
weeks.

Mrs. Ridgemont made a comment on the pleasant setting, ending, "Beech Hill is so rigidly formal."

"Yes," agreed her hostess. "Beautiful and gracious though such places undoubtedly are, they were built for another age and style of life."

Tea was brought in almost immediately, and small bursts of conversation rang out while it was being dispensed, along with sherry and Madeira, by the butler as Lady Eversley prepared it for her guests. Trays of tempting jam tarts and slices of cake were greeted with pleasure, especially by the gentlemen.

A footman entered with a message for Lady Eversley, who heard him out and then said, "Will you ask the doctor to join us for tea, Martin, if he can spare the time?" When the footman had gone out again, she explained to those within earshot, "Our housekeeper of many years is laid low with a severe case of influenza. I sent for Doctor Rydell an hour ago because it seemed to me her temperature was higher and she was even more restless."

Sarah could not help contrasting Lady Eversley's pleasant manner with Doctor Rydell as she inquired about her housekeeper and then waited upon him herself when he chose tea over sherry to the condescension displayed by her Aunt Townsend the previous day. The doctor had looked a little overwhelmed at the horde of people watching his entrance, but his tactful hostess put him at ease at once, indicating the place beside Sarah on the long sofa. Obligingly, Sarah made room for the latest arrival by edging closer to Lady Eversley, and the three were soon chatting comfortably of the minor outbreak of influenza in the village and surrounding area that was keeping the doctor constantly on the move.

"You are looking tired yourself, Doctor Rydell. You must try to get more rest," Lady Eversley kindly advised him. "It would not do for you to succumb to an infectious complaint at this crucial point. We should have an epidemic on our hands."

"I am hoping we are over the worst of it, ma'am. To my knowledge, there have been no new cases since Saturday."

Sarah asked after Grace Medlark's little daughter, who was still seriously ill. She was listening to Doctor Rydell's reply

when her eyes strayed to Arabella, who had been exerting all
her considerable charm to monopolize her host's attention since
their arrival. For a second she was taken aback by the glance
of pure venom directed at her by her cousin until she realized
that she had earned it by virtue of her place beside the doctor.
Since the only way to placate Arabella would be by being rude
to the doctor, she could only pretend ignorance of the message
in her cousin's speaking eyes. Arabella's response was to turn
her shoulder on the party on the sofa and redouble her efforts
to charm Lord Eversley, who, conscious of his duty to all his
guests, was not about to cooperate in her scheme.

The viscount smilingly extricated himself with the excuse of
refilling the men's glasses, and some shuffling of places
occurred in the next few minutes. Balked of her prey, Arabella
turned her attention to Cecil, who was seated nearest, but that
young man, alerted by a dangerous glitter in her eyes that belied
smiling lips, cravenly made his escape by claiming to be dying
for another piece of cake.

William, taking pity on his pretty cousin, slid into Cecil's
vacated chair and set about drawing her fire.

The doctor's manners were far too good to let him appear
anything but pleased with his company, and he remained by
Sarah even after the conversation, led by the viscount, became
more general. If he cast one or two discreetly admiring looks
at the effervescent young girl, who seemed oblivious to his
existence, Sarah could only sympathize. If she could have
released him to approach Arabella by going over and engaging
William's attention herself, she'd have been happy to oblige,
despite a conviction that the attraction was fated to be crushed
by parental disapproval. She was trapped on the sofa by her
duty to her hostess, however, so she could only pretend
ignorance of any undercurrents and carry on politely.

His responsibilities as host notwithstanding, the viscount had
been making some observations of his own during the party and
drawing some unpalatable conclusions. Not having had the
advantage of witnessing the first meeting between Arabella
Townsend and Doctor Rydell, Mark had only the evidence of
his own eyes to go on. His eyes told him that Sarah and the

handsome doctor were already on comfortable terms with each other and that each was perfectly content to remain in the other's company. This was unwelcome news enough but not the worst the afternoon had to offer.

His nerves had prickled warningly at the outset this afternoon when he had seen William Ridgemont tenderly assisting Sarah down from the carriage, and his eyes had regularly sought out that young man almost without his brain's direction ever since. He had been aware each time William's glance had strayed to Sarah, which had happened frequently despite the fellow's exemplary behavior in acting the perfect guest. The result of this concentrated observation was the unwelcome conviction that William was in love with Sarah after knowing her for less than a sennight.

Mark liked William Ridgemont better than any member of the general's family. He had character, intelligence, and kindness, and was remarkably free of the pride, arrogance, and selfishness that characterized the others. He would undoubtedly make some fortunate woman a good husband.

Having said all this, Mark was conscious of a burning desire to take this virtuous and inoffensive young man blindfolded into some huge dark forest and leave him there to find his own way out in a few years' time.

It was not lost upon him that his own attitude didn't bear scrutiny. He was not yet ready to pin down his uncomfortable feelings for Sarah; therefore, he had no right to complain that another man had seen and appreciated the prize and was willing to make an immediate commitment. Granted, William was fortunate in that, not having had his trust betrayed in the past, he had the confidence to act on his judgment and feelings now, but who had ever decreed that fairness was an element in courtship? Fairness was for horse-racing, where weight handicaps could be assessed. The heart knew no such rules of fair play.

By the time Mark had gone to see their guests into their carriages, Lady Eversley was fairly sure that today's gathering had not come up to her son's expectations. He was acting the perfect host to the end, but his mother sensed frustration in him. She supposed from the standpoint of information that the tea party had proved more satisfying to her. She now knew that her son's interest did not lie with Arabella Townsend, which was an incalculable relief. She had not been happy to think of him entangled with a girl brought up by Adelaide Townsend, with her false values. It must be Sarah Ridgemont then, but she had had no opportunity to evaluate their reactions to each other for the simple reason that the two had not come within arm's length or tongue's reach of each other during the entire span of the tea party.

Lady Eversley had been predisposed to like Sarah for her grandmother's sake, but it was still a relief to find she could do so unreservedly. For Mark's sake, his mother was prepared to accept a dumpy little thing with a squint or even a hump if she made him happy, but this young woman was truly lovely in a quiet way that did not seek to call attention to itself. Her looks would wear well also because part of her appeal lay in a natural sweetness of expression that would remain when youth had faded. The girl had a frank way of looking at everyone out of clear honest eyes. There was no affectation about her, a welcome rarity in these days, and her conduct today had revealed a well-bred ease of manner and consideration for others. She had patiently submitted to being questioned about her life before her father died and about her brother, and she had done her best to set Doctor Rydell at ease.

Lady Eversley's lips quirked into a private smile as she added the mental qualification that it was hardly a sacrifice on any young woman's part to devote time to the handsome doctor. Certainly the coquettish Townsend chit had been well enough aware of his attractions to begrudge her cousin his attention, but then she automatically set out to captivate every personable male in the room. It was a natural reflex in one of her type, though not a characteristic calculated to endear her to her own sex. The little smile on Lady Eversley's lips deepened as she began to plan some future entertainments with the object of giving matters a nudge in the right direction.

It was a determinedly cheerful Sarah who accomplished her simple preparations for dinner in a mechanical fashion that evening. As might be expected, her thoughts were much taken up by a recapitulation of the afternoon's outing.

For someone who had scarcely poked her head out of doors for a sennight, the short drive to Eversley had provided a welcome opportunity to see something of the neighborhood in which she would henceforth be residing. Eversley itself had both surprised and delighted her: surprised by its complete contrast to Beech Hill, and delighted by the unconventional charm expressed in its picturesque but unregulated sprawl. Beech Hill was like a beautiful piece of sculpture, conceived and accomplished in its entirety in a single frenzy of creation, and thereafter remaining unchanged for more than a century. On the other hand, one had the impression that Eversley was still evolving, still creating itself daily. It was not as impressive as her grandfather's house at first sight. The visitor came out of the avenue of copper beeches and feasted his eyes on the beautiful structure of Beech Hill in all its architectural purity, set like a single perfect jewel against a black velvet drape. The visitor almost sneaked up on Eversley, hiding and nestling among a lush and sometimes overgrown natural setting, revealing itself wing by wing as the drive curved. From her all-too-short inspection of the complicated and varied facade before the viscount had sewpt his guests inside, Sarah was bound to speculate that its creators had never heard of symmetry, for the building had obviously been expanded and altered at the whims of succeeding generations of owners. Still, the house's visual interest and attractiveness were undeniable, whatever its probable shortcomings as good architecture.

Sarah would have welcomed a tour of the interior of Lord Eversley's home but had had to content herself with intriguing glimpses into open rooms on the way to the lovely drawing room where their hostess had welcomed them. Again, the atmosphere was in startling contrast to the formality of the beautifully proportioned and elegantly furnished rooms at Beech Hill. Perhaps it was the proximity of the outdoors that was responsible for the air of informality prevailing in the delightful room where the tea party had taken place.

It had been a pleasant interlude, largely owing to the warmth

and charm of their hostess. Sarah had liked the viscount's mother
at once and had come away with the happy confidence that Lady
Eversley had returned the feeling. If the afternoon had fallen
a little short of her expectations, she had only herself to blame.
It was inexcusable for someone of her advanced years to indulge
in the schoolgirl folly of spinning romantic daydreams. Best
to get the shaming confession out into the open. The bronze-
green bonnet, the new coiffure, the unadmitted eagerness had
all been for Lord Eversley's benefit.

And with what result?

Sarah's entire share of Lord Eversley's attention today had
consisted of a smiling welcome upon meeting and a firm hand
assisting her into the carriage to accompany his smile at parting.
It was true that he had seemed to elbow William out of the way
in order to extend this assistance, but in all probability the
gesture was prompted by the slightly guilty conscience of a good
host who has suddenly realized that he has neglected one of his
guests.

A timid knock on the door provided a welcome interruption
to her unsatisfactory reasoning. It was Maria, wondering why
she had not received a call to do Miss Ridgemont's hair for
dinner.

"I had planned to leave it in the coil you arranged this
afternoon, Maria," Sarah replied with a swift glance at the clock
on the mantel. "Unless you feel it needs to be repinned?"

Maria promised that it would be the work of an instant to
redo the coil, and less than five minutes later Sarah ran
downstairs to see whether her grandfather still intended to dine
with the family.

Sir Hector, resplendent in a burgundy velvet coat and satin
knee breeches, was accepting a large ruby ring from Somers
when Sarah entered in response to his invitation.

"Ah, here is my granddaughter, Somers. I won't need to
trouble you, after all. You may give me your arm to the dining
room in a moment, Sarah. I have promised my keeper"—with
a darkling look at the imperturbable valet—"not to attempt the
stairs just yet. The man was prepared to plague me to death
until I agreed."

"And quite right too, Grandfather. How elegant you look."
Sarah's smile was for both master and servant, who both gazed
back at her with similar expressions of approval.

Then Sir Hector growled, "In my day the way a man dressed
told you something about him. None of this boring black and
white. Even military uniforms have more variety and appeal
than this uninspired passion for anonymity that that ass
Brummell has decreed."

Sir Hector regaled his escort with his views on the recent
decline of elegance in the sartorial habits of both sexes as they
walked slowly along the corridor past the chapel and west
staircase before turning into the great hall to enter the dining
saloon at the end of it. Sarah made appropriate murmurs, though
she was preoccupied to some extent with the physical presence
of her grandfather. He was a head taller than she and held
himself admirably upright, but she was nervously aware that
she was taking more of his weight by the time they had gained
the dining room, a distance of perhaps a hundred feet. She
caught Millbank's eye as they entered, and he hurried to pull
out the chair at the head of the table. Once she had seen her
grandfather seated, she volunteered to fetch the others from the
drawing room, hastening away on the words to spare him any
conversation.

Out of sight in the hall, Sarah lingered on the bottom step
for a few moments to give her grandfather time to recover his
breath before she went upstairs to announce dinner. He would
absolutely hate to have the rest of his family know what this
effort to preside at his own table was costing him.

As a happy family event, the dinner was doomed from the
moment Sir Hector demanded that Sarah be seated opposite him,
explaining with a malicious smile directed at his daughter, who
was about to take that place, that as his granddaughter was
making her home with him, she would naturally assume the role
of his hostess. He quelled the appalled protest that rose to
Sarah's lips with a raised hand and a brusque remark that it
would save a lot of trouble to begin as they meant to go on.

From the instant of meeting her aunt's malignant glance as
the latter passed her in tight-lipped silence while the seating

arrangements were adjusted to suit the general's pleasure, Sarah's appetite deserted her. She sat rearranging the food on her plate while struggling to respond in turn to her uncle and Vincent, who were seated on either side of her. Arabella, looking enchanting in a frothy confection the color of a raspberry ice, pulled out all the stops in her efforts to charm her grandfather, whom she had run to greet with a delighted kiss on his dry cheek on entering the room. Sarah, trying to swallow tiny morsels that wouldn't choke her, could only pray that her cousin would prove entertaining enough to keep Sir Hector happily occupied till the penitential meal had ended.

She had dared set her hopes too high, however, for her grandfather dashed them down during a pause while the dishes from the first course were cleared away. He had been eyeing his ebullient young granddaughter with benign interest as she gestured with a well-kept hand sparkling with rings below a delicate wrist bearing a bracelet of large gold links.

"I like that rig of yours, Arabella," he began with a deceptive amiability that brought Sarah's eyes up from the contemplation of her plate as he went on. "One thing I'll say for your mother, she's got good taste. Between the pair of you, you ought to be able to outfit Sarah in style. And no nipcheese notions of economy, mind you. I can stand the damages."

It would have been difficult to tell which of the three ladies included in Sir Hector's masterly plan was most disconcerted. Sarah did not utter a sound, but the color drained from her face and she gripped the edge of the table with her thumbs for support. Arabella's pretty mouth hung open for a second or two until she mastered her surprised dismay and snapped it shut. Her mother, who had contributed nothing beyond monosyllabic responses when directly addressed during the first course, lowered her eyes, but not before Sarah quivered under the quick flare of anger that had struck sparks in the dark depths at the general's casual presumption. Two hectic spots of color burned in Lady Townsend's cheeks, and it was she who found her voice first.

"Sarah is not a marriageable young girl to be dressed by her elders for her presentation to society," she said, a hard edge to her voice. "She may prefer to select her own wardrobe."

"Oh, yes, Grandfather. I would not wish to impose on my aunt or my cousin," Sarah put in quickly. "Lottie can help me acquire whatever is necessary."

"You'll do as you're told, girl," snapped Sir Hector, then his tones became suspiciously bland. "Why should you—or they—consider it an imposition to expect your closest female relatives to assist you in the task of assembling a wardrobe? Shopping is meat and drink to females."

"I did not say it was an imposition, Father." Lady Townsend's frost-edged voice rang out clearly. "I merely questioned the necessity of bringing other opinions than Sarah's into the business. At her age she is entitled to suit herself in the matter of clothes."

"She can't be expected to know all the latest follies and fancies current among the so-called cream of society. That's where you and Arabella come in. And that's all I'm going to say on the subject," he finished with a rising choler that no one wished to intensify.

William, ever tactful, asked his grandfather's opinion on the latest news from France, where Wellington's army was reported to be on the brink of a decisive victory.

As the men, eager to leave the embarrassing subject of Sarah's wardrobe behind, began an animated discussion of the army's position, Sarah shrank further into her shell, miserably conscious that her grandfather's high-handed championship had resulted in an augmentation of the animosity already borne her by Aunt Townsend and Arabella. Her cousin, ignored at present, was frankly sulking since her attempts to lure Cecil away from the men's war talk had been unsuccessful. Lady Townsend was absorbed in her own thoughts, which, if her sour expression spoke true, were anything but pleasant. Of the women, only Mrs. Ridgemont continued to eat her dinner as if nothing untoward had occurred. Sarah had given up any pretense of eating. Without knowing it, her features assumed the stillness of a portrait, her habitual defense whenever a situation became unbearably hurtful.

Much as she had longed for the uncomfortable meal to be

over, the immediate aftermath might be likened to escaping from
the frying pan into the fire as she followed the ladies up to the
drawing room on reluctant feet. Arabella and her mother instantly drew apart for private converse, both of them making
clear their disinclination for the least share of her company.
Aunt Ridgemont took pity on her and initiated a gentle conversation about trivialities, which they managed to sustain until the
gentlemen reappeared. Her grandfather had retired directly after
the port, she learned from William, who joined her where she
sat on the sofa next to his mother's chair. Sarah could only thank
a belated providence for removing a potential source of further
dissension from their midst.

Gradually over the next hour she relaxed under the calming
influence of William's society. He cheered her at the start by
directing the conversation toward the expected arrival of her
brother, and she soon entered into his enthusiasm for planning
activities to interest a boy of eleven who was unused to country
living. If by the time she sought her bed she had not entirely
forgotten the aggravated tension that would continue to exist
between herself and her cousin and aunt, at least it was no longer
so uppermost in her mind as to destroy her rest.

11

Richard and Lottie arrived the next day.

Until the post chaise hired by Mr. Coke in London pulled into the drive in midafternoon it had been a dreary day. Yesterday's sunshine was only a memory as the day dawned with overcast skies and an unwelcome chill in the air. Seeking to avoid a similar chill indoors, Sarah breakfasted at an hour when her aunt and Arabella were still in their beds. William, at last able to get into his riding boots, went off with the other men, leaving her to her own devices, which she decided, at least for the morning hours, should not include the doubtful companionship of the other women. When she had conferred with the housekeeper and cook and visited her grandfather, who was a trifle fatigued after his social evening, she whiled away the time remaining before lunch in making sketches of gowns she would like to have made and lists of accessories to buy.

The presence of the gentlemen at lunch diluted the air of cold enmity emanating from her Aunt Townsend. The men also served to distract Arabella from contributing to her mother's determined snubbing of Sarah. For her part, Sarah refrained from offering any opportunities for the exercise to her aunt's caustic tongue, to the point of sitting nearly mumchance throughout the meal. This pusillanimous policy had little to recommend it over any considerable length of time and would, if detected, be roundly condemned by her grandfather. For the moment, however, her diffidence kept the situation from erupting into greater unpleasantness.

She fled thankfully to her own apartment when the meal was

over. She attempted to read a book she had taken from the library shelves the day before, but her state of mind was such that concentration on the printed word was a feat beyond her capabilities. It was a relief, therefore, when William knocked on the door to her antechamber and proposed a tour of the grounds. Sarah accepted the offer with alacrity, donning her black pelisse and bonnet while her cousin waited in the great hall.

Mrs. Ridgemont emerged from her apartment just as Sarah joined William, so they paused on their way out to tell her of their intention to explore. Mrs. Ridgemont's vague blue gaze dwelled on Sarah for a second with a bit more interest than she usually displayed before she smiled and wished them an enjoyable outing.

The cousins were rounding the side of the house in a companionable silence an hour later when the post chaise came into sight at the end of the drive.

"It's Lottie and Richard, I know it is! Hurry, William."

Sarah set off with the speed and purpose of an arrow in transit, arriving at the foot of the double flight of steps just as the postilion opened the carriage door. By the time William, going more cautiously on his still-weak ankle, reached the scene embraces had been exchanged and Sarah was listening to her young brother's enthusiastic account of the journey with a fond smile on her lips. A tall straight-backed woman wearing a black pelisse and hat and an uncompromising aspect was surveying her immediate surroundings with a judicial eye as William silently joined the group. He essayed a smile, and the lady unbent sufficiently to give him a polite nod and a direct look that reserved judgment.

"Oh, William," Sarah said, catching sight of him at last, "please forgive our poor manners. Stop a minute, Richard, and get your breath back. I'd like you to meet one of our cousins."

As Sarah proudly performed the introductions, William realized that he was being regarded with great interest by both members of her immediate family. He found himself hoping they liked what they saw. He certainly did. Both Richard and

Miss Miller gazed at the world with the same honest approach that he had noticed in Sarah.

"How do you do, sir? Sarah wrote that you were the nicest of our cousins," Richard said, naïvely carrying frankness too far.

"Richard! Where are your manners?" cried his sister, aghast, while Miss Miller tutted disapprovingly.

The dark Ridgemont eyes of the youngster turned on his sister in puzzlement. "But naturally I would not say this in front of the others, Sarah."

William laughed and clapped his young cousin on the shoulder. "Of course you would not, Cousin Richard, and I am highly honored to have earned your sister's regard, believe me." He could feel the measuring quality in Miss Miller's look and was not displeased that Sarah suggested going inside at that moment.

Joseph was directing the removal of the baggage as they ascended the long flight of steps to the accompaniment of Richard's awed comments on the size and grandeur of his grandfather's house. Sarah told William that she was going to take the newcomers in to meet her grandfather. He nodded and proceeded on to the drawing room.

Leaving Richard and Lottie with Somers in the drawing room of Sir Hector's suite, Sarah burst into the bedchamber on a quick knock and then drew up short, stammering a surprised apology as she saw that he was not alone.

The tall man in the dark-green coat and fawn-colored trousers rose to his feet on her entrance. "That's all right, Sarah," he said easily, appearing not to notice her raised eyebrows at the informal mode of address. "Your grandfather has just finished wiping me off the board, and I for one am delighted with the interruption."

"Your mind was not on the game today, Eversley," the general allowed magnanimously. "Did I hear sounds of arrival outside, Sarah? Does that account for your air of suppressed excitement?"

"Richard and Lottie are here, Grandfather. Will you meet them now?"

"Bring them in," he said shortly, rising slowly from the wing chair beside the chess table.

Lottie dropped a stiff curtsy when Sarah presented her, but her grandfather held out his hand and said with a graciousness she had not before suspected in him, "Welcome to Beech Hill, Miss Miller. I am well aware that I owe you a huge debt of gratitude for taking care of my grandchildren these many years. I hope you will be happy here."

Only when he had heard her conventional reply did Sir Hector permit himself to turn his attention to the quietly waiting child. He was very inch the general as he examined the boy, but Sarah was proud to see that Richard's interested gaze did not waver under the intent scrutiny.

"How do you do, sir?" he said politely.

"Well, you are certainly a Ridgemont if your sister isn't," the old man conceded.

"Not a Ridgemont? What can you mean, sir?" Alarm spread over Richard's countenance and his eyes flew to his sister's face.

"Nothing to make heavy weather about, boy. I meant merely that you look like the Ridgemonts and Sarah doesn't."

"Oh," said Richard, enlightened, "I see. My father looked a lot like you, sir," he added, following this line of thought to a not entirely felicitous conclusion, judging by his grandfather's sudden scowl.

Sarah broke in to make the newcomers known to Lord Eversley. While the three exchanged amenities, her grandfather sank back into his chair. Guessing that he was more tired than he wished to admit, she proposed taking Richard and Lottie up to the drawing room for a general introduction, adding politely, "I trust you will stay to tea, Lord Eversley."

He bowed. "I'll be delighted, Sarah."

Again that bland use of her given name seemed to disconcert Sarah, who swept the others out of the room after promising to send Somers in to her grandfather.

Lottie, whose keen eyes had not left Sarah's face for the last few moments, took advantage of Lord Eversley's question to Richard about the journey to speak for the girl's ears alone as she deliberately slowed their steps along the corridor. "I'll have to meet the rest of your family sometime, so it might as well be now, but I won't be staying to take tea with them.''

"Of course you will, Lottie!"

"No, Sarah. I am not a member of your family and I won't be eating with them.''

"You are my . . . my companion, and companions dine with the family." Sarah's gentle countenance had assumed its rare mulish look.

Lottie said patiently, "Look, my dear, I know your concern is all for my feelings, but I am not of the gentry and that's all there is to it. Believe me, I would feel awkward and unhappy to be pushed in among my betters—''

"They're not your betters!"

"Not in heaven's eyes," Lottie agreed with a tart smile, "but genteel society and heaven are two different places, and genteel society is not for the likes of Lottie Miller. I would not like it one bit, not for a minute.''

Sarah still seemed disposed to argue as they reached the west staircase, but Lottie changed the subject with an admiring comment on the sweeping wrought-iron railing. Lord Eversley answered her and continued to point out features of the staircase as they ascended, depriving Sarah of any chance to reopen the discussion.

All family members were present in the drawing room when they entered. Fortunately, boyish curiosity about his unknown relatives provided a shield that protected Richard from subtle evidence that his presence was not greeted with unanimous goodwill. Sarah was prepared for Aunt Adelaide's patent disinterest. In the excitement of meeting so many people at once, Richard didn't even notice. He was most interested in his splendid male cousins, although when he was presented to Arabella, he blinked and said, "Sarah was right. You are very pretty, Cousin Arabella.''

Arabella laughed out spontaneously. "I think I am going to like you, Cousin Richard," she replied, twinkling an impish smile at him and looking more appealing, Sarah thought privately, than she ever did when concentrating all her efforts to charm.

"And what did Sarah have to say about the rest of us, Cousin Richard?" Vincent asked, wearing the smile of an amiable tiger.

Sarah's nails bit into her palms as she sucked in a breath, but Richard had not been fooled by Lord Townsend's assumed innocence.

"She just said we had three male cousins and a very pretty girl cousin," he replied, gazing at his oldest cousin with candid dark eyes, adding parenthetically, "I already knew about Aunt Adelaide and Uncle Horace from my father."

Sarah expelled a relieved breath and waited for the next hurdle, but all went smoothly from that point.

When Lottie had been presented to all the Ridgemonts, she glanced significantly at Sarah, who hesitated as the tea tray was brought in. Lottie made a tiny negative movement of her head, and sighing, Sarah excused herself to take her old friend up to the room that had been prepared for her, after ascertaining that Richard was happy enough for the moment answering William's questions about his journey.

It was fully twenty minutes before Sarah returned to the drawing room. She and Lottie had had much to catch up on and she had stayed to introduce her to Clara, who would be waiting on the nursery suite. Promising to return with Richard after tea, she left her old nurse directing the willing Clara in the unpacking of the most essential baggage before she would take any refreshment herself.

A slight shadow of anxiety for Richard's fate at the hands of his new relatives faded as she reentered the drawing room to see him happily munching on cake and listening to a discussion between William and Cecil. Aunt Adelaide was seated behind the tea table talking to Vincent. When she did not appear to notice that her niece was once more in their midst, Sarah squared her shoulders and abandoned her recent posture of self-effacement in her aunt's presence.

"May I have some tea, Aunt?"

Lady Townsend filled a cup without even glancing up.

Lord Eversley, who had been seated beside Arabella, sauntered over to the tea table and took the cup from Sarah's hand when it was prepared. "I'll carry this for you, Sarah," he said, indicating the chair he had been occupying.

Presented with a Hobson's choice of calling attention to herself with a refusal or obeying Lord Eversley's direction, Sarah took the chair beside her cousin with a murmur of thanks. Arabella promptly turned her shoulder on her, but her attempts to ignore Sarah's presence were foiled by Lord Eversley, who saw to it that Sarah was included in the limping conversation that followed.

If he were intuitive enough to sense that all was not well between Arabella and herself, then he should have been intuitive enough to know that his intervention would only annoy both women, Sarah concluded, hardening her heart and refusing to put up more than a minimal show of civility as she racked her brain for an acceptable way to disengage herself. She had not been visited with an inspiration when William came to the rescue once again.

"Sarah, do you ride?" he asked, leaning across his brother to attract her attention. "Cecil and I are going to teach Richard to ride starting tomorrow. Will you come with us?"

Sarah shook her head, smiling at the excitement on Richard's face. "I'm afraid I do not ride, nor do I possess a habit, but I am persuaded Richard will be thrilled to have you take him out. Thank you both so much."

"Bella, you and Sarah are about the same size. Do you have something you can lend her for riding?" William asked with a regrettable lapse from the exquisite tact that generally characterized his behavior.

Arabella stiffened and glared at her cousin. "I have only one habit with me," she replied shortly.

"In any case, I should prefer to postpone any riding lessons until I have acquired the proper clothes," Sarah said, looking directly at William.

"I would estimate that my mother is near your size, Sarah," Lord Eversley said, unexpectedly entering the lists. "She will be more than happy to lend you a habit until you can have one made."

"I would not dream of asking Lady Eversley to lend me her clothes," Sarah was scandalized.

"You would not be asking, she'll be offering," he pointed out.

"Absolutely not. It is unthinkable."

The decision in Sarah's tones finally silenced Lord Eversley, who pulled in the corners of his mouth as he eyed her expressionlessly. This had the effect of making her feel gauche and ungrateful at the same time. Goaded, she plunged into an ill advised attempt to soften this impression that had her talking in circles until his eyes began to dance wickedly. She stumbled to a stop, reddening at a sudden conviction that he must find her both childish and amusing, but any incipient resentment was rendered stillborn by the endearingly boyish smile he sent her suddenly, a smile that took years from his age and hinted at the existence of another side to this enigmatic and compellingly attractive man. The smile Sarah gave him in response was, all unknowingly, an expression of complete capitulation to the strange attraction he had always exerted over her.

Afterward, Sarah could not have said with truth whether she was relieved or disappointed that Arabella reasserted her claim to Lord Eversley's attention at that moment. There were no more private looks exchanged between the viscount and Sarah, at least partially because she was careful to avoid looking directly at this gentleman during the discussion of the availability in the neighborhood of suitable mounts for novice riders that reigned until Lord Eversley took his leave a half-hour later.

With the advent of her brother and Lottie, life at Beech Hill became much more tolerable for Sarah. Nothing of a positive nature had occurred to alter the personal feelings of the rest of the Ridgemonts toward the existence of their brother's children, but with her family present, she no longer felt exposed and isolated in an alien environment. Also, she was so busy showing Richard and Lottie over the house and grounds and planning her new wardrobe that she spent far less time in the uncongenial company of the Ridgemont females. Actually, it was only Aunt Adelaide's society that she found invariably unpalatable. The mercurial Arabella could be quite good company when not under her mother's quelling eye, and Aunt Ridgemont, though inclined to dwell inexhaustibly on the multiple virtues of her son William, was never actively unkind to Sarah or Richard.

Richard blossomed under the excitement of country life. He had a happy child's ability to adapt to changing situations and had accustomed himself to the cramped living quarters and dirty streets of London, but he flourished at Beech Hill like a plant long starved of sunshine. Not only did he have spacious grounds, woods, and a village all within exploring distance, but his new cousins were introducing him to the previously arcane secrets of horsemanship. For a boy whose entire acquaintance with these wonderously beautiful creatures had consisted of surreptitious pats on city streets when the opportunity offered, heaven could promise no sweeter joy. His progress in riding was measured in gigantic strides, and his glowing happiness settled forever the self-doubts about the rightness of her decision to come to Beech Hill and the niggling sense of disloyalty to their father that had pricked Sarah's conscience since her arrival. For the joy of witnessing Richard's contentment she would serenely endure a thousand snubs from her relatives.

Though Richard spent most of his time outdoors, the unpredictable early spring weather provided enough inclement periods to confine him to the house occasionally. After exploring all the possibilities the nursery offered for entertainment, he discovered the rich resources of the library, which his grandfather had put at his disposal. He was content to spend hours surveying the contents of the shelves, and this was the first place Sarah looked if her brother's whereabouts were in question.

She had wondered a little uneasily if the presence of a lively child in the house would adversely affect her grandfather, but she need not have worried on that score. Fortunately, Richard showed no timidity in the presence of his irascible grandsire, a reaction that would have annoyed the general excessively despite the characteristic bullying designed, one would have thought, to produce just such a condition in his victims. From the second day of his stay when Richard had wandered into his grandfather's bedchamber with a book detailing Julius Caesar's experiences in Gaul and questions on his lips about this campaign, the oldest and youngest members of the family had apparently forged a bond of common interest in military history that no one could have predicted. Without ever defining a policy or intention, the boy slipped into a pattern of spending some time with his grandfather each day.

In the sennight following Richard's arrival at Beech Hill, Sarah was happier than she had been since the golden days of her betrothal, so many years ago that she had difficulty summoning that halcyon period to mind. Though strangely reluctant to dwell on it, she was too honest to deny the similarities to that period of her life in the present situation. Certainly the sense of anticipation with which she greeted each day on arising was in large measure connected with the possibility of a visit from Lord Eversley. The pounding of her heart and her moist palms were immediately familiar despite the years that had elapsed since she had last experienced these signs of insecurity in the presence of one particular man.

Lord Eversley dropped in nearly every day. He generally began his call with a brief visit to Sir Hector unless the latter felt up to a session of chess or piquet. If not pressed for time, he would end up in the drawing room exchanging civilities with whichever members of the family were present. On the first two occasions these had not included Sarah, who was generally busy in some other part of the house. Recognizing after the second visit that Sarah's relatives had no intention of apprising her of the presence of a guest, Lord Eversley had then removed the element of chance by instructing Joseph on his arrival each day to inform Miss Sarah of his presence in the house.

Sarah was thus in no doubt that he intended to see her when he called at Beech Hill, but her confidence in her powers of attraction was not of such a high order that she dared hope he came primarily to see her, perhaps even to court her. They were never alone for a moment, nor did they ever indulge in a conversation that could not have been heard by all and sundry. Sarah had too lately been living from hand to mouth, weighed down by fears of the future, to cavil at a period of delicious uncertainty. There was no hurry to bring matters into the open.

Her relatives' visit would not continue too much longer with the imminence of the London Season to draw them away from Beech Hill. Meanwhile there was a warm look in Lord Eversley's dark eyes when they settled on her that filled her with secret excitement.

To Sarah's relief nothing more had been said by her grandfather on the subject of acquiring a fashionable wardrobe under Aunt Adelaide's guidance. She suspected that his pleasure in getting to know his youngest grandson had driven the matter out of his head, and she was duly grateful. Before leaving London, Lottie had had the foresight, when informed of their radical change of circumstances, to dip into their small capital to purchase several lengths of fabric and some accessories that Sarah would need in refurbishing her wardrobe. Before closing the shop she had also packed up the prettiest of the hats in stock along with the rest of Sarah's wardrobe. Within a day of settling into Beech Hill, Lottie had cut out two dresses to Sarah's designs, using the nursery as a workroom. The two women had stitched steadily to finish the first one, a pale-green muslin sprigged with a pattern of darker green leaves, made up in a simple style but featuring a triple flounce piped in dark-green satin.

She knew the gown was a success by the silence that greeted her entrance into the drawing room, where the ladies were entertaining Lord Eversley late one morning. He rose with a smile and complimented her on her blooming looks, at which point Aunt Ridgemont had remarked, "Yes, that is a very pretty dress, my dear. William has always liked green."

Lady Townsend introduced a new topic at that point, but Sarah noted Lord Eversley's thoughtful glance at Mrs. Ridgemont before he replied to Lady Townsend.

The second dress was a heavy cream-colored silk suitable for evening, cut with a low bodice that showed off Sarah's smooth shoulders and lovely long throat. Sir Hector, dining with them that evening, had gazed on her for a long moment before saying gruffly, "Now that you have more color in your face, you are growing more like your grandmother every day. We must get you some pearls. Adelaide has all her mother's jewels."

Sarah had murmured appropriately, avoiding her aunt's resentful glance. She knew Lady Townsend considered that any gift to Sarah even a compliment, was made at Arabella's expense, but she had concluded there was nothing she would say or do to mollify such irrationality.

The next morning when she went in to see her grandfather, he presented her with an invitation he had just received for the household to dine at Eversley the following week.

"A sennight should be long enough to have a superb gown made in Marshfield. I'm well-known there. Just have the account sent here."

"You don't think the cream—" Sarah began.

"No. It's quite good enough in the ordinary way, and so I told Miss Miller. She's an accomplished seamstress, but this dinner at Eversley will more or less mark your bow to local society and I want you dressed to turn heads. Get something trimmed with crystals or beads or lace—Miss Miller knows the style I'm after. She has a sound head on her shoulders and a good eye for what becomes you. She'll see that you're well-turned-out."

Sarah was so flabbergasted to hear this second reference to Lottie, whom she had not suspected of being on familiar terms with Sir Hector, that she did not immediately perceive the tacit retraction by omission of her aunt as her fashion mentor, a point Lottie did not neglect to call to her attention when she demanded an explanation from her old friend a few moments later.

Thus it was that a still-bemused Sarah found herself accompanying Lottie into Marshfield the next morning in her grandfather's old-fashioned but solidly luxurious carriage. Since neither Arabella nor her mother ever came down to breakfast before seven, there had been no one to question or impede the expedition. Sarah quite looked forward to exploring Marshfield. She had liked what she had seen of the bustling town on her arrival despite her headache and preoccupation with the ordeal ahead of her. Watching the countryside roll past on the day that featured a fitful sun dodging in and out of bunchy clouds, Sarah had trouble convincing herself that less than three weeks had actually passed since she had come to Gloucestershire to seek help. It was nearly inconceivable that their lives could have altered so radically in that short span of time, but here she was, the pampered granddaughter of a wealthy man, living in a mansion and driving in her own carriage to commission an expensive gown in which to meet the local gentry. Small wonder she still felt a bit dazed and doubtful of her good fortune.

Marshfield was as prosperous-looking and active as she remembered. Her grandfather's coachman set them down at a hostelry favored by Sir Hector where they could get a good luncheon after their business had been completed. Sarah's spirits were on tiptoe with excitement as she and Lottie stepped into a nearby draper's shop to ask for the name of the best modiste. The middle-aged man, whom she took to be the proprietor, cast a knowledgeable eye over the bronze-green bonnet that had not come from a provincial town, pricing it within a guinea, Sarah guessed, and gave them directions to the establishment run by Madame Bouchard.

Madame Bouchard was located on a street parallel to the main thoroughfare. They headed down a pleasant side street lined with attractive small houses and shops. They had nearly reached the intersection they sought when Sarah glanced idly at the pretty stone house with a bow window that they were passing. The front door stood open, its opening filled by a broad-shouldered man in a dark-green coat. As he raised his hand to place a brown beaver atop crisp black hair, something about the set of those shoulders and the way he carried his head riveted Sarah's eyes. She saw two white hands sparkling with rings creep over his shoulders. The smooth-fingered hands clasped each other below delicate wrists at the back of the man's neck and brought his head down. The arm that had placed the hat on his head went around the unseen woman's body a second later as he acquiesced to the embrace.

Sarah's step had faltered for a split second, but now she leapt forward, pulling an astonished Lottie with her as she hurried around the corner.

"What's the matter? Why are you racing along like this?" gasped Lottie when she had recovered her breath sufficiently to speak.

"I . . . I saw a person I prefer to avoid," Sarah replied, unable to think up a convincing lie on the spur of the moment.

"Who? Who do you know in Marshfield?"

Sarah didn't answer immediately. She was continuing her rapid pace down the walkway, while at the same time looking back over her shoulder every second or two. Lottie repeated her question.

"No one. I know no one in Marshfield."

"Then whom are we avoiding?" Lottie asked in pardonable exasperation.

It seemed as if Sarah was not going to reply. Her eyes were fixed straight ahead now, having ascertained that the danger of being seen was over. After a moment, however, she said dismissively, "No one of any importance. Come, here is Madame Bouchard's shop."

12

S he recovered, of course.
One didn't break one's heart over an acquaintance of less than three weeks' standing, no matter how attractive.

Sarah was neither ignorant nor naïve. She had been a helpless witness to her father's grief when her mother had died so suddenly, pitying the deep loneliness that nothing and no one could assuage, and understanding the restlessness that could be soothed by other women.

Lord Eversley had been without a wife for several years. In theory she was not shocked that he should keep a mistress, but being confronted with the reality of the woman had taught her very quickly that she would never willingly share a man she loved. If, influenced by her own awakening feelings, she had read more into his manner than he intended, then she was the only one to suffer, and she could surely do that with dignity. If, on the other hand, it was his intention to court her for whatever reason, then the sooner she made her position clear, the sooner that farce could be ended.

Sarah was quite pleased with the way she had dealt with the situation. Within five minutes of seeing Lord Eversley taking fond leave of his mistress, she had herself well enough in hand to calmly discuss styles and fabrics with a dressmaker and bring her critical faculties to bear on examining with Lottie some examples of Madame Bouchard's work before they had committed themselves to engaging her to make up the gown she would wear to the Eversley dinner party.

Though disposed by instinct and affection to get to the bottom of Sarah's strange behavior on the way to the dressmaker's, Lottie had been given no opportunity until they had concluded their business with Madame Bouchard. By that time Sarah was able to throw her off the scent by conceding in a self-deprecating tone that she had displayed an excessive aversion to meeting someone who, while vulgar, was not so low as to justify avoiding a brief acknowledgement of his acquaintance by such an extreme measure. They had methodically accomplished all the items on Lottie's list, partaken of a better-than-average luncheon at the inn recommended by her grandfather, and returned to Beech Hill in perfect amity. If Sarah had to invoke all her acting skills to present a serene appearance, the result was worth it. The incident was allowed to be forgotten.

During the days that elapsed before the scheduled dinner party Sarah succeeded in avoiding Lord Eversley's visits by having urgent business elsewhere if she knew he was with her grandfather or in the drawing room. The sense of eager anticipation with which she had greeted each day had disappeared, but that could not be helped. There remained a great deal to be thankful for, as she constantly reminded herself.

When not with her grandfather or sewing with Lottie, she was most likely to be found with William. She had always preferred his company to that of her other relatives, and now there was the added factor of gratitude to him for his generosity in employing hours of his time in teaching Richard how to ride. He and Richard were already fast friends, and she was grateful that the boy should take William as a model rather than the more dashing and worldly Vincent. Cecil, having met some friends from his youth in the neighborhood, had rather faded from the picture as far as the equestrian tutelage was concerned.

Yes, she assured herself, life was going along swimmingly and would improve when her less congenial relatives removed themselves from the house and she made some acquaintance among the local families. She was looking forward to the Eversley dinner party. It would give her a chance, among other things, to make it inescapably clear to a certain party that she was not interested in receiving his attentions.

Actually, the opportunity to accomplish this necessary chore presented itself rather sooner than expected.

Grace Medlark's little girl, a five-year-old called Minnie, was making a slow recovery from the influenza that had assumed the proportions of a small epidemic in the locale. Sarah had insisted that Grace remain home with the child during her fretful convalescence. One sunny afternoon she had the cook make up some gingerbread men and gathered together a few delicacies from the still room to tempt the little girl's appetite, which Grace said was sadly lacking. Thinking Richard might wish to accompany her on her walk into the village, she checked the library and her grandfather's rooms. Not finding him, she headed upstairs and entered the day nursery, where Lottie was busily sewing on some fabric they had not been able to resist in Marshfield.

Richard was there also—playing spillikins with Arabella!

From the slightly defiant look her cousin shot her, Sarah must have looked as astonished as she felt, but Richard said easily, "Do you know, Sarah, that Cousin Arabella never learned to play spillikins when she was a child? She has clever fingers, though, and is getting to be a dab hand at it already."

Arabella scrambled to her feet. "Mama is resting and all the men have ridden off somewhere," she said by way of explanation.

"I was planning to walk to the village with some things for Grace's daughter," said Sarah. "I thought Richard might like to come with me." Something about Arabella's downcast face prompted her to add, "Perhaps you'd care to take a walk, cousin? It's a lovely warm afternoon after all that rain this morning."

"Too nice a day to spend indoors," Lottie said comfortably. "Go along with them, Miss Arabella."

Darting a look at the clock on the wall, Arabella surprised Sarah by assenting. "I'll run down and get my bonnet and pelisse." She added with a grin to Richard, "I'll beat you next time."

When Arabella had gone to fetch her wrap and Richard was

picking up the spillikins, Sarah said, raising her brows at Lottie, "Well, that was a surprise. I never thought she'd come with us."

"That poor child is just plain lonely," Lottie gave as her opinion. "She never sees her brother and sees too much of that mother of hers and her cronies. If you ask me, she needs friends of her own age."

"Has she come up here before?"

"Once or twice. She likes Richard. He taught her to play cribbage last time."

Sarah, a basket over her arm, was occupied in revising her ideas of her young cousin as the three set off in the direction of the village. Richard and Arabella chatted away, unconcerned with their companion's silence as they strolled down the lane that wound its way between greening fields to come out eventually at the common in the village. Apparently absorbed in the pleasant scenery, Sarah stole a long look at the pretty, dark-haired girl from time to time.

Arabella's manner toward the boy was not that of an adult condescending to a child but of two persons meeting on equal conversational ground. Though Richard's insecure and eventful life had matured him beyond his years in some ways, he retained a child's enthusiasm and bright outlook. Arabella was the surprise. Gone were the affected mannerisms and flirtatious style that sought to fix all attention on her admittedly appealing person. With Richard she was unselfconscious and genuinely interested in his impressions of the neighborhood, revealing a sweetness and empathy that Sarah had not so far suspected in one whom she had considered completely self-centered. Her heart warmed to Arabella for liking her little brother. Could Lottie be right in her contention that the girl was lonely? Her life would seem to be a continual series of social engagements, but if these were all with her mother's circle of friends, she might indeed feel emotionally isolated. Perhaps all this desperate flirting was an unconscious search for someone of her own to be close to.

Sarah was so preoccupied with the new picture of her cousin that was taking shape and color in her mind that Richard had to speak to her twice to capture her attention. She shook off

her introspective mood and made an effort to join in the others'
conversation for the rest of their walk.

They were quite a merry little party by the time they entered
the scrupulously neat cottage that Grace shared with her
husband, little Minnie, and Minnie's two elder brothers. Grace
was almost tearfully grateful for the visit as she apologetically
ushered the callers into the homey kitchen, where a pot of something savory simmered over the fire.

"I'm sorry to bring you into the kitchen, Sarah, but it's the
warmest room for Minnie, and she won't let me out of her sight
since her illness."

"Of course, Grace. She wants spoiling a little at this stage.
Hello, Minnie," Sarah said softly to the anxious-looking little
girl lying on a sort of daybed set near the fireplace. "I am a
friend of your mama's. My name is Sarah, this is my brother,
Richard, and our Cousin Arabella. We've come to visit now
that you are getting better, and to bring you some gingerbread
men."

The winsome child, with the free-flowing fair hair and
delicately pointed features of a Botticelli angel, was too overwhelmed by shyness to speak. She stared at them through gray
eyes like her mother's that widened with delight at the iced
gingerbread figures, her pale little face brightening as she
realized the basket of treats was meant for her. Her joy knew
no bounds when Arabella produced a sumptuously dressed doll
she had snatched up from a cabinet in the nursery on their way
out. In lieu of words, of which she was plainly incapable, the
moppet threw her thin arms about Arabella's neck as the girl
bent to place the doll in her lap. Arabella laughed and sat down
on the daybed, gathering child and doll onto her own lap while
she explained that the doll had belonged to her mother when
she was a little girl like Minnie.

Arabella was softly embroidering on this theme to a rapt little
girl while Sarah conferred with Grace in low tones when Richard
brought Doctor Rydell into the room a moment later. No one
but the boy had heard the knock on the front door.

Grace apologized profusely, but it was doubtful if the doctor
heard a word. His amazing dark-ringed gray eyes were fixed

on the young woman cuddling the sick child in an unguarded stare of adoration that caused Grace and Sarah to exchange a shocked glance of understanding and dismay. Arabella went slowly pink as her eyes clung to the doctor's.

"Doctor Rydell comes to see Minnie every afternoon, no matter how crammed his schedule," Grace said hurriedly, her voice sounding unnaturally loud in the charged atmosphere of the cosy room.

At least it had the effect of releasing everyone from the tableaulike postures in which all but Richard had been frozen. Arabella replaced the little girl against the pillows and straightened away from the bed, stepping back to give the doctor room to approach. Minnie suddenly regained her power of speech and proceeded to regale the doctor, an obvious favorite, with a list of the gifts her visitors had brought. Her fluting voice lisped as she thrust the doll under his nose while he took her pulse and went over her with a professional eye and a gentle touch.

A flustered Sarah began saying their good-byes, hoping to effect an escape before the doctor was finished, but her efforts were stymied by Minnie, who included Arabella in all her remarks and kept that young lady pinned to her side—not unwillingly, Sarah was convinced. In the end, she abandoned her futile attempts to drag Arabella away, and it was she who left the cottage last, lingering to say good-bye to Grace on the doorstep as Arabella and Doctor Rydell walked on ahead with Richard in attendance.

This was the position when a man cantered down the street on a magnificent black stallion. Two magnificent animals, Sarah amended with a sinking heart. She noted that the human one was wearing the same dark-green coat he'd worn in Marshfield. There was no way of avoiding a meeting. Grace had gone back into her house at a call from Minnie.

Lord Eversley had already dismounted and saluted Arabella and Doctor Rydell and had laughingly relinquished his reins to Richard, who had offered to walk the beast with transparent hopefulness.

They met at the gate to the Medlark front garden as Sarah

approached on reluctant feet, having seen that, instead of walking back toward the gate, her cousin and the besotted doctor had remained talking together where Lord Eversley had greeted them. Neatly trapped, she summoned up a social smile that froze in the warmth of Lord Eversley's pleasure in the meeting.

"At last, Sarah. I had begun to think fortune meant never to favor me with a glimpse of you again."

"Good afternoon, Lord Eversley."

"Can you not manage Mark?" he asked with a beseeching smile that would have melted her reserve a week ago.

"On a fortnight's acquaintance? Heavens, I am not so forward," she declared, producing a light laugh with a supreme effort. It must have sounded as false to him as it did in her own ears because his brow creased slightly and his look grew searching.

"You've known me longer than you have William Ridgemont, whom you seem to have no qualms about addressing by his Christian name. Am I less deserving of your favor?"

Sarah swallowed nervously at the sincerity in his quiet tones. "But William is my cousin, sir," she protested, still trying to maintain a careless air.

"Are you saying you prefer not to accord me the same privilege?" he asked, refusing to accept his cue to play the scene lightly.

"It . . . it is too soon."

"No, it's more than that," he replied, reading the evasiveness in her face. "You and I have never stood on ceremony from the moment of our first meeting, so why now? What have I done to offend you?"

"Nothing. Of course you have done nothing to offend me!" She was rapidly losing the struggle to remain cool and composed.

"Methinks the lady doth protest too much," he said with a bitter curl to his lip. "There is more to this than a simple wish to proceed more slowly down the path on which we have embarked. Everything about you is screaming 'stop.' I have grievously offended you in some way, though I promise you it was unintentional.''

"Nonsense, sir,'' she cried, feeling more harassed by the moment. "Of course you have not offended me. It is not for me to be offended at anything you might choose to do. How can you think it? We are the merest acquaintances.'' Her voice was under commendable control when she finished this speech, but Lord Eversley impatiently brushed aside her words.

"Fustian. We've been more than mere acquaintances from the moment we met. There's something eating away at you, all right, something you consider heinous, and you've no intention of telling me what it is. In fact, now that I come to think of it, it wasn't bad luck that has kept us from meeting this week, was it? It was intentional on your part. You needn't bother to frame the lie, because I know I am right.'' He ran a rough hand through his hair from forehead to nape, squeezing his neck muscles as he gazed at her in impotent exasperation.

"Sir, this conversation is getting us nowhere. Perhaps we had best agree to disagree?'' Her glittering smile set a muscle twitching in his cheek.

"By God, we won't! It is too vital. I can never get a moment of privacy with you at Beech Hill, so we'll have it out here and now, in front of half the village and your brother and cousin if necessary.''

"Won't you please believe me when I say you have not offended me, but . . . but it is for the best that we remain casual acquaintances?''

Distressed amber eyes pleading with him, as well as trembling lips, calmed the flames that had been burning in his near-black eyes, and he said more gently, "I'm afraid I cannot accept that, my lovely one. It's too crucial to our ultimate happiness to get to the bottom of this misunderstanding. Your brother is approaching. I'll come to Beech Hill tomorrow . . . No, I forgot. I have business in Marshfield tomorrow.''

"Yes, I am sure you have,'' Sarah said unwisely, but she was at the end of her emotional tether by then.

Mark's gaze, which had been on the gatepost as he mentally went over his schedule, snapped back to her face, alerted by something in her voice. "Now, what did you mean by that?" he inquired with soft menace, taking in her rising color and shifting glance.

"Nothing at all."

"Has someone been telling tales about me and Marshfield, by any chance?"

"No," she said with convincing conviction, but he was not put off.

"No one has told you I have a mistress there?"

Sarah gasped at his effrontery, and the look she sent him could have ignited a woodpile in a hurricane. She'd have left him then, but he stood squarely in front of the gate. She'd have needed a squad of cavalry to budge him.

"He's a wonderful horse, Lord Eversley. What's his name?"

Two pairs of eyes swung around to focus with difficulty on the eager boy holding out the reins of the handsome stallion. Lord Eversley accepted them mechanically and said, "Heracles," producing a faint smile for Richard.

"Oh, that suits him right down to the ground," Richard said approvingly, smiling impartially on the pair on either side of the gate. "He looks strong enough for anything."

Richard's timely intervention had served to extricate his sister from the most embarrassing ten minutes of her life. Her relief took the form of falsely bright remarks on the lateness of the hour, which caused Doctor Rydell, wandering nearer with Arabella, to take reluctant leave of the party. Lord Eversley bowed too and said all that was proper to the occasion, his attractive baritone so laced with irony that it was a wonder no one save Sarah seemed to notice. His parting glance at her had a biding-my-time quality about it that had her frantically searching her wits for a way out of going to his mother's dinner party, now only two days off.

There was no way, short of a last-minute indisposition, as a few fruitless hours of cogitation told her. A few more hours devoted to the subject convinced her that she would merely be delaying the inevitable confrontation between them. Lord Eversley was clearly not a man to let a few social conventions deter him from pursuing an objective. Her outraged sensibilities weren't going to count for much against that determination. Actually, the longer she considered the subject, the closer she came to agreeing with him. Embarrassment aside, only frankness would serve in such a vital matter as her future happiness.

It was with a fatalistic calm therefore that Sarah entered the Eversley house on the night of the dinner party. She knew she was looking her best. Madame Bouchard had created a deceptively simple gown of a champagne-colored gossamer silk that floated and drifted when she moved; it sparkled at each shift of light, thanks to hundreds of beads, ranging from gold through amber and several shades of brown, that had been sewed onto the abbreviated bodice that revealed more of her supple body than she would have deemed quite proper before she had returned to England.

Maria had been ecstatic over the gown, begging to be allowed to try a more elaborate style of coiffure to do justice to its elegance. The result was a high top knot from which long curls descended in a frivolous and utterly charming cascade that made her look not a day older than Arabella. A feathered fan dyed shades of amber, which she displayed with the consummate grace imparted to her years before by her mother, earned strong approval from her grandfather, who was forcibly reminded of his wife's alluring use of these lovely adjuncts to a woman's toilette. As for Lottie's reaction, her old nurse had blinked back tears of regret that Alice Ridgemont had not lived to see her daughter so finely decked out in a manner worthy of the full flush of her beauty.

Sarah would have been less than human to remain ungratified by the compliments on her appearance elicited from her Uncle Horace and her male cousins. For once the admiration expressed by Vincent seemed genuine, and he had the grace to look slightly rueful as he met her cool, measuring glance. Her Aunt Ridgemont, managing to appear dowdy even in a relatively attractive gown of deep sapphire-blue satin by virtue of an inappropriate shawl of a predominantly bilious green print and an ugly pale-blue turban that she had perched precariously on crimped locks, approved her niece's new coiffure with a vague smile. Her expression sharpened as she intercepted William's reaction to Sarah's enhanced loveliness, and her blue eyes flashed to Sarah's face in time to witness a slight rise in color before long lashes descended in protection as William continued to regard his cousin with silent but speaking devotion.

As on the previous occasion when the Beech Hill residents had gone together to Eversley, Sarah traveled in the carriage with William and his parents. She and her uncle carried on a desultory conversation during the drive. William was uncharacteristically absent in spirit, and Mrs. Ridgemont did not once open her lips until they were in sight of their destination.

Despite her best intentions to remain cool and uninterested in Lord Eversley's reaction, a feminine urge born with Eve lifted Sarah's eyes to his face, and she derived immense satisfaction from the excitement that flared up for an instant before he became the perfect host, greeting her as if they had not parted on a quarrel at their last meeting.

Lady Eversley, looking ten years younger than her age in a gown of cerulean blue that deepened her eyes and flattered her coloring, welcomed her guests in a more formal drawing room in another wing on this occasion. Sarah could see Aunt Adelaide's avid eyes evaluating the superb diamond necklace her hostess wore. She herself was wearing a small fortune in rubies and diamonds that flashed about her strong neck and in the raven locks that as yet contained very few gray strands. Arabella was entrancingly pretty in an all-white costume and her pearls. For once Sarah did not feel at a disadvantage in her relatives' company, though the only jewelry she wore was a pair of long earrings studded with pieces of amber in an intricate gold filigree setting. They were attractive rather than valuable, but she had kept them when the rest of her mother's jewelry had been sold because her father insisted they must have been designed to complement her eyes. She'd not had occasion to wear them for more years than she cared to recall, and she could not help moving her head occasionally just for the pleasure of feeling them swing away from her neck. Arabella had admired them enviously, then conceded with rare generosity that they would not have become her half so well as her cousin.

Sarah glanced at her cousin now and saw a radiance come over her face. She did not have to turn her head to know that Doctor Rydell must have entered the room at that moment. She had not been so immersed in her own dilemma these past two days that she had forgotten Arabella's blissful state as they had walked home from the village after the accidental meeting with the handsome young doctor. At the time the painful contrast between the results of the two accidental meetings that had occurred during their errand of mercy had occupied her mind almost exclusively, but she had gradually come to a realization that Arabella's plight was more to be pitied than her own. Her decision about Lord Eversley was hers alone to make. She also knew her grandfather would be delighted to see her married to his dear friend.

Arabella, on the contrary, was under the thumb of a parent who intended her to make a brilliant match. Though a gentleman, Doctor Rydell was far removed from her in birth and fortune, and his devotion to his profession would render him completely ineligible in Lady Townsend's eyes. Arabella's present radiance as she gave her hand to the doctor and gazed up into his eyes was destined to be the brief precursor of deep unhappiness if her heart was involved. That this affair was more than her cousin's usual flirtation, Sarah knew beyond doubt. Arabella didn't flirt with Simon Rydell. She had tried ignoring him, perhaps out of a sense of self-preservation at their first meetings, but this defense had failed her in Grace's cottage. As for the doctor, he had no defenses where Arabella was concerned, and Sarah feared for both when Lady Townsend became aware of the situation.

A touch on her arm brought Sarah back to a sense of her surroundings and she smiled in mute apology at her hostess, who was about to present her to the squire and his lady. Sir Randolph and Lady Mortimer were kind-seeming people, perhaps a few years younger than her uncle, who welcomed her affably. Only the eldest of their numerous progeny, a pretty girl of seventeen or so with a mop of sandy curls, was with them this evening.

Lord and Lady Calderby, whose estate was on the outskirts

of Marshfield, were a bit more reserved than the Mortimers but quite affable. Their son looked to be about Cecil's age and appeared all but tongue-tied when presented to Sarah and Arabella. His sister, copper-haired and green-eyed, whom Sarah shrewdly surmised to be the reigning belle in the area, did not suffer from the same shyness. She eyed the Ridgemont young ladies in the assessing manner of an athlete rating the field of competition, smiled prettily, murmured politely, and glided off purposefully toward the corner where Lord Townsend and William Ridgemont were speaking with their host.

Sarah, smiling at such blatant tactics as she patiently answered the squire's concerned queries about her grandfather, ceased smiling when she noticed that Arabella, far from having her competitive spirit aroused by Miss Calderby, had failed to mark the latter's departure from her position by Doctor Rydell's side. She was only partially reassured on locating Lady Townsend with her back to her daughter while she answered the same questions about Sir Hector put by the Reverend and Mrs. Henry Tallant, who completed the dinner party. If Arabella were to continue to demonstrate her marked preference for Simon Rydell's company, her mother would not long remain in the dark.

Sarah, seated between the vicar and her Cousin Vincent, enjoyed a very good dinner. She could handle Vincent's nonsense with ease by now and she made the happy discovery that Mr. Tallant had lived in America for several years before his marriage. He proved a most entertaining dinner partner as they compared their experiences in the former colonies. From time to time she was conscious of Lord Eversley's brooding eye on her, but she was careful not to meet his glance directly. Her survival instincts were still intact. She could not know that the flickering candles in branched silver candelabra deployed down the length of the table set alight a myriad of gold and copper glints in her rich bronze tresses, that her eyes gleamed with light that rivaled the amber pieces winking in their gold settings depending from her ears, but she could sense the intensification of that brooding regard as the meal progressed. She was not released from its grip until the ladies adjourned to the large drawing room, leaving the men to their politics and port. There would come a reckoning between them soon, but a dinner party where he had a host's responsibilities was not the occasion.

Sarah went quite unsuspecting to her fate. She did wonder briefly why Lady Eversley had brought her into the intriguing glass conservatory at one end of the long room to see an exotic flower called an orchid before the men returned from table, but she followed her hostess willingly and profusely admired the brightly colored blossoms she'd been shown. She was still bent over the plant in fascination when Lady Eversley excused herself a trifle breathlessly, "Mark will bring you back, my dear. I must return to my guests now."

Caught off guard, Sarah whirled to find a scant foot of space between herself and the fiery-eyed man who filled her thoughts, as a drift of cerulean blue vanished into the dim reaches of the sparsely lighted conservatory.

"As you may recall, our last conversation was interrupted at a most interesting point. We are going to finish it now."

Sarah was astonished at her own calm. She experienced no return of the dismayed embarrassment that had gripped her in the village. She even produced a small smile as she observed, "You have a very devoted mother."

She had succeeded in surprising him. She saw his jaw relax as she became aware of piano music coming from the drawing room. All her senses were alerted suddenly. The musky odor of vegetation and moist earth assailed her nostrils, she felt the coolness of damp air on her skin and the heat coming from Mark's body as he closed the gap between them to inches. Instinctively she retreated, but he caught her by the shoulders.

"Mama knew I had something urgent to say to you. Sarah, whoever told you I kept a mistress in Marshfield was correct except in one vital particular—the tense. It should have been the past tense. I did keep a mistress, I do not any longer."

She was shaking her head, refusing to look at him.

"Dammit, Sarah, you are not a child. You know men aren't saints. Until you came into my life I was determined not to remarry. I didn't think a woman like you existed except in my imagination. You cannot deny us this chance at happiness simply because I haven't been celibate for the past five years."

"It's no use, Mark," she said sadly. "No one told me anything about a mistress. I saw you with my own eyes. And it was very much the present."

"You saw me?" His voice was mystified. "You saw me what? When?"

"Please, Mark, let's not prolong the agony with more lies. We must return to the party before we're missed."

"What did you see?"

The grip on her half-bare shoulders tightened, and she wondered fleetingly if she'd be trapped out here for hours with telltale red marks on her skin. She lifted her chin and said steadily, "I saw you taking leave of her earlier this week in Marshfield. You were embracing in the open doorway for the whole world to see." She could not prevent a trace of bitterness from becoming evident in her voice.

To her surprise he did not look abashed but annoyed as he administered a small shake to the shapely shoulders in his slackened hold. "That's exactly what I was doing, taking leave of her permanently. And if you saw that much, you should have seen also that the so-called embrace was more or less forced on me—"

"*Less!*"

The indignant cry had barely left her lips when they were ruthlessly covered by Mark's mouth. His arms had gone around her shoulders, one hand pinioning the back of her head to keep her mouth in position, but thoughts of escape, indeed thought of any nature, were beyond Sarah at that point. After the first moment of shock, the desperate passion in his kiss had awakened long-dormant feelings in her, and then, as the embrace lengthened and his lips began to move coaxingly over hers, quite new and insistent feelings. She flamed into response, whimpering softly in her effort to enclose as much of him in her own embrace as her tightening arms could encompass.

Mark was trembling slightly as his lips ceased their thrilling depredations long enough to whisper on an unsteady breath, "Sarah, my darling love, after this you cannot deny—"

A loud hiss of surprise jerked both heads around in alarm,

but the only lights in the conservatory were in their vicinity. Neither could distinguish anything as they heard footsteps hastily leaving the other end of the conservatory.

"Someone saw us," Sarah said, jumping out of his arms in alarm.

"It doesn't signify." Mark was reaching for her again, but she eluded his grasp as she frantically pulled the small puffed sleeves of the champagne silk farther up on her exposed shoulders to cover the faint marks made by his fingers.

"Of course it signifies! Please don't follow me out this entrance. Wait a moment and go out the other door." Sarah was heading for the closest exit as she spoke, repinning a couple of curls that had become disarranged. She was stepping through the doorway on the action, leaving him glowering in frustration.

Sarah's entrance went unremarked through a stroke of luck she knew she didn't deserve. The doorway at the end of the wall that backed the conservatory was partly concealed by an artistic display of potted trees and plants placed in the corner of the room. Sarah had the good fortune to be gliding through this miniature forest at the moment when a song had just ended and there was much milling about the pianoforte as the two young ladies who had been performing smilingly made way for the vicar and his wife, who were about to sing a duet. Sarah sank onto a chair amid applause and movement, being careful to choose one near where Mr. Tallant had been sitting, in the hope that the removal of his comfortable girth would account for her sudden visibility to curious eyes. She did not possess the requisite nerve to look around the room to seek out the eyes of the one person who knew she had just reappeared—the inadvertent witness to that impassioned embrace in the conservatory.

She was tinglingly cognizant a moment later of Lord Eversley's quiet entrance from the more exposed door as she willed him not to sit in her vicinity. Truth to tell, now that her racing pulses were coming back to a normal rate, Sarah's primary reaction was total shock at her own wanton behavior. She had been kissed by her former fiancé on any number of occasions, and she had mildly enjoyed the contact, but she had never imagined anything remotely resembling the assault on her senses that Mark's marauding mouth had provoked. As her heartbeat slowed, the memory of her recent abandonment to needs and pleasures of whose existence she had been entirely ignorant brought a suffusing heat to her cheek and she could meet no one's eyes.

Sarah was unnaturally quiet for the remainder of the evening, too busy avoiding Mark to be capable of any but the simplest responses to conversational overtures. How could she concentrate on producing witty repartee when her appalled intellect was trying to figure out what magic arts he had employed to elicit such wantonness from someone of her cool temperament?

She was no closer to a conclusion when Lady Eversley bade her good night with a twinkling look that covered her with confusion again. She was not sure whether she was thrilled or afraid when Mark whispered that he would see her tomorrow as he handed her up into her uncle's carriage. She was so pre-occupied with her own chaotic thoughts that she never noticed that the conversation on the ride home consisted entirely of general observations by her uncle and quiet brief replies from William.

13

Breakfast was Sarah's favorite meal at Beech Hill because Lottie and Richard invariably shared it with her, the other ladies never did, and the men's participation depended upon the weather and their morning plans.

On the morning after the Eversley dinner party the sole occupants of the dining saloon when Sarah entered were Lottie, Richard, and Cecil, who gulped a final cup of coffee, wished her a hasty good morning, and departed—to meet some friends in Marshfield, Richard informed her before he and Lottie began firing questions at her about the party. Sarah tried to satisfy them; Richard was mainly interested in the menu while Lottie was preoccupied with the persons in attendance, Sarah's reaction to them and theirs to her. Lottie had never gone in much for subtlety when she wished to know something, though she had always possessed an intuitive sensitivity for the sore spots to avoid during Sarah's painful adolescent years when the family fortunes had fluctuated so rapidly that all sense of security was endangered. Sarah smiled at her with deep affection as she did her best to recall the friendly or flattering things that had been said to her during the course of the evening.

A lifetime's intimate acquaintance with her old nurse left Sarah in no doubt that Lottie's primary concern was Lord Eversley's reaction, and she did her best to satisfy this while still hugging her precious secret to herself. At this stage she was too unsure of what would be for the best in the future to share her feelings, even with Lottie. She knew what she wanted—a few glorious moments in Mark's arms had shown her that—but this might not be the best thing for all concerned in the long run.

In order to distract Lottie from her friendly inquisition when Richard had gone off to visit his grandfather and the two women had accepted second cups of coffee, Sarah told her about Arabella and Doctor Rydell, starting with her earliest observations and going into the details of the meeting in the village and their subsequent behavior at the dinner party.

"Aunt Adelaide appeared not to have recognized her daughter's state, although I cannot conceive how she can remain blind after the degree of particularity Arabella demonstrated last night. She sat beside the doctor at dinner, all but ignoring the Calderby lad on her other side. Everyone must have remarked her behavior. If it had not been for Doctor Rydell's innate good manners, which led him to circulate and pay his respects to his other friends when the men rejoined us after dinner, I am persuaded no thought of propriety or her mother's displeasure would have induced Arabella to leave his side."

Lottie shook her head. "No good ever came of fixing one's interest outside of one's own class."

"Well, as to that," Sarah countered hesitantly, "Simon Rydell is certainly a gentleman, but there's no denying the disparity of their circumstances."

"Mayhap they'll all be leaving here before the affair progresses too far," Lottie said with an optimism Sarah could not believe was justified. She said no more on that head, however, deeming it time to go and give her grandfather an account of the party, a greatly expurgated account, she decided as she finished drinking her coffee. At least she could pass along all the kindly inquiries and messages from his neighbors.

Following her call on her grandfather, Sarah was crossing the great hall heading for the east staircase when William came out of the dining room. Her cheery greeting was met with a disturbingly intent stare before William said abruptly, "Sarah, may I speak with you privately?"

"Of course, William. What is it?"

"Not here. Will you come into the library? We won't be interrupted there."

Sarah accompanied her silent cousin, concealing her reluctance beneath a brief smile as her eyes skimmed his serious countenance. Already she knew that the coming interview was going to be difficult and painful.

Her instincts did not betray her.

William opened the library door and stood back for her to precede him inside. He did not speak immediately when he had seen her seated in a leather chair in front of an ornately carved and much-scarred desk. Instead, he took a few restless steps away, his back to her. Staring at that taut posture, Sarah experienced a wave of compassion, but there was nothing she could do to avert what was coming. Though convinced in theory that she had nothing to reproach herself for—she had always been honest and sincere in her dealings with William—there was no escaping the weight of his probable disappointment and pain. She cringed internally from the necessity of inflicting it.

William turned a tightly controlled visage to her. "I do not suppose you can be in any doubt about the way I feel about you, Sarah," he said quietly. "It seems to be obvious to everyone else." He paused then, searching her compassionate features for some encouragement he did not find, for his gaze flickered, then hardened.

"We . . . we have been the best of friends, William," Sarah said, rushing to fill the uncomfortable pause.

His lips tightened briefly before he went on with leashed emotion. "I know that, and the fear of losing your friendship has kept me silent thus far, but it's no use, Sarah. I cannot play the coward indefinitely and let another man walk off with the prize I dared not aim for. I love you, and I must put my hopes to the test. Will you marry me? I won't rush you into a decision," he went on when she bit her lip and did not speak at once. "I know that Grandfather loves having you here, and there is Richard to settle into school in the next few months, but I have to know if you could care for me enough to consider marrying me."

Sarah was gripping her hands together in her lap, hating herself for what she was going to do but recognizing the necessity. She swallowed dryly and said, "I am so sorry,

William. I do care for you, but it is not the right kind of caring, not the kind on which to build a marriage.'' She stopped then, torn by an urge to explain away the pain she was inflicting, but realizing the futility of more words to the same end.

Their eyes clung for an uncomfortable eternity, the blue ones searching the amber for signs of weakening.

''Is there someone else?'' William asked at length, as though the words were dragged out of him.

Sarah's lashes flickered, though her gaze did not waver. ''The only thing that has any significance is my feeling for you, William,'' she said gently. ''I hope you know how honored I am to receive your proposal. I am dreadfully sorry for any pain my decision causes you. I hate the idea of bringing you unhappiness even for a little while, but you deserve a wife who will give you so much more than I could.''

William held up a staying hand, taking in a deep slow breath. ''Do not go on, my dear,'' he said with a wry twist to his sensitive mouth. ''I cannot stand your pain at causing me pain. I think I always knew what your answer would be, and I meant what I said earlier: it was the thought of losing your friendship that has kept me silent these past ten days.''

''You will never lose my friendship, William,'' Sarah assured him, eager to make whatever small reparation was in her power.

For the first time he looked away from her, saying at last, ''May I beg a favor of you, Sarah, in the name of that friendship?''

''Of course.''

''I have tried to disguise my feeling for you from my mother once I began to fear it was all on my side, but I doubt I've been successful. She is too aware where I am concerned. You must have noticed that she cherishes an unrealistic opinion of my worth and talents.'' His smile was rueful and drew a sympathetic chuckle from Sarah. ''She likes you, but she can be . . . difficult if she believes anyone is acting against my interests. I do not wish her to know you've turned me down, Sarah, for her sake and for yours.''

''I understand, William.''

''I know there is generally some awkwardness attached to

the situation in which we now find ourselves, but if we can
manage to carry on for the rest of our stay as if this morning
never happened, it would save a lot of strain. I'll sound out my
father on bringing our visit to a close, today if possible.''

"Of course I'll do as you think best, William." Sarah was
desperately eager to bring the torturous interview to a close now,
before she disgraced herself and made her cousin even more
unhappy by bursting into tears.

With his usual sensitity to her moods, he smiled crookedly
and walked over to open the door for her. "Thank you, Sarah,"
he said quietly.

Sarah was incapable of more than a swift stretching of her
lips in response as, eyes lowered, she passed him and headed
for the closest staircase at a near run. In her room she indulged
in a short, restorative bout of tears before she trusted herself
enough to go back into company. Fearing Lottie's sharp eyes,
she washed her face and hands and put a dab of powder on her
shining nose before deciding her appearance would pass muster.

Sarah and Lottie were sewing in the nursery a half-hour later
when Joseph knocked with a summons for Sarah to go down
to her grandfather at once.

"Is anything amiss, Joseph?" she asked, folding up her work.
"When I left Grandfather scarcely an hour ago, he seemed
fine."

"Now, Miss Sarah," Joseph replied, smiling at her as she
walked down the west staircase with him, "Somers would have
mentioned it if Sir Hector had taken one of his turns." The
footman's cheerful demeanor was most reassuring, but Sarah's
footsteps were purposeful as she parted from him at the bottom
of the staircase. He headed back to his post in the great hall
and she went down the corridor that led past the chapel to her
grandfather's apartment.

She was passing the open chapel door when a strong arm in
a blue coat reached out and hauled her inside. Before she could
utter more than a tiny squeak of protest, Sarah found herself
in Lord Eversley's arms being soundly kissed as he nudged the
chapel door shut with his foot.

So last night had not been an aberration brought about by

moonlight and a romantic setting, Sarah had time to think before she surrendered to the thrilling sensations Mark's lips on hers produced all along her nervous system. She strained to him, untutored in the ways of passion but gratifyingly obedient and quick to follow where he led. It was broad daylight now and the chapel, with its frescoed ceiling, could not qualify as a romantic setting, but the results were the same as on the previous night. As Mark released her lips lingeringly, he looked somewhat dazed, and his breath came unsteadily.

"I had to make sure last night really happened, that what flared between us was not wishful thinking or a figment of my imagination."

A smile quivered on Sarah's lips as she stared up into his bemused face, all shyness forgotten. "It felt very real to me," she said softly. Looking her fill at her lover, she marveled at the difference happiness made in his stern aspect. At times his eyes had seemed hard enough to remind her of gleaming lumps of obsidian; now they were more like melted chocolate. The harsh lines in his cheeks had faded away and his stern mouth was relaxed and beautiful. She placed a tentative finger on his lips to trace their line, and he laughed and kissed it. Then he seized her hand and brought it to cup his cheek while the fingers of the other hand lifted her chin as he returned her scrutiny with fascinated thoroughness.

"You are so incredibly lovely," he breathed against her lips before straightening up once more to say with some difficulty, "I have no wish to beat what I hope is a dead horse, my darling, but I'd like to think you could understand how it was with me and the woman in Marshfield."

"You do not have to explain, Mark." There was no shadow in the glowing eyes that looked back at him, and somehow that emboldened him to proceed.

"I would like to tell you." Hearing the questioning inflection, Sarah nodded. "For the first two years after my wife died, I was so filled with rage that I would not have cared if I never saw another female for the rest of my life. I must have tried my poor mother's love to the utmost, I was so impossible to live with. Most men, most normal men, need women sometimes even if there is no affection between them, and not just for lovemaking. A woman softens the rough edges of a man's temper, a woman can keep a man sane. It may sound a strange thing to say, but I think we would not be standing here today if I had not kept a mistress these past three years. Certainly I'd have grown even more cross-grained and crabbed than I am. I am persuaded you'd have found me so disagreeable as to take me in irremedial dislike on sight instead of forgiving me for my severity to you at first.''

"You are not cross-grained and crabbed," protested Sarah lovingly. "Autocratic and dominating perhaps, but not crabbed.''

Mark laughed outright. "I shall study to mend my ways, ma'am," he said, gathering her into his arms once again. "You have nothing to fear on that score, Sarah, and I promise you never will. I am not a philanderer by nature. I thought I was in love with the girl I married. She was pretty and gay and fun to be with. Though I soon discovered I did not know her at all, I was never unfaithful to her, here or in Portugal.

"Darling, I am supremely confident that you and I will build a wonderful life together. What I felt before pales in comparison with the love I have for you. I adore you, Sarah.''

She returned his embrace with fervor but said uncertainly, "Are you so sure you really know me, Mark? Three weeks ago you were unaware of my existence.''

His steady eyes on hers gave her the reassurance she sought. "I may not yet know your favorite color or food, or if you are testy in the morning, but I recognized and respected your essential honesty right from the beginning. I know that you are kind and brave and generous and loyal—''

"Oh, Mark!" Two tears slipped over her cheekbones, and he gave her a gentle shake.

"If you are going to cry each time I tell you why I love you, you will severely cramp my style in compliments, sweetheart.''

"Oh, Mark!" This time she laughed, and was promptly kissed.

"You will marry me, Sarah? Soon?''

She drew a little away from him. "What do you call soon?''

"Tomorrow," he replied promptly. "I'll get a special license."

Sarah laughed again, rather shakily, and blushed. "I am flattered by your eagerness, but I could not leave my grandfather on the instant like that after just . . . Oh, my goodness," she cried, her eyes widening. "My grandfather! He sent for me, and I forgot everything the moment you—I mean, we—"

This time Mark's laugh was young and carefree. Sarah looked at him uncertainly, then something about the impish lights in chocolate-brown eyes registered in her brain.

"Mark," she scolded, trying with little success to keep her lips firmed primly, "it was you who sent Joseph to me with that message. I wondered why he did not simply head down the back stairs, which were nearer the nursery. It was a trap."

"And an ambush," he admitted shamelessly. "Shall I apologize?"

The impish lights were in amber eyes now. "I shouldn't believe you," she declared with a toss of her head.

"Let us go tell your grandfather our news. He can make the announcement to the others this evening."

Sarah had grown very still at these words.

Mark's hands on her arms above the elbows tightened spasmodically. She winced, and he loosened them, muttering a short apology. "What is it, Sarah? Is something wrong? Tell me."

The tip of her tongue made a quick nervous circuit of her upper lip. "It's about the announcement, Mark. Would you mind very much if we didn't make an announcement yet? May we wait until after the family leaves Beech Hill? That should be any day now, I would imagine. Doctor Rydell says Grandfather's condition is fairly stable, and the Season will be starting soon in London, will it not?"

"Why do you wish to delay the announcement of our betrothal? Your family must know sooner or later." His eyes were probing hers, and Sarah feared he would find her explanation inadequate, but she had to try to make him understand.

"I think you know that the situation here has been a bit difficult. There is some resentment of our presence, Richard's and mine—indeed of our very existence—and I do not wish there to be any shadows or dissension cast over our happiness.''

Mark's eyes did not cease their probing. ''I do understand, darling, and I hate seeing that ill-natured Townsend woman treat you like an interloper and worse, but there is something else I understand that makes it imperative to let them all know how things stand. William Ridgemont is in love with you. The longer we delay an announcement, the more likely it is that he will declare himself. I am persuaded you would not wish to have that embarrassing situation to deal with.''

''It is too late,'' Sarah said on a sigh, accepting that only the truth would suffice now. ''William did propose this morning, and when I had to refuse him, he begged me to go on as we have been in order to spare his mother's feelings.''

''His *mother's* feelings?''

''Yes. You know how Aunt Ridgemont dotes on William. He is sure she has guessed that he wishes to marry me. If she knew I had turned his offer down, she would be very upset, and things would be even more difficult for me. I . . . I promised I would go along as if nothing had happened.'' Mark's brows drew together in a thunderous scowl, and she said hastily, ''It shouldn't be for more than a few days, dearest. William is going to suggest to his father that they all wind up their visits at Beech Hill. Indeed, he may already have done so. Please, Mark, may we leave matters as they were and keep our betrothal a secret for a few days? I really cannot face the idea of more unpleasantness on top of Aunt Adelaide's attitude.''

Mark was extremely reluctant to postpone making his claim on her official, but he was not proof against the pleading in those lovely eyes. Before he left, they agreed to say nothing to Sir Hector under the circumstances. The general's nature fitted his name too well to trust that he would refrain from gloating over this coup.

Sarah went a little warily into lunch, unsure what to expect, but she need not have worried that William would permit any awkwardness to develop between them. He was already seated at table when she entered. He half-rose and patted the back of the chair beside him in smiling invitation as she issued a general greeting. There was actually more danger that she would reveal the happiness bubbling inside her, thus arousing curiosity. It was necessary to banish all thought of Mark and concentrate on the easy conversation between William and Richard, in which they included her from time to time.

Lottie refused to eat at the family table except for breakfast. She and Richard shared the evening meal in the nursery and she ate at the housekeeper's table in the middle of the day. The only other person to pay any attention to Sarah at lunch was Arabella, who chatted nonstop about the Eversley party, addressing most of her remarks to her cousin as if they'd been bosom friends in their cradles. Sarah noted with amusement that among a plethora of comments on the food and decor, and snippets of information about the neighbors, not a single reference to Doctor Rydell dropped from her ready tongue. She had seated herself at a distance from her parent and seemed to her cousin to be studiously avoiding that lady's eye. Neither Cecil nor Vincent was present, and the elder ladies, perhaps a bit fatigued from the late evening, were more than usually silent that day.

The only awkward moment was caused by Richard, who mentioned that he was sorry to have missed Lord Eversley's visit because he particularly desired to ask him something about a recent news account of the campaign in France.

"Lord Eversley hasn't been here today," Lady Townsend said shortly.

"Yes, he was, Aunt," Richard insisted innocently. "I saw Heracles in the stables this morning."

Sarah could sense William's quick look at her and prayed that no rise in color betrayed her as she addressed her brother. "I daresay he just dropped in briefly with a message for Grandfather. Why do you not save the article to show him on his next visit?"

Though she had been careful to keep her gaze trained on the boy, she encountered Aunt Ridgemont's eye as she returned her attention to her plate. The contact was so brief that afterward Sarah could not be sure that she had really glimpsed a degree of malevolence she would never have credited in one habitually so divorced from the concerns of others. Her heart seemed to miss a beat before galloping on while a guilty presentiment ran through her mind that Mrs. Ridgemont knew about her and Mark. Despite William's superb performance, he had not managed to throw dust in his mother's eyes.

Compelled against her will, Sarah shot a covert glance at the woman calmly eating pudding, the mild blue eyes as vague as ever in her apple-cheeked countenance. Most likely a trick of light and shadow and her own guilty knowledge had caused her to see something that didn't exist, Sarah told herself, but she was more than happy to leave the table shortly thereafter for an hour or two of blessed privacy in her own quarters.

Despite a lingering concern for William's unhappiness, Sarah's solitary musings were eminently satisfying that afternoon. She thought—she hoped—that Lady Eversley was disposed to like her and would approve of her for a daughter-in-law. For her part, she had no doubts that her grandmother's friend would prove to be one of the benefits of the marriage. She was an incredibly fortunate individual. A few weeks ago life had seemed all challenge and struggle and uncertainty about the future. Suddenly the future was full of the promise of love and happiness. Richard would have his fair chance to make a good life for himself, her grandfather had the healing promise of the gratitude and companionship of his older son's children at the end of his life, and she would have Mark's love.

Thoughts of Mark and visions of a happy harmonious life together, hopefully blessed by children, filled Sarah's mind as she rested on the chaise longue in her room with an unopened book of poetry lying in her lap. She was only distracted from a particularly appealing image of herself holding a little boy with his father's deep-brown eyes and black hair when a stray glance at the clock brought her back to reality with a crash. She was already late for the daily ritual of tea in the drawing room, and she particularly desired to give no cause for criticism until this family gathering could be brought to a close.

Sarah tidied her hair and freshened her appearance in record time and headed off at a brisk pace to the drawing room. She forced herself to an artificial composure as she entered, a composure that was immediately shattered by the sound of Aunt

Adelaide's commanding voice directed at herself. This in itself was so unusual that Sarah blinked.

"I beg your pardon, Aunt?"

"I asked you where Arabella is."

"I'm afraid I do not know, Aunt Adelaide. Perhaps she is in the nursery playing cards with Richard. Once Richard gets involved in a game, he is extremely loath to let his victims escape," Sarah said with an indulgent smile meant to invite a like response.

Her invitation was not accepted. Lady Townsend fixed her niece with a basilisk stare and stated accusingly, "Arabella told me that you and she had made plans to walk to the village this afternoon to visit Grace Medlark's little girl."

14

Sarah's insulating bubble of happiness burst with a pop as she took in the sense of her aunt's words, and her mind began to function at double speed.

Drat Arabella!

Obviously the girl had sneaked off to meet Simon Rydell, whether by prearrangement or not did not concern Sarah for the moment. Her domineering aunt was expecting an explanation.

"I . . . I fear that after our late evening at Eversley I succumbed to the lure of my bed this afternoon, Aunt, and fell fast asleep. Not wishing to disturb me, Arabella would have gone by herself to visit Minnie so as not to disappoint her. The child is vastly taken with my cousin and no doubt begged her to remain. Arabella is wonderful with Richard too," she went on chattily. "She has a real affinity for the young."

If Sarah hoped to divert her aunt's thoughts with praises of her daughter, she had sadly misjudged her woman. Lady Townsend began to catechize her about previous visits to the Medlark house. Sarah, replying with seeming candor, came to the dismaying realization that Arabella had probably been using visits to Minnie as a cloak for assignations with the doctor since that first accidental meeting. Fortunately, before she had been pushed to the point of perjuring her soul, her cousin appeared in the doorway, somewhat breathless but sweetly apologetic.

Before Lady Townsend could open her lips, Sarah nipped in to say warningly, "I am so sorry you had to go alone to Grace's because I fell asleep this afternoon, Arabella. Had I been there,

I'd not have let Minnie make you late for your tea. That child has you wrapped around her little finger.''

"She has me wrapped around her heart, actually. She's really the most enchanting little creature with her big eyes and funny little lisp.'' Arabella had rallied fast and had even produced a creditable little laugh, but she had looked stricken for an instant to see the battery of eyes expectantly turned on her, and some of her rich coloring had drained away.

Vincent was studying his sister with a speculative expression that promised trouble in the near future. Though she gave no sign, Sarah was aware when his gaze shifted to herself, and she made a mental note to avoid her eldest cousin for a time.

Dressing for dinner in her own suite later, Sarah reflected with a significant lack of complacence that a crisis had been narrowly averted, though perhaps for the present only. Thanks to William's efforts, which she had striven to abet, the conversation at tea had been firmly focused on subjects unlikely to provoke any controversy. Lady Townsend had been uncharacteristically silent, not seeming to notice her daughter's attempts to wait upon her comfort. Mrs. Ridgemont had been more abstracted than ever, her attention concentrated on a heap of tatting in her lap. They may have brushed through today's situation without a confrontation between Arabella and her mother, but unless the temporary residents left Beech Hill immediately, Lady Townsend was going to learn of her daughter's involvement with Doctor Rydell. Sarah would have preferred to remain completely ignorant of the issue, but by using her as an alibi, Arabella had plunged her right into the middle, as it were. Though she did not relish the task, the idea of having a talk with her cousin was taking hold in her mind, though what advice she could hope to offer was beyond her at the moment.

As Maria slipped the cream silk over her head and began to do up the buttons, Sarah stood rather limply before her. Too much of a highly emotional nature had already occurred today. Any further scenes would wait upon the morrow.

Alas, for such cowardly shrinking from confrontation . . .

* * *

Insulated by his isolation from the undercurrents swirling within his house, Sir Hector chose that evening to announce that his lawyer would be arriving at Beech Hill the next day.

Sarah noted that Horace Ridgemont, seated on her right, tightened his fingers around the handle of his knife involuntarily, but he gave no sign that his father could have seen from the other end of the table that this news disturbed him. Lady Townsend, however, had never learned the wisdom of concealing her reactions to her father's baiting, nor did she on this occasion.

"Why should you want to summon a lawyer all the way from London?" she asked, glaring at him. "What do you intend to do?"

"I should have thought that would be obvious, my dear Adelaide," replied her parent with a purring quality to his bland tones that must have set his daughter's teeth on edge. "I am going to change my will, of course."

Having enjoyed the effect of this little bomb in the sudden cessation of conversation down the length of the table, Sir Hector returned his attention to his dinner, choosing that moment to articulate fulsome praises of the quality of the veal scallops in mushroom sauce. "Be sure to pass on my compliments to Mrs. Hadley, Sarah, my dear," he ordered at his most debonair as he smiled at her.

"Yes, Grandfather." Sarah's tones were wooden, but she choked back rising hysteria, convinced that invisible waves of antagonism were rolling across the table toward her from all her relatives, with the single exception of William. Not for a moment did she credit that her grandfather intended to make a new will in favor of herself or Richard, but true to the spirit of his name, he took a fiendish delight in setting his family at odds. It was all she could manage to remain decently upright for the rest of the meal and try not to dwell on the depressing notion that her very existence was deplored as an affront and an evil by those who should be closest to her by ties of blood. So much for her hopes of a quiet peaceful evening!

Sir Hector commanded Sarah's escort when he retired to his rooms directly after dinner, declaring his preference for brandy and solitude over port and endless contention. He had the satisfaction of seeing his son's lips set tightly at this gibe, but Horace made no reply except to wish his father a good rest. Sarah, silently waiting for the old man to rise and leave, could not suppress the ungenerous thought that her grandfather was secretly disappointed that his daughter, at a look from her brother, had not pressed him for details of the changes he intended to make in his will, thus depriving him of the pleasure of refusing to disclose his intentions. Demanding his grand-daughter's company rather than accepting the arm of his son or one of his grandsons on the trek to his rooms was just another maneuver in his endless campaign to discomfit his family.

Sympathy for her grandfather's frail state of health warred with a desire to protest the unenviable position his blatant championing always placed her in *vis-à-vis* the rest of the family, but as usual, she could not bring herself to complain to him about her treatment at the hands of the others, fearful that any retaliation on his part would only serve to exacerbate the situation and further alienate her. How was it going to end? she wondered, not for the first time. The situation was all the more deplorable because she truly felt that with a little goodwill on all sides the source of contention could be removed. Her relatives were not depraved and evil by nature, but greed was not an ennobling characteristic. They invariably showed them-selves at their worst when questions of inheritance came up.

By the time she left her grandfather in Somers' capable hands after a short discussion about preparing accommodations for Mr. Hammond, Sir Hector's attorney, Sarah's reluctance to join in the after-dinner farce of conviviality was heightened by her disturbing reflections. Any company was to be preferred to that of her current thoughts, however, so she forced herself to enter the drawing room with the appearance at least of composure.

The room was not very well populated at the moment. The only man present was Cecil, lounging in a chair talking to Arabella. Lady Townsend was also absent, Sarah noted, just as Arabella, catching her roving eye, explained blithely, "Mama has retired early with a headache."

Her cheerful manner bespoke a sad want of filial sympathy, but Sarah, giving her cousin the benefit of the doubt, decided it was more likely an expression of her relief at evading the possibility of being taken to task by her mother over her disappearance this afternoon.

Mrs. Ridgemont was seated in a corner of a long sofa, almost buried in a heap of tatting, which she must have fetched from her rooms after dinner. Sarah hesitated, then seated herself beside her aunt, who did not look up from her work. She appeared to be having difficulty getting it untangled, and Sarah asked, "May I help you with that, Aunt?"

"No, thank you, I can manage," Mrs. Ridgemont returned shortly, her eyes never leaving the untidy mass beneath her fingers.

Stung by the decided rebuff, Sarah edged farther away on the sofa just as William came into the room, followed a few seconds later by his father. He seemed to size up the situation at a glance because he joined Sarah with a smile, asking, "Do you play the pianoforte, Sarah?"

"Not really," she said, explaining with a rueful smile, "Mother tried to teach me, but every time we suffered a reverse in our fortunes, the pianoforte was the first thing to be sold. I have not touched an instrument in years, though I would dearly like to resume lessons sometime when . . . when . . ." She faltered..

He finished smoothly, "When your life settles into more of a routine? I hope you will. Shall we ask Bella to play for us, then?"

The next hour passed quite pleasantly with Arabella playing and then singing some very accomplished duets with her brother when Vincent wandered into the drawing room. It wasn't until Millbank appeared with the tea tray that she looked up and said, "Goodness, Sarah, it must be well past the hour when you usually go up to say good night to Richard. Here is the tea tray."

Sarah jumped up. "So it is. I was enjoying your music so much I lost track of the time. Will you excuse me, everyone?"

She hurried from the room, amazed that she could have forgotten what had settled into a nightly routine of dropping in to say good night to Richard after he had drunk the hot milk and honey Clara brought up to the nursery suite each evening.

Generally, on leaving the drawing room, Sarah went right up the west staircase and down the long corridor toward the nursery quarters above her apartment in the front of the house, but she had promised to bring Richard a book she had been reading, so tonight she detoured by her own rooms first, intending to use the back stairs in the hall outside her apartment.

She had her foot on the second step when a rustling sound drew her eyes upward in the dimly lighted hall as Clara appeared at the top carrying a tray. "You shouldn't have made a special trip for the tray, Clara. I would have brought it down to the kitchen as usual. I am quite late tonight, I know."

"That's all right, Miss Sarah. I didn't come—"

Clara's words were lost in a shriek of terror as she suddenly pitched down the stairs, the tray flying out of her hands to bounce and roll down the flight to the added sounds of clanking metal and breaking china. Sarah sprang forward, her book joining the other debris as she flung it down to free her hands as she instinctively dashed up the stairs to break Clara's fall. She was never quite sure where she found the strength to grab the hurtling girl and hang on to the railing without the impact sending them both down the rest of the flight. Her arm felt like it was being pulled from her body and she was jostled off one step, but she managed to right her balance on the one below without letting go of Clara. With one shoulder and the hand that had been gripping the rail, she gently eased the maid's inert figure back safely against the stairs, leaning her weight forward into this task to keep from overbalancing and going over backward herself now that she had no hold on the railing.

By the time Sarah, breathing heavily, had eased herself slightly away from Clara's slumped form, the stairwell was full of noisy humanity, or so it seemed to her in her dazed state. Actually, the crowd consisted only of Somers, puffing up from the floor below, and Richard and Lottie, dashing to the top of the staircase from the nursery suite. Though the din had seemed loud enough to wake the dead to one in the echoing stairwell at the time, the house was too well built and too large to transmit sounds from one section to another.

Trying to examine the now-weeping girl for injuries was no

simple chore. Sarah's gentle exhortations to Clara to tell her where she hurt met with no response except an intensification of her sobs. It took Lottie's stern command to stop "wailing like a banshee" to penetrate Clara's hysterics. Meanwhile, Sarah sent Somers to fetch Joseph and reassure her grandfather in the apartment below hers that the accident had not been serious, her reasoning being that Clara could not possibly produce so much noise if she were seriously injured.

It was nearly a half-hour later before order was finally restored. In that time, Clara's weeping was stemmed by the sheer force of Lottie's personality and she was found to have suffered no more than a wrenched ankle and a thorough shaking up. Joseph carried her up to the room she shared with Maria, where Mrs. Glamorgan skillfully bound the ankle after hot and cold cloths had been applied for a time. A restorative pot of tea containing a generous tot of brandy was produced by Sarah, who delivered it personally while the mess was being cleaned up by two of the maids. She wished to assure herself that Clara would drink it and settle down as comfortably as her throbbing ankle would permit. Other than repeating that something seemed to grab her leg, the girl could not explain the accident, but the emotional fury of her weeping had worn her out, and Sarah went back to the nursery suite convinced that the accident victim would sleep soundly.

Her intention was merely to reassure Lottie and Richard as to Clara's improved condition before seeing that her brother went to bed, but the gravity of their expressions as she entered the day nursery warned her that something else was amiss.

"Richard found this tied around one of the balusters at the top of the stairs," Lottie began without preliminary, holding out a coil of some material.

"What is it?" Sarah overcame a strong reluctance to accept whatever it was, and held out her hand.

"Thin picture wire, I should imagine. On the wall side of the staircase it was fastened to a tack that was pulled out of the wall, no doubt by the impact when Clara hit the wire. Richard found the tack too."

Sarah closed her eyes for an instant, wishing to scream a

denial. She had to clear her throat twice before she could produce any sound at all as she stared from one grave face to the other. "Are you saying that Clara's fall was not an accident, that someone tried to . . . to injure her?"

"Not exactly. Here, sit down." Alarmed by Sarah's loss of color, Lottie pushed her down onto a straight chair that Richard brought forward.

"What do you mean, not exactly?"

"Think, Sarah. That wire was obviously put there to hurt someone, but it is not Clara who usually comes down this staircase every night carrying a tray." As Sarah's hand crept up to her throat, fear looked out of the eyes that clung to Lottie's. She wanted to deny the truth staring her in the face, but the words would not come.

Instead, she murmured inanely, "Poor Clara."

"Fortunate Clara, you mean. If you had not been coming up the stairs at that precise moment, it is likely the girl would have broken her neck. The stairs and the landing are stone, and she would have fairly flown down them headfirst."

"Would not Clara have seen the wire when she came up to get the tray?"

"She did not come up for it. When she brought up the milk over an hour and a half ago, Richard inveigled her into playing a game of spillikins with him. She was up here with us the whole time. Since you were late, Clara decided to take the tray down when they finished. That wire was put there during the time Clara was in the nursery."

"By whom?"

Sarah was shaking now, and Lottie urged, "Come and have some hot tea, love. I had Maria bring it to Richard's room after the mess was cleaned up."

Sarah allowed herself to be led through to her brother's bedchamber, where a small table had been set near the fireplace. Obediently, she sat where indicated and drank the strong tea Lottie prepared for her.

"What are we going to do, Sarah?"

Sarah started. Richard had not spoken a word up to now; in fact, he had been so quiet she had forgotten his presence in the horror of the discovery that had just been reported to her. Her eyes flew from his set features and anxious eyes to Lottie's in mute protest, but Lottie merely shrugged.

"I could not very well keep it from him when he found the wire. Richard was as quick as I to make the correct deduction."

"What are we going to do, Sarah?" the boy asked again.

"Nothing," she replied decisively. Seeing the stubborn protest in his face, she went on before he could speak. "Whom do we accuse, a servant? One of the family? Which one?" As his expression became more troubled and uncertain, she continued, "You see? There is nothing to tell us who did this horrible thing. We must simply trust that when the perpetrator hears how the plan misfired and injured someone, it will shock him—or her—into a realization of the enormity of this misdeed."

"But we must tell Grandfather at least. He will send them all away, and then you will be safe," cried the boy, clearly demonstrating where his thoughts were directed.

"No, Richard, that is the last thing we must do. Grandfather is a very frail old man and it would upset him greatly to have to think a member of his family capable of such a deed. The doctor warned that we must at all cost ensure that nothing is permitted to upset him."

"He'd be more upset if you were killed!"

"I am persuaded nothing of this nature will happen again. Promise me, Richard, that you will not speak of this to Grandfather—or to anyone else in the house either." As he hesitated, she took his hand in a comforting clasp and compelled his eyes with hers. "Promise me, my dear."

"All right, Sarah. I won't speak of it to anyone in the house. But everyone will know anyway. The servants are bound to talk about Clara's fall," he added as she looked at him doubtfully.

"Yes, but Clara does not have any idea how the accident happened, and no one has seen the wire except we three."

"And the person who put it there," Lottie said grimly, having the last word.

It was the last word only because Sarah refused to discuss the matter further. She saw Richard into bed, advised Lottie to do the same, and went directly to her own suite. She could not face those people in the drawing room again tonight.

For the first time in her life Sarah locked every door that led into her bedchamber, four in all. She did not even attempt to get into her bed until she had conquered a recurring tendency to shake like a blancmange every few minutes. Instead, she huddled into a boudoir chair by the fireplace. There was no possibility of sleep in any case because her mind insisted on behaving like a mechanical toy: it would no sooner run down than a new worry would act like a key that wound it up again.

She had meant every word she said to Richard about her grandfather. The shock of learning that a member of his family was capable of cold-blooded murder—she shivered as her mind stumbled over the phrase—might well bring on a fatal heart attack. So might the news of her own death at the hands of one of her relatives, she acknowledged with another bout of shivering, but she was not going to let that happen.

Luck had been with her tonight, and with Clara. It was a spine-chilling thought that it might favor a murderer the next time. She huddled deeper into the chair, admitting and confronting her fears on that head. She had not convinced Richard there would be no more attempts, not surprising when she could not convince herself.

She must take precautions. The locked doors would protect her tonight, but what about tomorrow? And the day after? Taking a deep calming breath, Sarah decided that she could not afford to look beyond tomorrow for the sake of her sanity. What precautions could she take tomorrow? She forced her numbed brain into a rational mode and tried to consider coolly. Of a certainty she would watch where she planted her feet at all times. She could also see to it that she was never alone with any member of the family. That much she could do.

But could she? Unbidden, a picture of Mark hauling her into the chapel this morning came into her mind. He had admitted gleefully that he and Joseph had conspired together to get her to the spot of the ambush. The results had been delightful this morning, but another conspiracy, even an unknowing one on the part of a servant, could prove lethal.

Tomorrow would be the critical day. Mr. Hammond arrived

tomorrow. His business with her grandfather should not take very long. Presumably, Sir Hector had sent for his lawyer only after settling in his own mind the way he wished to leave his fortune. She shivered again. It could not be a coincidence that the attempt on her life had occurred within an hour or two of her grandfather's announcement that his attorney was coming for the purpose of writing a new will. If the perpetrator of that fiendish act was convinced that Sarah would be the principal heir, then he or she would try again tomorrow. Sarah faced this squarely and decided her best defense was to stay close to Richard and Lottie all day.

She was growing very cold. She chafed her arms below their brief sleeves and got stiffly out of the sheltering chair to prepare for bed. As she crawled beneath the covers a few minutes later, she wondered if the guilty party would reveal his or her identity in some fashion tomorrow when confronted with an intended victim in perfect condition. On the heels of this optimistic thought came a realization that it was a forlorn hope. Of course the assailant already knew his intended victim had survived the "accident." Her death or injury would have raised a hue and cry throughout the house. There would be no giveaway starts of surprise or facial tics on her appearance before her family tomorrow, when tomorrow finally came. She only hoped her enemy was spending as miserable a sleepless night as she was.

As she persued this avenue of thought, it occurred to Sarah that though her enemy knew the wire had not succeeded, he would not know whether it had been discovered. If it had, the crucial advantage of an unsuspecting victim would be lost in future attempts.

A sudden conviction jolted through her like a bolt of lightning and jerked her upright in the bed. The person who had strung that deadly wire across the stairs would go back sometime during the night to retrieve the evidence of the attempted crime if possible. If no one had discovered the wire, Clara's "accident" would remain just that. If it had been removed—(as it had)— the perpetrator would know that greater caution would be required on any further attempts. She had pushed aside the bedcovers and extended one foot over the edge of the mattress when she began to shake with fright. She sat poised on the edge, struggling to gain command of her fears for what seemed like an eternity before a small whimper escaped her lips and she fell back onto the pillows.

It was no use. She was trembling and sweating at the mere idea of going back to those stairs tonight. Even if there were a place of concealment from which she could watch the top of the stairs unobserved, she would not be able to muster the requisite degree of courage to do this thing. If she'd only been using her wits earlier when Richard and Lottie showed her the wire, she might have sent a message to William. He'd have been willing to set a trap for the attacker. It was too late now. In fact, it could be literally too late to catch the person returning. Sarah groped for the tinder box on the bedside table and managed to light her candle after several tries. Almost one-thirty in the morning. The household had been asleep for hours. It was far too late to think of setting traps. The person would have acted hours ago.

Sarah blew out her candle again and resumed staring into the darkness. The plan would not have worked anyway for the simple reason that she could not afford to trust any member of her family, not even William, who, until he had revealed his deeper feelings for her today, had slipped so comfortably into the role of the older brother she had never possessed. A picture of the drawing room as she had entered it tonight after seeing her grandfather to his rooms flashed across her memory. Only Arabella, Cecil, and Aunt Ridgemont had been present when she had arrived. Any of the others might have strung that wire across the stairs before joining the party in the drawing room. It was only the matter of a few minutes to set it in place. Aunt Adelaide had never returned at all, and the others had wandered in separately. In fact, she groaned, now that she really thought back, she had no way of knowing how long those already in the drawing room had been there when she arrived. Aunt Ridgemont had stopped by her rooms to get her tatting, unless she had sent a servant for it, and for all she knew to the contrary, Arabella and Cecil might have arrived just seconds before she did.

Which one? Who hated her enough to deprive her of life? The enormity of the action, of the decision to take another's life somehow seemed beyond the scope of ordinary human behavior. Which of her relatives, her ordinary-seeming relatives, was capable of conduct outside the parameters of normal behavior? Or was it strictly a case of material gain and no personal animosity at all? The fact that the attempt had been made on the heels of her grandfather's declaration of his intent to change his will would seem to indicate this motive. In which case, it was not at all necessary for her enemy to bear her any personal dislike to decide to remove her from his path. Which of her seemingly normal relatives was beyond the reach of universal moral precepts? Sarah devoted uncounted sleepless hours to the problem but was no closer to an answer when she drifted into an uneasy slumber shortly before dawn.

15

In a contradictory fashion, the very air of normalcy prevailing the next morning contributed to Sarah's sense of moving through a dream—or, in the present situation, a nightmare.

Maria appeared with morning chocolate at the usual hour, which had never seemed more ungodly. Sarah looked upon the smiling girl with a jaundiced eye, having struggled up from the depths of oblivion in order to run and unlock the door to the hall after heaven knew how much racket Maria had created with her persistent knocking. She returned a reluctant grunt to the maid's cheery greeting before practically diving back into bed.

Maria was instantly all sympathy. "Don't you feel well this morning, Miss Sarah? Why was the door locked?" After putting the tray on a side table, she bustled over to open the draperies without waiting for an answer.

Sarah made use of the delay to rub the sleep out of her eyes and try to reassemble what wits remained to her after the most wretched night of her life. By the time Maria turned back to her she was ready with two lies, one of which turned out to be only too true, unfortunately. "I have a headache, and all the doors are locked because I intended to sleep late this morning."

"I am so sorry for disturbing you, Miss Sarah." The crest-fallen girl approached the bed with a cup of steaming chocolate.

The sight of her sweet little face added remorse to Sarah's other problems. "It was not your fault, Maria," she said hastily. "I neglected to leave a message that I did not wish to be disturbed this morning. That smells good."

Her false brightness as she accepted the unwanted chocolate had the desired effect of bringing a smile back to Maria's face. Sarah forced herself to take a sip and smile approval, thus freeing the maid to set about gathering up the discarded clothing lying in a heap on the floor, a task she was rarely called upon to perform for her generally neat mistress.

"How is Clara this morning?" Sarah remembered to ask.

Maria's lengthy report on her friend's spirits—high—and her ankle—sore and swollen—took them through the chocolate phase, by which time Sarah was feeling nearly human again.

She took special pains with her appearance in a vain attempt to disguise the purple shadows under her eyes, a legacy of a largely sleepless night. She paid extra attention to her hair, deepening the soft waves at the temples to draw attention away from her pinched features. It seemed the right moment for the debut of her new morning gown also, fashioned from the shiny cotton fabric in the rosy-tan shade of the breast of a mourning dove that she and Lottie had bought in Marshfield.

Sarah pinned a smile on her face as she knocked on her grandfather's door. Was it only yesterday afternoon when her task had been to disguise her happiness at accepting Mark's proposal of marriage? Events at Beech Hill moved with a speed that set her head spinning, but she had best guard against that. She was going to need all her wits about her to get through this day.

Sarah exchanged amenities with Somers, who eyed her closely but made no comment on her ruined looks. No consideration of tact or delicacy had ever been known to set curbs on Sir Hector's tongue, however. He watched his granddaughter's approach through narrowed, still-keen eyes.

"What ails you this morning, Sarah? I've seen troopers who looked better after a night of roistering about town."

Sarah smiled palely and responded in the same spirit. "I promise you I touched nothing beyond a half-glass of wine at dinner. I have a bit of a headache this morning, that's all." She dropped a kiss on her grandfather's cheek and glanced at the empty tray in front of him. "You've made a good breakfast," she said with approval.

Sir Hector brushed aside the obvious attempt at diversion with an impatient twitch of his head. "I hope you have not been so idiotish as to let this business of my will upset you." His voice was gruff, but there was a faintly anxious look in his searching eyes, and Sarah realized this was as close to an apology as her grandfather would ever come. Fortunately, since she could think of nothing to say, Sir Hector gave her no chance to reply as he went on, "I also hope you have not been cherishing any grandiose notions of becoming a great heiress, because you'll be sadly disappointed if you have."

This time she actually laughed at his bellicose expression and was rewarded by a relaxation of the ferocity. "I never thought you were such a wet goose, but that misguided daughter of mine has been indulging in monumental sulks and high fidgets ever since she learned of your existence. Just because I'm tied to these rooms doesn't mean I do not know what's afoot in my own house, never think it. If she chose to believe me a romantic old dodderer in my dotage, to be swayed by a pair of amber eyes and a pretty face, even if the face is your grandmother's, then the more fool she. I did not see why I should hasten to disabuse her of her cherished fantasies—or the others either. Let them think what they will."

Oh, Grandfather, Sarah thought with mounting distress as she listened to this rambling rationale, if you only knew what you've done! She was brought out of her unhappy musings by the sudden cessation of his voice and an expectant expression on his aquiline features.

"I . . . I am sure you have been most equitable, Grandfather," she murmured.

"That's more than the rest of them will think. They're a greedy lot, my loving family."

Sarah felt incapable of addressing the bitterness in his voice, so she remained silent, and after a brief hiatus Sir Hector resumed in a businesslike manner.

"This place will go to William eventually. He's the only one of 'em who cares a ha'penny for it. It takes a mint of money to maintain it, and it will take a lot more to bring it into the nineteenth century, but that won't be my problem, thank God. It will do for me as it is."

"What about Uncle Horace?"

"Oh, Horace will have tenancy and the use of the income for the immediate future. He is my son, after all, whether or not he's the son I'd have chosen. If he wishes to live here, well and good; if not, he'll have the wherewithal to stay in London and keep in with the political set, which is what he's always yearned to do. He doesn't have a feel for the land like William does. Well, for that matter, neither did I. The army was always my first love. But William's children will grow up here, whatever arrangements Horace chooses to make."

"I'm glad, Grandfather," Sarah said softly. "It was William who really introduced me to Beech Hill, though Grace showed me around when she thought I was the new housekeeper."

"And I let you take a crack at being the housekeeper," Sir Hector chortled with his devilish grin. "You were none the worse for the experience either."

"Not at all," she agreed with an impish smile of her own. "I enjoyed it."

"The decision to leave the estate to William won't be popular in all quarters," admitted Sir Hector, "though why Adelaide thinks I should ever feel responsible for Vincent when he stood to succeed his father, has always passed my understanding. The only thing I'm giving Vincent is that black stallion of mine he's been after since I stopped riding. He wants to breed him, and I'll say this for Vincent: he may be the complete town beau without two ideas to rub together, but he does know horseflesh."

"My aunt will be disappointed, I fear," Sarah put in hesitantly.

"Adelaide would be disappointed if she and her children received less than one hundred percent of the estate. That's simply the way she's made. She's already got her mother's jewelry, which is worth a small fortune. To keep the peace, I've arranged for her to have a modest annual income, though Townsend left her very well fixed. It will go to Arabella eventually. I've provided a healthy dowry for both of you girls, and you needn't look for more afterward. I see no reason to further enrich Eversley at the expense of my grandsons."

Sarah turned bright pink as she stared into mocking dark eyes.

"I told you not to expect me to be blind and deaf just because I'm stuck within these four walls," her grandfather reminded her with gleeful satisfaction.

"Do you approve, Grandfather?"

"You could go farther and do worse," he said, patting her hand in the most demonstrative gesture of affection he ever permitted himself. "Eversley comes from good stock and he's sound to the core. His father was a good friend of mine, and I'm not sure but what Mark isn't a better one. He had a bad experience with his marriage, but it hasn't soured him. I wasn't sure about that until the second time I saw him with you. That's when I knew he'd recovered his faith in women. I'm pleased with your choice, Sarah. I just wish I could have kept you here longer, that's all."

"There's no mad rush, Grandfather."

"If there isn't, then he's not the man I took him for."

Sarah giggled at the indignation on her behalf expressed in her grandfather's tones, and received a slight tap on her cheek in rebuke.

"Little liar. There's no need for a long engagement. If I cannot keep you in this house, then I'll settle for having you both three miles away."

"I play chess too, Grandfather," she said demurely.

A speculative gleam came into his eyes. "Ah, methinks I scent a challenge. I'll remind you of that when this lot clears out." He cleared his throat and said, "Now, where was I when the room became permeated with orange blossom? Ah, yes, the dowries. I'll fix it so you have an income of your own, but I am tying Arabella's up in her children. They'll need protection if she exercises the same amount of intellect in choosing a husband as she does in her conversation. Of course, if her mother has her way, the child will be bartered for a title and bags of gold, with no say in the matter at all."

"I would not worry too much about Arabella, Grandfather. I do not believe she subscribes to her mother's requirements for choosing a husband, and I should think she intends to have a say in the matter."

"You say this with authority, but I am seeking no information," Sir Hector remarked, holding up his index finger and wagging it from side to side. "She's her mother's problem, not mine, I am happy to say. I thought one of her cousins might do, perhaps, but Cecil is still too young and William will not be in a great hurry to fix his interest again, I warrant."

Sarah's eyes fell, her expression concealed by thick crescents of dark lashes. She did not speak, nor, in a rare instance of tact, did the general pursue the subject.

"You may have noticed that I have not yet mentioned the boy," he invited.

"Or Cecil."

"We'll come to him in due course. About Richard . . . Did you speak the truth when you said you came here to ensure his education, no more?"

"Yes, Grandfather." Sarah's eyes remained steady on his. "Richard is a wonderfully alert, capable, and energetic person even at this tender age. I have every confidence that he will make a successful life for himself."

"I happen to agree with you. That boy is destined for a military career."

Alarmed, Sarah's mouth dropped open, but she was given no opportunity to protest.

"Now, you keep quiet and hear me out, girl. This is none of my doing, I promise you. I hope I have learned my lesson on that score. As it happens, the inclination skipped a generation. I knew in less than a sennight that the lad was a natural for the military. He knows more about military history than I did at his age, and I had a father in the army."

"Richard has never given any indication that he would like a military career," Sarah said, still doubtful.

"He might not know it yet, or it may be he feared the money would not be there to buy him a pair of colors. It is now, but it can wait upon his schooling. I won't push him toward it. I've already set the wheels in motion to get him entered at Harrow."

"Thank you, Grandfather. I could not have hoped for more."

"Oh, there is more. I'll settle a sum on him as I will for Cecil, who has been sounding me out about buying him a commission this visit. The war in the Peninsula may be all but over, but the Americans want reminding of their place. He'll see some action over there unless I miss my guess. They won't get the principal until they are thirty, but they'll have the income to supplement their army pay.''

''You've been very generous, Grandfather, and thoughtful too of what is best for each person.''

Sarah carried a picture of her grandfather's gratified face with her as she went on to breakfast. He might insist that he cared nothing for the opinions of his family, but he had certainly given much thought to the welfare of each individual member when deciding how to leave his fortune. She felt light-headed with relief that now it could never be claimed that she or Richard had cast a spell over an old man whose conscience tormented him over his treatment of his elder son.

The worried faces Richard and Lottie turned to her as she entered the dining saloon brought her back to reality in a rush. At present she was the only person who knew the provisions of the new will, so the danger that had threatened her life yesterday remained, and she would do well to remember this.

''I am so sorry to be late,'' she said with quick repentance to Richard and Lottie. ''I stopped in to say good morning to Grandfather.''

What conversation there was at table that morning was a stilted affair. The men were all present, but even William seemed disinclined for light chatter.

Lottie, having obviously come to the same conclusions as Sarah concerning her safety, said meaningfully, ''I trust you still plan to help me finish your new dress today, Sarah?''

Sarah hastened to reassure her old nurse on this point, but in the end she did not immediately accompany Lottie to the nursery for a day of sewing. To everyone's surprise, Arabella drifted in toward the end of the meal. She greeted everyone with a dazzling smile and chatted away brightly—a bit too brightly, Sarah decided as she studied her cousin, looking pretty as a picture this morning in red-sprigged white muslin dress. The chatter was designed to hide the fact that she was making a poor pretense at eating, though she consumed two cups of coffee and crumbled a muffin on her plate when anyone glanced her way.

As the men went about their various affairs and Lottie was preparing to leave, Arabella asked Sarah in an undertone if she could spare her a few minutes before she busied herself about the house. Aware that Lottie had stiffened, Sarah sent her a reassuring smile before agreeing to her cousin's request.

"Shall we go into the library?" Arabella suggested.

"Let's make it the chapel instead," Sarah countered. She considered herself more than a match for her delicate cousin, but it would ease Lottie's mind to hear that she had foiled any unlikely conspiracy involving attackers stationed in the library by simply changing the place of the meeting that was obviously the whole reason for Arabella's rare presence at the breakfast table. Arabella nodded agreement, watching with barely contained impatience while Sarah finished her coffee as Lottie, satisfied that no immediate danger threatened, left the saloon with her own version of a meaningful look directed at Sarah.

Studying her silent cousin nibbling nervously at her lower lip as they crossed to the chapel, Sarah knew past doubting that Arabella cherished no lethal animosity toward her. The poor child was concerned exclusively with her own complicated romance. She smiled encouragingly at the girl as they sat in two of the straight chairs placed in the chapel.

"I . . . I wish to thank you, Sarah, for covering up for me with Mama," Arabella began with a rush. "I suppose you guessed that I went to the village to meet Simon Rydell?"

"Yes," Sarah said simply, her sympathetic eyes on her cousin's half-defiant, half-fearful countenance.

"And I suppose, like Vincent, you believe I am conducting some mad flirtation to relieve the boredom of a stay at Beech Hill?"

"No, I certainly do not believe you are flirting with Doctor Rydell. Did your brother challenge you with this?"

Arabella nodded unhappily and fell into a brown study. After a lengthy pause, Sarah probed, "If you are not engaged in a flirtation, what are you doing with Doctor Rydell?"

"I . . . I am in love with him, and he loves me!" There was a challenging tilt to Arabella's dimpled chin.

Sarah merely nodded. "What do you plan to do about it?"

"We wish to marry, of course!"

Sarah nodded again, accepting both the sincerity and the bravado in the bald statement. "Have you given any thought to what your life with Doctor Rydell would be, Arabella? Very different, I think, from the life you have been leading."

"I am sick to death of the life I've been leading. It was fun at first to make my bow to the queen and go to parties and flirt and become one of the successes of my Season, but I have had two Seasons already, and I have grown to hate the everlasting round of social events, seeing the same people at each one, and each one exactly like the one before it."

"And yet I believe I have heard you describe your existence at Beech Hill as tedious and boring also."

Arabella flushed. "I know, but that was before I met Simon."

"You do not believe there would come a time when you might find life with Doctor Rydell boring also?"

"No! And so I told Vincent when he tried to paint a depressing picture of my life as the wife of a country physician. When you love someone, you become interested in their concerns, and Simon has the sole responsibility for the health of everyone in this district. It's a dedicated life and I wish to help him, and I know I can help him. You said yourself that I was very good with Minnie."

"But not all the doctor's patients are as attractive as a charming little child," Sarah felt obliged to point out.

"No, of course not, and I am not so simple as to think squalor and wretchedness are anything but deplorable, but Simon does things to help people. Oftentimes it is depressing work because he cannot always help, but he feels the rewards are great. And I know I can make his home comfortable and happy for him."

"Do you think of him as a noble character?"

Arabella's chin went up again, but she answered forthrightly, "Yes, I do, though Simon would scoff at such a high-flown description. At the very least he is dedicated to the best interests of the people of this district, and I honor him for it and I wish to be by his side."

"You do not think you will regret the parties and social activities that make up your life at present?"

"No, and anyway, it is not as if this were a desert or some uncivilized locale. I know all the local families, and Simon also is welcome everywhere. There will be ample social life, Sarah. He is not penniless, you know. He has a modest income apart from his practice, and a comfortable house in the district."

"Well, you seem to have matters settled nicely in your mind. Am I to wish you happy?"

For the first time, Arabella's eyes shifted and her assurance slipped away from her as her soft mouth twisted unhappily. "I think you know my mother will be adamantly opposed to our marriage. Vincent too suspects Simon might be a fortune-hunter, and he has gone to confront him this morning. I don't mind that. Simon will acquit himself well, and it matters only a very little if Vincent refuses to believe in him. Vincent is a very worldly person. How can he be expected to have anything in common with Simon?"

How, indeed? Sarah's respect for her seemingly feather-brained cousin's inherent shrewdness and understanding of all the ramifications of her romance was growing by leaps and bounds, but she probed a little further. "Do you believe you will in time be able to obtain your mother's consent to the marriage, Arabella?"

"If you really knew my mother, you would not ask that question. I doubt she could reconcile herself to the fact that her daughter married a mere physician even if Simon were to become the king's medical adviser. We shall have to wait until I am of age, of course, which is in six months. Will you stand my friend, Sarah, though I have no right to ask it of you after the way I treated you in the beginning?"

"Yes, of course. But surely you are aware that my opinion carries no weight at all with your mother?"

Arabella smiled a little mistily at her cousin. "No, but it carries weight with Grandfather, and I should not wish him to think poorly of me, though I know he already thinks me a flib-bertigibbet with more hair than wit. I was used to think it rather fun to tease him, but I shall be well-served now if he disapproves and decides to rescind the dowry he promised me. I have a little money from my father, but I have more of a practical nature than Simon, and I would like to ensure my children's future education at least.''

Sarah studied her "practical" cousin and was hard-pressed to contain her amusement, though she conceded her point. Arabella had indeed thought the matter through and was exhibiting a ruthless single-mindedness of purpose that did credit to her mother's training, though Lady Townsend would never be brought to see the virtue of it.

''As soon as Simon applies to Mama for my hand, she will begin packing and whisk me away from here, Sarah. I would take it as a great favor if you will write to me and give me news and, if your conscience will permit, messages from Simon. Mama will see to it that we have no direct communication for the next six months. I shall be paraded before every eligible *parti* in the kingdom.''

Arabella sighed and Sarah continued to marvel at just how far off the mark had been her first impression of her cousin. She had no qualms about promising what the younger girl asked of her because she was persuaded Arabella did indeed know her own mind and heart. Moreover, she agreed with her cousin's decision and wished her well.

It would be pleasant to have Arabella residing in the district where she would be living, Sarah exulted as she set off to check with Mrs. Glamorgan on the accommodations being readied for Mr. Hammond.

On the way back from this errand she happened to pass through the great hall at a moment when Richard and Joseph were standing together engaged in serious conversation. The fact of their engagement was not surprising—Richard had become great friends with the likable footman—but Sarah was a trifle surprised to note that neither had apprehended her presence, so absorbing was their talk. She did not bother to speak to either, feeling she would disturb their concentration, but headed up to the nursery, where Lottie proceeded to scold her severely for wandering about the house unattended when she well knew a hidden danger lurked. Aware that Lottie's snappishness was a measure of her anxiety, Sarah bore the strictures meekly and settled down to a session of determined stitching.

16

M r. Hammond arrived before lunchtime and had already left Beech Hill before Sarah wandered into the drawing room for tea. Evidently the landlord at the inn in Marshfield where he had spent the previous night had just received some fine Scottish salmon, and enticed by promises of a feast, Mr. Hammond had made arrangements to dine and stay there before proceeding back to London the next day.

All this was explained by her grandfather when she checked on him before heading for the drawing room. To her consternation, Sir Hector decided to accompany her. Though initially concerned that he should attempt to climb the stairs, Sarah found that he did very well with some support from Joseph's strong right arm as she hovered anxiously in the rear.

Admittedly, her anxiety was not all on her grandfather's account. Richard had not put in an appearance in the nursery since lunchtime. This, coming on top of his absorption in his own thoughts during the meal, had caused Sarah to arrive at the logical conclusion that he was up to something. She took advantage of the flurry of activity to make her grandfather comfortable in the drawing room to ask if anyone knew her young brother's whereabouts that afternoon, but no one admitted seeing him since lunch. Nor had he told anyone of his plans. Everyone else was present when she and Sir Hector arrived, with the single exception of Arabella, who slipped in a moment later while the others' attention was on the fuss being made over her grandfather. Arabella shook her head when Sarah inquired if she had seen Richard that afternoon.

As soon as Millbank left the room, an expectant hush descended on the gathering, as though they were members of a church congregation waiting for the service to begin. As Sir Hector proceeded without roundaboutation to outline the provisions he had made for his family, he had the rapt attention of all in the room save one. Sarah was growing more anxious about Richard by the moment, her normal concern at the length of his unexplained absence augmented by the horrors of last night's attack. Having already been told of her grandfather's intentions, what attention she spared from her worry about Richard was directed at the avidly listening members of her father's family. She witnessed Aunt Adelaide's frustration and William's astonished delight when her grandfather explained his rationale for disposing of the house in the unorthodox manner he had chosen. When her cousin's eyes sought hers involuntarily, she was ready with an unclouded smile for his good fortune. She knew by the slight dimming of his eagerness as he turned away that he understood that it did not change her decision not to marry him. There was a strange glitter in his mother's usually mild gaze as she listened and watched her son, but she did not seem as transported by triumph as Sarah might have expected. Perhaps Mrs. Ridgemont felt the slight to her husband, though Horace admirably concealed any disappointment he might have felt at not inheriting Beech Hill outright.

Sir Hector did not pause for comment but proceeded to list all his arrangements in a dry uninflected voice, not even pausing when Cecil let out a whoop at the offer to buy him a commission in the army. When he came at last to the end of his recital, it was Vincent who spoke first.

"Do you mean I am to have the Hellion immediately, Grandfather?" His dark Ridgemont eyes shone with anticipation.

"You may take him away with you when you go. He's been getting fat and lazy since I gave up riding, but the breeding's there. You may just get yourself a champion from him."

"I know just the mare to breed him to, the loveliest little bay with beautiful conformation." In his enthusiasm, Vincent turned to William, seated beside him on the sofa, and gave his shoulder a resounding smack. "Well, you dull old dog, I wish you joy of this great ark. I may have just acquired a Derby winner.''

"How dare you insult William and strike him like that, you ill-bred, jealous oaf! Were you not content with making his childhood miserable with your rough, bullying ways?''

Every eye in the room was fixed on the taut figure of Mrs. Ridgemont, her round face contorted with rage, her posture proclaiming an intention to spring upon her stunned nephew with outstretched claws.

"Madeleine, control yourself!''

"Mama, please, my dear! Vincent meant nothing by his remark; it was said in jest.'' William's voice carried over his father's sharp command.

"Yes, Aunt, pray forgive my boorish attempt at a joke. I freely confess that I bullied William unmercifully during our youth, but you will be glad to know that all ended when he turned sixteen and developed a punishing right hand that kept me in my place from then on.''

Hearing the remorse in his voice and seeing the concern on his face as he made his aunt this handsome apology, Sarah liked Vincent better than she ever had before, happy to detect a spark of humanity in his makeup at last.

"There, you see, Mama?'' William's tones were coaxing and gentle.

"Yes, yes, I am sorry too, only I have such a frightful headache. If you will excuse me, I shall go to my room.'' Mrs. Ridgemont was pale and shaking as she got awkwardly to her feet.

"Shall I come with you, Aunt? I can get you a powder for your headache,'' Sarah said.

"No, not you!'' Mrs. Ridgemont put up a shaking hand to her forehead and attempted to control the note of hysteria in her voice. "William will come with me, and my maid will mix me a powder. Thank you just the same.'' The last words were nearly inaudible as she leaned on her son's arm and allowed him to lead her from the room, past the two figures who had entered in time to witness the embarrassing scene just ended.

"Richard, where have you been all afternoon?" Sarah cried, perceiving the newcomers for the first time.

Her voice seemed to release everyone from the trancelike state induced by the recent unpleasantness. A collected breath was expelled and murmurs of conversation broke out.

Lord Eversley, who accompanied Richard into the room after holding the door open for the departing mother and son, said easily, "Richard rode over to Eversley this afternoon and brought me back for tea. I trust I have not come at an inconvenient time?"

Inconvenient! Sarah swallowed back a hysterical giggle at the thought as her grandfather said cordially, "Not at all, my boy, come in. Sarah will give you a cup of tea, unless you'd prefer sherry?"

"Tea will be fine, sir." Mark's eyes followed Sarah as she prepared the tea Aunt Townsend poured out. He accepted the cup in one hand and took her elbow with the other to steer her to a settee at a little distance from the main grouping.

Sarah felt they must be the center of all eyes, but her grandfather began to question Richard about his afternoon's adventure, and some of the others started spontaneous conversations at that point. "Why did Richard ride to Eversley today?" she asked, though she was afraid she knew the answer before she finished uttering the question.

"He came to tell me what happened here last night. Thank goodness he has more sense than you seem to possess, Sarah. You must not remain in this house tonight. I have come to take you to Eversley with me. My mother will be happy to welcome you until this group leaves Beech Hill."

"Thank Lady Eversley most sincerely for me, Mark, but it won't be necessary for me to run away."

"I beg your pardon, but it is most necessary. I refuse to let you remain exposed to mortal danger." His expression was harsh with determination and anxiety.

Sarah hastened to reassure him. "No, you do not understand, Mark. Grandfather has just told everyone of the changes he made in his will. I'm to have a dowry, and he plans to settle a sum on Richard too, but no more than Arabella and Cecil will receive. If there was some fear that he would make either of us his principal heir, that is now removed. There is no longer any reason to try to . . . to—''

"To kill you? There was never a reason, not for a sane mind. Do you call stringing that wire across the stairs the action of a sane mind?''

"Perhaps not, but the danger is past, my dear. Please, don't look like that.''

They had been conducting their argument in low urgent tones, oblivious to everyone else in the room, but now Sir Hector called over to the engrossed pair, ''Did you hear that, Sarah? Horace had just told me he has made plans to remove from here tomorrow.''

Somehow Sarah managed to say what was proper to the occasion, though the greater portion of her intelligence was concerned with devising a convincing argument to ease Mark's anxiety.

At that point William came back into the room and headed directly over to Sarah and Lord Eversley, his expression strained as he dropped into a chair set at right angles to the settee. ''Sarah, I am the bearer of an apology from my mother for being short with you just now. She was not herself, but her maid has put her to bed and she will be better in a few hours. Sometimes she gets the most terrible headaches . . .'' His voice trailed off.

"That's all right, William,'' Sarah said. "I know what torment it is to suffer from the migraine. There is nothing for it except to go to bed and stay there until the pain goes away.''

There was no opportunity for the betrothed pair to resume their interrupted discussion during the remainder of Mark's call as William stayed planted in his chair while Mark sat in a simmering silence he broke only when directly applied to for comment. For once, William's flair for knowing when his presence was not appreciated did not seem to be operating, and Sarah, deliberately obtuse, refused to recognize the significant looks directed at her by her impatient fiancé. In the end, Sarah received a rather abrupt farewell from Mark, who then proceeded to isolate Richard in a corner for a lengthy private talk before he actually departed, leaving Sarah a prey to all the insecurities that can beset a newly betrothed girl.

She dressed for dinner that night with less than her usual attention, too depleted to sit patiently while Maria fussed over her hair. Her reaction was a bit odd, she told herself, considering that everything had worked out so wonderfully well. Only Aunt Adelaide had been disgruntled at learning the provisions of her father's will. Vincent, it seemed, had never expected anything; he had come at his mother's behest to present a picture of family solidarity. She pushed aside a stray thought of the effect Arabella's marriage plans would have on this pretty picture. Sufficient unto today were today's problems. The Ridgemonts would depart tomorrow if Aunt Ridgemont were up to traveling, and perhaps the Townsends would follow suit. Certainly they would if Simon Rydell made Lady Townsend a formal offer for Arabella's hand.

Thinking this could well be the last evening of enforced intimacy with her enlarged family, Sarah pinched her cheeks to encourage some color and went off to the drawing room wearing a determined smile.

Actually it turned out to be a pleasant evening. Now that her grandfather's arrangements were out in the open, there was a noticeable reduction in tension in the atmosphere. Mrs. Ridgemont did not put in an appearance that evening, nor did Sir Hector, whose big scene had left him too fatigued to wish to put forth the effort required to preside at his table. The others conversed easily on all manner of topics, with the upcoming London Season dominating Lady Townsend's conversation. In the course of the evening she even managed to address a few civil remarks to her niece, from which Sarah gathered that past hostilities were to be forgotten in future. She was grateful, though her father's sister would never be listed among her favorite persons.

Arabella was a bit subdued, no doubt anticipating the imminent parting with her doctor, but there was an attractive air of serenity about her that Sarah considered a tremendous improvement over her former frenetic vivaciousness. The only sad note was that William distanced himself a little from Sarah.

He was as kind as usual, but tonight he did not seek out her company. Even knowing in her heart that this was the wisest course, Sarah mourned a little for the loss of the delightful companionship they had enjoyed so briefly.

Oddly enough, she found herself reluctant to end the evening. A new chapter would begin tomorrow, a chapter alive with the promise of love and happiness, so it was strange to wish to prolong the present. What a perverse creature she must be!

She shook her head at her own foolishness as she entered her bedchamber. Solitude at last—and rest. She had not realized how tired she was until she had gone in to say good night to Richard just now. His air of suppressed excitement had struck her at once because it was in such marked contrast to her own feeling that it required more strength than she possessed just to keep her head upright on her neck. She had laughingly agreed to his request to read in bed for a while since he didn't feel sleepy at all. So much for the soporific properties of hot milk!

One thing was certain, she concluded as she slumped wearily onto a chair and bent to remove her shoes: there would be no need of hot milk to induce sleep for her tonight after going essentially sleepless the night before.

Sarah paused in the act of drawing off her shoe, her face frozen in its "portrait" look. She drew in a shaky breath. How could she have forgotten that she had spent the previous night and most of this day in a state of morbid fear that someone was planning to kill her? She expelled slowly and her mind began to function again. Of course she had not forgotten the hours she had spent cringing behind locked doors last night or her anxiety at facing her relatives earlier today. Had she not dropped into the nursery during Richard and Lottie's evening meal to tell them of the revelations her grandfather had made at tea in order to set their minds at ease?

As she resumed removing the other shoe, it was with a sense of unreality that Sarah acknowledged that she had not thought of her earlier fears once during the evening just passed in the company of these same relatives. She shook her head in wonderment, but total exhaustion was rapidly taking possession of her mind and body. She was beyond thinking or wondering at anything.

Sarah made short work of undressing, not even bothering to put her hair in the single braid she usually adopted for sleeping. She tossed a handful of pins on the dressing table, snuffed the candles, and crawled thankfully into her bed. She was asleep before the scent of the snuffed candles had dissipated.

At first the dream was lovely. Golden sunshine bathed her uncovered head as she wandered in a sweet-smelling meadow dotted with hundreds of daisies and buttercups. She was tempted to gather a few, but her feet took her onward. The field abutted a wood, a rather inviting sight since the sun's rays were growing hotter. The deep-green wood promised coolness and shade, and she could see glimpses of lovely flowers, an unfamiliar variety with enormous white blossoms with deep-red centers. Enchanted, she hurried forward, glad to escape the rising heat.

But she could not escape it. There was no cool air in the forest, no air at all, and strange vines were hanging from the trees. They seemed to be reaching out for her, and she could not evade them, try as she would to twist and turn. They were squeezing her, one was wrapped around her throat, choking her. Her efforts to tear away the vines so she could breathe were draining her of strength, and everything was growing darker. She was afraid of this darkness that was descending so rapidly. She tried to scream and could produce no sound. She could neither scream nor breathe, and her flailing arms were ineffective against the vines. Weak and desperate, she exerted one last frantic effort to pull them away, flinging her arms out madly into the suffocating silence.

Sarah became vaguely aware of sounds, in the far distance at first and then coming closer as she drew in great gulps of air. She heard her name called repeatedly by a man—Mark?— but there were other sounds too, strange guttural grunts and bursts of angry invective.

"Sarah, open your eyes. Are you all right? Stop that, you murderous bitch! Stay still."

Sarah opened her eyes on darkness and fought a consuming

panic, but though it was dark, she was breathing more easily. The darkness was not so enveloping as before, she realized shortly. There was a dim light somewhere off to the right, but it was enough to illuminate the struggling forms moving in front of her bed. Her bed! She was in her own bed in her own room, and others were in here too.

"Sarah, can you hear me? By God, if you've killed her, I'll strangle you here and now."

"I'm not dead, Mark," Sarah responded to the agony in his voice, though it hurt to speak.

"Thank God!"

Her dazed understanding made little of the movements around her, but the larger figure, which must be Mark, was half-carrying, half-wrestling the other to the hall door, which he succeeded in opening after more struggling. His loud voice calling for Somers echoed up and down the stairwell.

By the time Lord Eversley, marching his now quiescent antagonist before him, came back into the room, Sarah had managed to light the bedside candle, despite fingers that shook throughout the lengthy operation. She was dragging on the soft rose-colored wrapper that Maria had laid across the foot of the bed hours earlier when Mark appeared within the circle of light, holding a woman in front of him by her two arms. He then twisted her arms behind her back, gripping her wrists together in one of his hands. The woman thus imprisoned had her head down while she struggled for breath, but Sarah recognized her.

"Aunt Ridgemont!" Her hand went to her throat.

Slowly Mrs. Ridgemont raised her head while her labored breathing steadied. The two women looked at each other. Sarah flinched from what she saw in the other's face, and her eyes grew wide with horror and bewilderment. "Why?" she whispered.

"Do not play the innocent with me, you vile, deceiving wretch," her aunt spat at her. "Did you think I did not see the way you enticed William with your honeyed tongue and smiling ways? And then, when you had made him fall in love with you, you broke his heart because you had lured a richer fool into your net, you wicked, heartless jade." This passionate diatribe ended in a whimper of pain as Lord Eversley jerked on her arms when she tried to lunge at the shrinking girl on the bed.

"Sarah, what has happened?"

Three persons erupted into the room at that moment. Lottie, her gaunt figure tightly wrapped in a robe of maroon wool, two long salt-and-pepper braids dangling below an incongruously frilled nightcap, sent her voice ahead as she marched in behind the running boy. Bringing up the rear was the small erect figure of Somers, still dignified despite a badly tied dressing gown, whose collar was half inside, and thin ankles on view below his nightshirt. All three had obviously heard something of the screaming invective because their eyes were fixed on Mrs. Ridgemont in fascinated horror.

Lord Eversley took charge before any more questions could be asked. "Somers, go fetch Mr. Horace Ridgemont. Richard, check to see if the commotion has awakened your grandfather. If it has, reassure him that everything is under control, but do not under any circumstances allow him to come up here. Do you understand?"

"Yes, sir. I was right, wasn't I, sir?" Eagerness ran through the boy's voice.

The viscount said grimly, "I am glad someone is pleased."

"Oh," said Richard, deflated, "it is not that I am pleased, exactly." He cast an unhappy glance at the straining woman and swallowed. "I . . . I'll keep Grandfather away, sir." He backed toward the door, saying soberly, "I am glad you are all right, Sarah."

"Richard!"

"Yes, sir?"

"For what you did for your sister today, I thank you from the bottom of my heart."

"Yes, sir!" The boy hurried out of the room, obviously bursting with pride.

Somers, his face troubled, followed at a pace more befitting his years and station. When Mark turned back, he saw that Lottie had gone over to the bed, where she now sat with her arm around a quietly weeping Sarah. He made an involuntary move in that direction before, with lips clamped firmly together, he turned away and sought a chair across the room, into which he pushed his prisoner with a curt command not to move.

Mrs. Ridgemont did not appear to hear him, but she made no resistance. She too was crying by now, soundless, despairing sobs that shook her body as she rocked to and fro in the chair. Mark could hear Lottie murmuring soothingly to Sarah as she stood over Mrs. Ridgemont. It seemed an eternity before Somers returned with a bewildered Horace Ridgemont in tow, but no one spoke in the interim.

Horace, wearing a dressing gown of bright-green brocade, stopped short at the sight of Lord Eversley, dressed for riding and standing guard over the huddled figure of his wife. His eyes took in the two women seated on the bed before returning to his father's stony-faced neighbor. He cleared his throat and came slowly into the room, his reluctance palpable.

"Somers told me you were here with my wife, but I thought he must be mistaken. He would not tell me anything more."

"He did not know anything more. Thank you, Somers, that will be all."

The valet bowed and backed out of the room, closing the door softly.

"What is wrong with my—with Mrs. Ridgemont, Eversley? What are you doing here in Sarah's bedchamber?"

"I regret to tell you, Mr. Ridgemont, that a few minutes ago I was barely in time to stop your wife from killing Sarah. She was trying to smother her by holding a pillow over her face. I was hiding in the room next door"—he nodded toward the servant's bedroom—"but if Sarah had not knocked over the water pitcher on her bedside table in her struggle to resist, I'd have been too late."

"I . . . I don't believe this!" Horace Ridgemont had fallen back in horror at the other's terse pronouncement. Now he raised a hand to his face and rubbed it, disarranging his hair even more.

"I fear you will have to believe it, and more. This was not the first attempt on Sarah's life. Last night a wire was strung across the top of those stairs on the next floor to trip Sarah when she brought a tray downstairs to the kitchen as she was in the habit of doing each evening. Fortunately on two counts, one of the maids took the tray instead, and Sarah, who was coming up the stairs at the time, managed to break the girl's fall, or your wife would be a murderess at this moment.''

"Madeleine, have you nothing to say to these accusations?'' Horace rushed past the viscount to stare down at his wife, who was keening softly and rocking back and forth in her chair. "Madeleine!"

"I failed, Horace, I failed,'' the woman moaned. "She should be dead. She has broken William's heart. I knew she did not love him, but he wanted her. I would have let her live if she had agreed to marry William, but when I saw her kissing Eversley in the conservatory, I knew she had to die. How could I let her live, the wife of another man, in the very neighborhood where William will live? It would break his heart every day of his life to have her near with her children, *his* children. Do you not see, Horace, I had to kill her, but I failed. I failed my son.''

For a long moment the awful keening of the woman rocking rhythmically in the chair was the only sound in the room. Mark glanced over to the bed: Sarah had her head on Lottie's shoulder and the older woman was running a hand up and down her arm as she held her closely. His eyes went to Horace Ridgemont's ghastly countenance as comprehension forced itself upon him. Slowly the stricken man straightened up and faced Lord Eversley.

"What do you intend to do?"

Mark's harsh aspect softened marginally in the face of the other's suffering, and he said quite gently, "You know that she will have to be restrained?"

The older man winced, but his features firmed, those formidable Ridgemont nostrils flaring momentarily. "Yes. She will have to remain at Alderby, but it was her family home, and it is where she is happiest. We are leaving tomorrow. Of course I shall see to it that she is attended constantly until our departure.'' He turned his head and addressed his niece. "There is nothing I can say to you, Sarah, except that I am deeply sorry.''

"I . . . I understand, Uncle. I am sorry too," she replied, barely above a whisper.

Mark stood back while Mr. Ridgemont coaxed his wife out of her chair and eased her toward the hall door. He stationed himself to screen the figures on the bed, but Mrs. Ridgemont did not even glance in that direction as she left, complaining fretfully of a headache, which her husband assured her would be treated as soon as they gained their apartment.

The second the door closed, Sarah flew off the bed and cast herself into her fiancé's arms, arms that received her thankfully and closed about her in protective urgency. "You saved my life, Mark," she whispered into his neck.

"And now it belongs to me," he said fiercely, tightening his hold.

"Always."

They were just emerging from a passionate kiss when a dry voice stated, "I'm still here."

"So you are, Miss Miller." The viscount lifted his head and laughed, albeit a trifle shakily. "And here you will remain for the rest of the night, I trust."

"Nothing and nobody could induce me to leave Sarah alone in this room while that archfiend remains in this house."

"Oh, Lottie, I feel so sorry for her. She is so pathetic."

"Pathetic, is it? If Lord Eversley had not been next door, you'd be dead now at the hands of that wicked creature. And what were you doing hiding in that room, sir? Did you suspect her?"

"Not until this afternoon. When Richard told me about the wire, I tried to persuade Sarah to stay at Eversley until the family left Beech Hill, but she refused." He gave his beloved a token shake.

"I really thought the danger was past once it was known that neither Richard nor I was the principal heir. I must confess that I suspected Aunt Adelaide because she hated me so."

"Adelaide Townsend has many unpleasant characteristics, but she is not unhinged. When I witnessed the way Mrs. Ridgemont went for Vincent this afternoon, I realized that she was unbalanced, and an unbalanced mind is capable of anything.

Far from accepting that the danger was over, I felt that the woman hated Sarah on William's account. After all, he had urged Sarah not to let his mother know she had refused his offer—''

''Mark! Are you saying William knew his mother would try to kill me, and did not warn me? No, *never*!''

''No, darling. I am saying nothing of the sort, but I believe William knows his mother's love for him is obsessive. He probably feared some kind of frightful scene if she thought you had wounded him. I doubt he suspected she was capable of murder. Most of us would have difficulty accepting that anyone close to us could possess such a dark side.''

''So you decided to stay here to guard Sarah tonight, and Richard helped you,'' Lottie surmised.

''Correct, Miss Miller. We planned it at tea after Sarah refused to go to Eversley. I walked back here through the woods tonight so no one should see me arrive, and Richard let me in a side door. He had taken the key to the servant's room while the family was at dinner so that Sarah could not lock me out, but she didn't take the precaution of locking any doors tonight. If she had, she would have discovered that the key to the hall door was also missing. I assume Mrs. Ridgemont took it while she was supposed to be prostrated by a headache this afternoon,'' he added somewhat dryly, and Sarah's lip trembled.

''I really did believe the danger was over, Mark.''

''I know, sweetheart. It is over now.'' He smoothed the long tousled hair back from her wet cheek and bent to kiss her again. ''It tears me apart to leave you tonight,'' he murmured softly, but Lottie's ears were keen.

''Nevertheless, leave her you must, Lord Eversley, and right now too. Sarah needs to rest and recover from this hideous experience,'' she asserted, her arms folded in front of her meager chest in an aggressive stance.

Mark eyed her with respect and took a step back from Sarah. ''I'll go downstairs and bring your grandfather up to date and see Richard off to bed,'' he promised.

He had already opened the door and was framed in the doorway when Sarah suddenly ran after him, her bronze tresses flowing over her shoulders in enticing disarray, her soft rose draperies revealing the lovely lines of her body, a long length of leg and delectable bare feet. She slid her hands up over his shoulders and brought his head down for a final kiss.

"Ladies are forever embracing you in open doorways," she said with a glint in her eyes that foretold a quick recovery. "But this time you are well and truly compromised, sir. You'll have to marry me to save your reputation."

"Sarah Ridgemont," cried Lottie, mortified at such indelicacy from a girl she had raised.

"Name the day," challenged Lord Eversley, wickedly appreciative of this same indelicacy from his future wife.

Epilogue

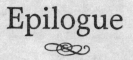

T here could not be a finer fall day than this one, the new Viscountess Eversley decided, smiling at the groom who helped her to dismount. She gave the chestnut filly a valedictory pat and a lump of sugar, gathered up the skirts of her elegant cinnamon-brown habit, tossed them over her arm, and started through the gardens that were still a riot of color, pulling off her gloves as she went. With little time to change before lunch, she hurried her step until, catching sight of her husband's dark head inside the conservatory, she promptly changed direction.

"Hello, Sleepyhead," the viscount greeted her when he turned at the sound of a light step.

Sarah pouted a little. "I know I overslept this morning, but you were gone when I got to the breakfast parlor."

"Couldn't help it, my love. I had an early meeting scheduled with my bailiff." He pulled her into his arms and kissed her lingeringly. "Good morning, Lady Eversley."

Though she had cooperated enthusiastically, Sarah still felt obligated to register a feeble protest in the name of decorum. "Mark, not here. We can be seen by anyone crossing the gardens."

"Let them look." He kissed her again. "Been to Beech Hill?"

"Yes, and at long last I feel able to claim fair proficiency as an equestrian. No aches, pains, or twinges after a six-mile round-trip, no moments of lost control, and my posture was perfect."

"I have never complained about your posture," he murmured with a provocative leer that dignity demanded she ignore.

"You did when you were teaching me to ride last spring. You said I looked like a lumpy sack of potatoes."

"I must have been out of my mind," Mark admitted, eyeing his wife's trim figure with masculine appreciation.

"I received two letters today," Sarah put in hastily, seeking to return the conversation to a rational basis, "one from Richard and one from William."

"And how is my esteemed brother-in-law enjoying his first weeks at Harrow?"

"You know Richard; he's like a cat. Wherever you throw him, he lands on his feet. He is fine and happy and has made several friends already. I rode over to read his letter to Grandfather, but he had received one also."

"I trust the general is bearing up under the separation?"

"He's a bit lonely after all the excitement of a wedding and having a youngster about the house, but he would never admit it, of course. We played chess."

"And?"

She wrinkled her nose at him. "He gave me an awful drubbing."

"I'll give him a game tomorrow and try to restore the family honor."

"Thank you, darling. He does love to have us drop in frequently." She hesitated a moment and he waited patiently. "William has been down to Alderby to visit his mother." Mark schooled his features to impassivity as Sarah went on, "She does not seem to recall anything of what happened in March, but William was more concerned with her physical health, which has deteriorated rapidly in the last few months. No one knew she had a weakness in the lungs. Mark, do you think it is very wicked of me not to hope for her recovery? I fear that William will never dare to marry while his mother lives." Her troubled eyes sought his, and he hugged her shoulders in wordless reassurance.

"William writes that his father feels that a great deal of the responsibility for what happened belongs to him because he never really loved his wife. It was an arranged marriage, you know. Uncle Horace believes that, in consequence, Mrs. Ridgemont poured all her affection on William to an unhealthy degree. He could see it but could do nothing to counter it except treat both boys equally himself. I wish—''

"Do not have that family on your mind, my love. There is nothing you can do. They must work out their own destiny.''

She sighed. "I know you are right, but . . . Oh, I nearly forgot! William had one piece of happy news to impart. He was present at a birthday dinner for Arabella a few days ago.''

Mark laughed. "Aha! I wondered where Rydell was off to when I saw him in Marshfield yesterday. I think we may safely assume that you will shortly have your cousin for a neighbor. Shall we get ready for lunch?'' He put down the pot plant he had been examining and dusted off his hands.

"In a moment. I have something to tell you first. This seems a fitting place. It is where you first kissed me,'' Sarah said, a dreamy expression spreading over her glowing countenance as she looked up rather shyly into chocolate-brown eyes that assumed a melting quality as comprehension dawned.

Mark gathered her hands together and raised them to his lips, his eyes never leaving hers. "Are you sure?''

"Well, I have not yet seen the doctor, but, yes, darling, I believe your mother will soon have that dark-eyed little grandson she has been longing to cuddle.''

Mark was heard to murmur that a little girl the image of her beautiful mother would be equally acceptable before he abandoned words for a more suitable demonstration of his happiness.

Sweet clear chimes rang out from the interior of the house, but the couple in the conservatory were happily oblivious of the sound. On a crisp, bright early-autumn day, Lord and Lady Eversley were about to commit the solecism of being late for lunch.